FRANKIE HOWERD

BARRIE GOSNEY

COX TWINS

DONALD HEWLETT

JIMMY PERRY

IAN CARMICHAEL

STARS IN BATTLEDRESS

By the same author

Promenades and Pierrots
By Royal Command
Dad's Army: The Making of a Television Legend
The Station Now Standing

STARS
IN
BATTLEDRESS

**A LIGHT-HEARTED LOOK AT SERVICE
ENTERTAINMENT IN THE SECOND WORLD WAR**

BILL PERTWEE

[handwritten inscription: To Roy / Best wishes / Bill Pertwee]

Hodder & Stoughton
LONDON SYDNEY AUCKLAND

British Library Cataloguing in Publication Data

Pertwee, Bill
  Stars in battledress.
  I. Title
  791.0922

  ISBN 0-340-54662-X

Published by Hodder and Stoughton,
a division of Hodder and Stoughton Ltd,
Mill Road, Dunton Green, Sevenoaks, Kent TN13 2YA.
Editorial Office: 47 Bedford Square, London WC1B 3DP.

Photoset by Rowland Phototypesetting Ltd,
Bury St Edmunds, Suffolk

Printed in Great Britain by
St Edmundsbury Press Ltd, Bury St Edmunds, Suffolk

The publishers would like to thank the following for the use
of the facial images featured on the jacket:
Michael Rowley (Russ Conway), Don Smith (Kenneth Connor)
and the Hulton Picture Company (Tony Hancock).
They would also like to thank Bryan Forbes for
permission to print the extract from *Notes For a Life*
(Everest Books, 1978).

Contents

Acknowledgments

Firstly, my thanks to the Right Honourable John Major for agreeing to write the foreword to this book. I am also enormously grateful to everyone I have either met, corresponded with, or contacted by telephone in connection with this book, and who have given me so much valuable information, pictures, programmes and posters.

I knew absolutely nothing of the events which I have tried to record in this book when I started writing it so I thank all those listed below for "remembering". After all, it was fifty years ago when most of these experiences took place, and for everyone a lot of water has flowed under many bridges since then.

Morris Aza, Norman Backshall, Jim Bailey, Ron Baybutt, Ken Behrens, Joe Black, Michael Black, Frank Broadley, Faith Brook, Janet Brown, Wilf Brunt, Bryan Burdon, Al Bush, Arthur Butler, Wyn Calvin, MBE, Ian Carmichael, Alex Cassie, Dennis Castle, Charlie Chester, MBE, Kenneth Connor, MBE, Michael Conway, Russ Conway, DSM, Alfred Cooper, Margaret Courtenay, Frank, Fred and Pauline Cox, Mike Craig, Ray Dalton, Michael Denison, CBE, Ken de Souza, Tom Drown, Clive Dunn, OBE, Denholm Elliott, CBE, Frederick Ferrari, Bryan Forbes, Tommy Frayne, Vic Gammon, Peter Garvin, Barrie Gosney, Lawrence Green, Stan Hall, Ivan Hanna, Jack Hardie, Doris Hare, Donald Hewlett, John Horsley, Eric Howe, James Howe, MBE, Frankie Howerd, Joan Hubbard, Roy Hudd, Maurice Jemmett, Cliff Jones, Geoffrey Keen, Pinkie Kydd, Audrey (Lupton) Lane, David Lodge, Len Lowe, Ernie Mack, John Macleod, Norman Macleod, Alfred Marks, Spike Milligan, Stella Moray, Arthur Moss, Sid Nayman, Patrick Newley, Nick Nissen, Richard Pasco, CBE, Alf Pearson, Walter Parrott, Jimmy Perry, OBE, Jon Pertwee, Bob Reader, OBE, Peter Reagan, John Rix, Jerry Roberts, Ken Robertson, Cardew Robinson,

5

Phyllis Rounce, William Ryder, Jack Seaton, Sir Harry Secombe, CBE, Eric Smith, Don Smoothey, Jack Stedman, Jack Steels, Clive Stock, Richard Stone, Stan Strutt, Frances Tanner, Bruce Trent, Jack Tripp, Sir Peter Ustinov, Reg Varney, Norman Vaughan, Vic Wales, Bill Wallis and Wilf Wyatt.

I must give a special thank you to Norman Macleod for his initial research and subsequent help during the putting together of this book.

What can I say about Geraldine Guthrie, my "nice lady up the road", that hasn't already been said by her neighbours when I arrive at her house at various times of the day and night with my handwritten scribble which she manages to type up into coherent text? Geraldine has suggested that she might write a book and I do the typing, but I don't want to get involved in "naughty" novels just yet. This is the fourth book she has worked on with me and it seems that my thanks to her get longer each time, and rightly so. Incidentally, Geraldine became a grandmother while we were doing this one and the baby has been christened Battledress!

My wife Marion as usual has contributed words and phrases in her usual generous way when my brain has stopped working in the early hours of the morning (a lot of people would say my brain seldom STARTS working). Marion's enthusiasm is always a source of encouragement.

Our son, actor James, has come into this one, helping me caption the pictures.

Note:

My comments within the contributions from other sources are enclosed in square brackets.

Foreword

I am delighted to have been asked to write this foreword for Bill Pertwee's latest book, *Stars in Battledress*. This light-hearted look at entertainment in the services during the Second World War is a worthy tribute to many brave men and women. They not only served their country in the front line, but also boosted the morale of their comrades by putting on shows and revues, sometimes in the most difficult and dangerous conditions. Many prisoners of war also staged theatrical and musical events, and their exploits are documented. The service personnel involved, many of whom went on to become well-known stars, made a unique contribution to the war effort. And now, all that remains to be said is, "Final call for beginners! Let the music begin, and enjoy the show!"

The Rt Hon John Major, MP
Downing Street
February 1992

Norman Macleod

Preface

This book was conceived during a sunny afternoon on the golf course with Norman Macleod. I knew that Norman had been in the entertainment business after the Second World War and I happened to ask him what he was doing before his demob, and he told me that for part of that war he was a member of the Stars in Battledress company. The name Stars in Battledress intrigued me, and I was happy to listen to Norman's explanation of its origin; it also helped to deflect attention away from my awful golf, a game which I find very pleasurable on a sunny day, with time to enjoy all the natural assets of a golf course – the trees, the wildlife, the birds – which explains why it can take me all day to complete twelve holes (my compromise of the usual 9 or 18) at a leisurely pace with a few balls and a couple of clubs. That particular game of golf with Norman Macleod certainly gave me food for thought, particularly those words Stars in Battledress.

I later contacted Norman again and told him of my idea to put a book together on the subject, though I didn't think I could proceed with it unless he was able to help me. He said he needed time to think about it. Thirty seconds later he said "yes", and so we were in business: at least I hoped we were. It was Norman's initial contacts with the people he had known during his period in Stars in Battledress that were to prove the starting point for

9

my research. Without this it would have been very difficult, if not impossible, to write this book. I didn't even have to promise Norman that I would try and improve my golf in exchange for his help. I have to say, by the way, that he is a fine golfer and a good tutor, I'm just a bad pupil.

Norman Macleod will enter the story again later, but for the moment let us go back to September 1939.

A Funny Thing Happened on the Way to the War

It is extremely difficult to be brief about any conflict, but certain events of the Second World War and beyond have to be recalled for the sake of younger people who may read this book. Older readers will hardly need reminding of them, as distinguished authors have meticulously covered the major upheavals of that period in great detail, and my brief introduction to the military events is purely a background to the activities of some service men and women who, by the nature of their professional calling, carried out a dual role in the hostilities as they developed.

In 1939 a chain of events began which changed the lives of millions of people over a long period of time. Some of them were actors, actresses, musicians and variety artistes of all descriptions – comedians, singers, jugglers, impressionists, dancers and technical personnel – who were to play their part in keeping up the morale of citizens in Britain and abroad.

As a nation we were to experience the Battle of Britain in the air, the possibility of an invasion, and huge night raids on our principal cities. Boundaries were redrawn in Europe, Africa and Asia, countries were occupied and reoccupied, and in many cases ravaged beyond recognition.

The Far East, which until then had only been presented as a mysterious and glamorous place in the pages of magazines or in Hollywood films, was to face at first hand some of the most horrific aspects of a war that went on long after the formal cessation of hostilities in 1945. Eventually the second front in France would, after bloody fighting, lead allied forces to the gates of Berlin and eventual peace, but even that was going to be fragile for a long time.

From the outbreak of war in 1939 morale in the UK was helped

11

considerably by BBC radio programmes like *ITMA* (*It's That Man Again*) with Tommy Handley and Co, *Happidrome* with Harry Korris, Jack Warner's *Garrison Theatre*, *Hi Gang!* with Bebe Daniels and Ben Lyon, and comedians such as Robb Wilton with his "The day war broke out" routines which were some of the funniest interludes in broadcasting.

At this time civilian entertainers, professional and amateur, were brought together to create some organised entertainment for military personnel, factory workers and other groups who were engaged in wartime activities. For a time, end-of-the-pier comedians found themselves shoulder to shoulder with the big stars of that period. These entertainers were enlisted by the organisation ENSA. Their activities have been well documented by the likes of Basil Dean, Vera Lynn, Joyce Grenfell, George Formby, Tommy Trinder, Noël Coward, John Gielgud, Ralph Richardson and the dear "Boo" Laye, so I do not intend to elaborate on what has been written by those artistes concerning their wartime experiences.

It is important however to mention what led up to the formation of the other entertainment organisations that are the subject of the ensuing pages. But first some explanation concerning ENSA. The Entertainments National Service Association was a direct descendant of the EFC (Expeditionary Forces Canteen) which existed for men and women of the services during the First World War. It was eventually reorganised and became big business, changing its name to the NAAFI (Navy, Army and Air Force Institutes). The NAAFI provided comforts for serving men and women away from home with canteens, low-priced food and, just as importantly, friendship for the lonely. Being a soldier could be very lonely at times, especially for youngsters. The NAAFI was so structured that they were able to make a profit, and in 1939 they became the basis for ENSA.

The job of creating an entertainment organisation to relieve the boredom of waiting for the war to materialise in the UK, France and the Low Countries in the latter months of 1939 and early months of 1940, fell to theatre and film producer Basil Dean. Dean had been involved with EFC during the First World War so he knew some of the difficulties ENSA would be up against. He had terrific enthusiasm and energy which he brought to his new job. He needed, and quickly obtained, the co-oper- ation of the NAAFI who could, among other things, help financially with the operation. Each performing member of ENSA would be paid £10 per week. Not a vast sum, but many actors and variety artistes in 1939 were not getting much more than that, some even less, apart from a few of the big names in the theatres, so £10 a week from ENSA would have been quite welcome.

By September 4th, 1939, the day after Britain went to war, Basil Dean was at work with a few theatrical friends, planning for the months and, as it turned out, years ahead. Theatres, particularly in London, were immediately closed, for a time anyway, so many professional artistes and stage staff were available to ENSA in the early months of the war, including a few very big names, and large numbers of amateurs who felt they had something to offer the organisation. Incidentally, quite a lot of the amateurs did become professional entertainers when the war was over. In 1939 it was Dean's task to mould all the various entertainers into groups, either as service parties or casts for plays which could be presented in NAAFI canteens, factories, shipyards, small provincial halls, and hospitals, and later during the blitz in the communal air-raid shelters.

At the outset Dean was invited to use the then vacant, famous Drury Lane theatre as his headquarters. Within a week or so of the war starting he had all the facilities of this marvellous theatre at his disposal, a large stage area for rehearsals, workshops for making scenery, storerooms and offices.

Almost at once certain star names had made themselves available at the various war departments, to entertain the service personnel through their own, or their agent's contacts, so these artistes were at that point not available to ENSA. Therefore parties being sent out to various service depots, whether it be army, RAF, naval ships or other establishments, had few well-known personalities heading the casts. Anyway, artistes had to sign at least a six-month contract with ENSA and this was not possible in most cases as far as the star names were concerned. Basil Dean's immediate needs were fulfilled by "no name" concert parties who were very professional in their own field because they had been working in theatres round the country before the war started.

As a member of the Concert Artistes Association from the mid 1950s I heard first-hand from people like Reg Lever, Cecil Johnson, Henry Lutman, Clifford Hensley, Brandon and Pounds and Rex Newman just how good those early concert groups were.

In fact the unknowns, like Clifford Hensley and others, worked for ENSA for most of the war, and after hostilities in the Far East ended, toured India and Burma. Hensley was my tutor, as it were, during my early days in seaside concert party, and his friendly approach to an audience was an inspiration. Later, when I began to move into radio and television, he became quite a fan of mine, which I very much appreciated, and during the making of *Dad's Army* I was able to suggest him for a small part in one of the episodes, which I know he thoroughly enjoyed. But to get back to Basil Dean.

There were just not enough professional performers to fill his increasing needs, so a lot of the amateurs and inexperienced professional artistes recruited by Dean and sent out in parties did cause some problems. Dean took the brunt of the criticism but it wasn't always justified. His aim was to bring live entertainment to all the military services and war workers wherever they were, and this was impossible with the artistes at his disposal at the beginning. The personnel at the various venues thought they were entitled to see big names heading their entertainment. Perhaps it would have been better if Dean had tried for more quality and less quantity. One has to say, though, that audiences were not disappointed for long once the good shows got started, even if they lacked stars. The poorer shows, however, were quickly given the bird and sent back to base.

Basil Dean, in his quest for more co-operation from the War Office and local battalion commanders, trod on a few toes and undeniably upset people with his brusque manner. He wanted better accommodation for ENSA artistes and better organisation at the venues, which at times was non-existent. Perhaps it was not surprising that ENSA became known as "Every Night Something Awful"!

One of the criticisms of mismanagement was justified on an occasion when Reg Lever was given sealed orders. He took a chance when his party was rumoured to be headed for the north of England, and he went to King's Cross station. Once on the train he opened the sealed orders and more by luck than judgment he was right. He could of course have gone anywhere, had he not been aware of the rumour. This sort of thing was not an isolated case and it was not the best recommendation for ENSA. On the other hand, Basil Dean was not responsible for signposts being taken away and place names being painted out to confuse possible

German invasion troops. This caused some performers to drive all over the countryside looking for their venue, and getting there either too late, not at all, or performing to a bunch of lads and lassies who were rounded up at the last minute by their sergeant-major and told to laugh when he gave the order, "otherwise you'll be on a charge". It couldn't have been easy to carry out the order on one such occasion. The solo artiste was the celebrated pianist Myra Hess.

Alf Pearson, one half of the popular double act he did with his brother Bob ("My brother and I") for over fifty years, remembers an ENSA party they were with called *The Joysticks*. A performance was to be given at a large gun site near Helensburgh in Scotland.

It was a very wet period and a piano had to be brought in to the Nissen hut where the party was to perform. A detachment of soldiers on the site was ordered to carry the piano to the hut and put it on top of some trestle tables which were supported by ammunition boxes. On the way the soldiers dropped the piano on the marshy ground, and when it was eventually put in place it was covered in thick slimy mud. The officer in charge ordered it to be hosed down and when Bob started to play it produced funnier noises than you'd hear in a farmyard.

I am sure Bob Pearson would have had some wonderful comment on the situation. He had a marvellous sense of humour.

Post-war the "boys" became one of the best-known radio and recording acts in this country. I know the dapper and charming Alf well; I also remember his late brother Bob with great affection.

Let there be no doubt that Dean's intentions were whole-heartedly directed towards providing entertainment for many different people, and although he may have been misguided at times, he did try to make life as easy as possible for the performers. On occasion the organisation at the venues let him down. This was the case again with *The Joysticks* in Scotland. ENSA parties sometimes included a well-known guest artiste and at Greenock, Gracie Fields, one of the biggest attractions in the country, joined the party at John Brown's shipyard on the Clyde. When they arrived there was no stage or platform available so the concert was given on the back of a lorry to an audience of six thousand workers. They shouted to Gracie, "We can't see you." She immediately got on top of the upright piano and knelt in a crouching position for the whole of her thirty-five-minute act. When she had finished she could hardly stand up straight with cramp. She had already done two shows that day and was flying (literally) straight off to do another.

Gracie, even though she had her own personal problems with her husband-to-be, film director Monte Banks who was about to be interned, did all that was asked of her with regard to morale-boosting concerts. When she took Monte to America, however, to avoid his internment because of his Italian ancestry, Gracie was immediately criticised for what people called deserting her duties. But she wasn't doing anything out of duty, she just wanted to help the nation's morale, and this she did. She immediately embarked on a long tour of the States and Canada promoting the "War Bonds for Britain" scheme. Gracie travelled thousands of miles giving concerts for the project, and then came back to England for an exhausting tour of service bases, factories and war charity events, all this when she wasn't in the best of health. Gracie took a long time to get over the hurt of the criticism of her trip to America, a criticism shared by only a few, as the following letter I received recently will illustrate.

Sid Nayman of Ilford in Essex was stationed on the Cocos Islands, a small group off the west coast of Australia, south of Sumatra, in 1945.

One of the islands was just big enough for an airstrip, a sort of staging-post for Singapore. The war in the Far East had just finished, but RAF and army personnel had to stay on the islands until further notice; we almost felt like a forgotten force. Then one day the island news-sheet announced that Gracie Fields would be interrupting a visit to Singapore to visit us. She arrived with her husband Monte Banks and gave us a wonderful show. I have never forgotten it to this day. Gracie told us our island reminded her of Capri, her island home in the Mediterranean. This visit kept us happy for a long time.

George Formby was another popular artiste who threw himself into tours entertaining all and sundry. George, like Gracie, had been a popular film idol in Britain before the war; in fact both of them had a bigger following here than the famous film stars of that time – Clark Gable, Ronald Colman, Myrna Loy and Betty Grable. With his topical songs such as "Mr Wu's an Air Raid Warden Now" and "Guarding the Home Guard's Home" George continued the great rapport that he had with the public. He was soon in France entertaining the services there, and in fact, like many other artistes, he just got out before the Dunkirk evacuation. Back in this country he proceeded to raise thousands of pounds for war charities while still continuing his film career and theatre dates in London and the provinces at the height of the blitz.

George later toured the Middle East with the same enthusiasm that he had brought to all his performing activities. However, Alan Randall and Ray Seaton, in their book *George Formby*, say this tour did cause some storm in England. Formby accused all the big show names of staying at home and filling their pockets when "there was a great need for them in the dust of the desert and elsewhere". George might have been justified in a few cases, but many stars had been giving their services to the war. I suspect he might have regretted his public comments. George was not a spiteful man, he was a popular entertainer and a kind man. He came back from the Middle East to fulfil professional contracts and was then off again to tour military bases in India.

Noël Coward certainly encouraged other artistes to go out to entertain the troops after he had done a long tour of the Middle Eastern zone. Producer Peter Daubney recalled his meeting with Coward in Charles Castle's excellent biography of the master, *Noël*.

I had been wounded at Salerno and I was in hospital at Tripoli and he came there to entertain the troops. After we'd been there a week, the matron came round and said that Noël Coward was going to entertain the troops. "The one thing is that you mustn't get out of bed, because you've only been here a week," she added. I was absolutely determined to go to this concert. So as soon as she'd left, I started dressing – it took quite a long time because I was completely encumbered by bandages. And when I entered the hall it was like being on board ship. The room seemed to sway about. There were about five hundred people who were all wounded sitting there, very truculent and ill at ease at having been forced into the auditorium. I don't think a lot of them had heard of Noël Coward. When the curtains parted, and we saw him, there he was – a Desert Rat, as we all were, but this was a Cartier Desert Rat, and he looked absolutely superb. Cool, clean, elegant and very dynamic. Well, this didn't enhance him at all in the eyes of the suffering five hundred, but he started off, and it wasn't just the sort of sorcery of his genius that he has on the stage, but his sheer determination, his battering willpower that made that audience absolutely one million per cent with him, and at the end they were choking with emotion. They stood and cheered and cheered.

I stayed behind after the performance because I wanted to go round and say hello. I went into Noël's room where he was washing, and when he saw how heavily bandaged I was, he said, "What's the matter with you?" "I've lost my arm," I said. I shall never forget this because I felt that he was much more compassionate than I was, and I think that through the sort of liquid heat and strain, and seeing all these wounded people, he was so deeply moved. "Which ward are you in?" he asked, and he insisted on taking me back to the ward himself. That was one of the great encounters I had in the war, and he was doing this to a lot of people, and certainly as an enhancer of the spirit and not a diminisher in any way. I think he's absolutely unique and he helped me enormously to get well.

Tommy Trinder, at that time a hugely successful stage and screen personality, was another artiste in France in 1939 and early 1940, and with his catchphrase "You lucky people" played to service men and women of the British Expeditionary Forces.

Tommy did his first tour under the banner of ENSA along with other artistes in southern Italy in 1944. He had been involved in some ENSA shows in Britain, but he also put an enormous amount of energy into various theatre shows during the height of the blitz in London when people remained determined to go to the theatres that were still open, and audiences included many service men and women.

It could never have been easy entertaining the theatre public during that period. When the air-raid sirens sounded audiences were asked whether they wanted to make for the shelters; most of them declined, which meant the show went on. Because they had to wait for the all-clear before going home, several shows finished before the raids did. Extra entertainment was improvised to fill the time and this is where Tommy Trinder came into his own. He was a master of the ad lib and was prepared to talk as long as he had an audience. I did quite a long tour with Tommy in the 1960s and he hated going straight to bed when he got back to the hotel; on several occasions I would still be drinking tea (Tommy was teetotal) and swapping yarns with him at four in the morning.

Trinder was a favourite with the royal family, and entertained them on many occasions. I visited him two or three times just before he died and he had several elegantly framed photos on his piano indicating his association with the royal family. On one occasion King George VI gave him a lovely pair of cuff-links of which Tommy was very proud.

Those charming sisters Elsie and Doris Waters, always elegantly dressed, and quite belying those favourite characters Gert and Daisy they created to huge effect on radio, were the first big-name stars to tour India and Burma. Talking to them many years ago in their lovely home at Steyning in Sussex, they said, "We were quite a hit with Orde Wingate's Chindits." That was an understatement if ever there was one. Incidentally, Elsie and Doris were the sisters of Jack Warner of *Dixon of Dock Green* fame and, as I've mentioned, *Garrison Theatre*. Jack was also a very fine cabaret performer.

Vera Lynn was certainly everyone's sweetheart along with Anne Shelton, and their enormous popularity was to prove long-lasting in the eyes of the audiences they entertained. Vera Lynn, in her autobiography *Vocal Refrain*, tells of her four-month tour of the Burma battle zone in 1944 accompanied by her pianist Les Edwards. She describes the constant moving about in the jungle, travelling on rough roads accompanied by a jeep carrying the piano and very basic sound equipment. They would perform two or three times a day, and visit makeshift hospitals, talking to severely wounded soldiers who had been fighting in indescribable conditions, giving them words of encouragement, all of which, as she says, seemed inadequate.

Lack of washing facilities, and all the time the feeling of fatigue at the end of each day, if not before, and knowing you will be doing it all again tomorrow, because that's what you've come out to do, to see the lads, give them some entertainment for just a short period of their very basic exist-ence, and to bring them a little bit nearer home by being with them.

And didn't the boys love Vera? All this for a young girl to cope with, to say nothing of the sometimes fraught flying conditions in all weathers in a strange selection of aircraft.

Will Hay, Max Miller, Arthur Askey and Richard Murdoch were also prominent in their own way in many of the ENSA tours in the UK and Europe.

One person who does deserve a mention, and who might poss-ibly be forgotten, is actress Bebe Daniels. She and her husband Ben Lyon, of *High Gang!* fame and several pre-war Hollywood movies, spent most of the war in London and Bebe used to go out entertaining on behalf of many organisations, travelling round at the height of the blitz with little regard for her own safety, and she and Ben always kept an eye on their neighbours' welfare in

London. In fact when Ben went on his trips to America he used to bring back goodies that were unobtainable over here for the whole street. Bebe was into Normandy within a few days of the allied landings in 1944 to entertain American service men, at times within a few hundred yards of the front line. Incidentally Ben had enlisted in the US army and became a colonel, along with Majors James Stewart and Clark Gable who were also posted initially to Britain. Bebe and Ben really loved Britain and Britain certainly loved them.

Joyce Grenfell was a tireless worker, entertaining the troops in the Middle East, Central Europe and India, and how they appreciated it. Joyce and her pianist Viola Tunnard put up with some very uncomfortable accommodation and working conditions, but seldom grumbled. Her diaries concerning those tours make exhausting reading. In and out of aeroplanes, several concerts a day, plus visits to hospitals make up a quite unique collection all gathered together by James Roose-Evans in his entertaining book *The Time of My Life*, which is what Joyce Grenfell called those tours in 1944–45. A paragraph in the book seems to sum it all up.

Together Viola and Joyce travelled to Algeria, Tunisia, Malta, Sicily, Italy, Egypt, Jerusalem, Jordan, Syria, the Lebanon, bits of the Arabian coast, Bahrain and all over India. The crying need all over the Middle East was for entertainers who could be truly mobile, go anywhere, and do their stuff in a hospital ward, from a jeep, or on top of a mountain pass; and so Joyce and Viola set off with a few suitcases, no scenery or props. She sang, she did her monologues, and, above all, she made the audiences sing. Joyce Grenfell always said that she learned her job by doing it. "The war was my training school, my university, and my learning time."

In the NAAFI canteens and factory warehouses, actors and actresses such as Godfrey Tearle, Edith Evans and John Gielgud braved the bombing to take their talents to many people who, up till then, had not had the opportunity to sample any sort of theatre drama. Because of it some of those audiences became drama fans, and all because of the war.

Many artistes who had got away from Dunkirk in 1940 were given the chance to return to France soon after D-Day in 1944. Many others will cross our path before we finish.

Punch Publications Ltd

By 1941 Army, Navy and Air Force Welfare authorities had an important part to play in the morale of the services. The army that had been rescued at Dunkirk was being rearmed just as quickly as the factories could manufacture their equipment, but it was becoming clear to Army Welfare that the service men and women who were waiting for involvement in future land conflicts required to be catered for with regard to entertainment, in a particular way. ENSA was doing a good job, but for various reasons, some of which I will explain later, they did have their limitations, although this was not necessarily their fault. So I hope this book will not diminish in any way the part played by the civilian entertainers who performed in many home and overseas areas, sometimes at great risk to themselves.

Introduction to Service Entertainment

A suggestion was made to the War Office by Army Welfare in 1941 that there should be a pool of professional performers who had enlisted in the services who could entertain the troops both at home and abroad. The idea was to have a "flying squad" of entertainers whom Army Welfare could send to the fighting zones prohibited to civilian entertainers, and entertain the service personnel, but at the same time be ready at a moment's notice to "perform" their regular army service duties. The scheme, if it could be put into practice, had one great advantage. It would enable those service men and women who were entertainers, or would-be entertainers, to ply their trade during their period of enlistment.

For the army it was a certain Lieutenant-Colonel Basil Brown, himself a Dunkirk escapee, who instigated the formation of Stars in Battledress. He thought the idea of service men and women entertaining their comrades might eliminate some of the problems that ENSA had incurred. The word battledress is usually associated with the army, but of course applies to all three services.

Squadron-Leader Ralph Reader, who had been in the air force since before the war, had already realised that air force personnel with entertaining abilities could be a very useful part of the RAF's contribution to service entertainment. He was approached in the late 1930s by a member of the Air Staff who suggested that if he would like to enlist in the air force he could be granted a commission, and later, under cover of his entertaining activities, do some Special Branch investigation work for them. So Reader was eventually to serve not only the need for service entertainment, but also play an important part in the hostilities in his work for British intelligence. Reader was to become a tremendous influence in the careers of several young RAF service men, as will become obvious as the story of the RAF Gang Shows unfolds.

The navy quite naturally had the difficulty of producing entertainment at sea; nevertheless this was overcome in several instances. Towards the end of the war all three services amalgamated to produce Combined Services Entertainment, and this organisation continued for a very long time.

"You're in the Army Now"

Stars in Battledress may well be regarded as the logical outcome of the divisional concert parties. The latter drew on the best talent in a division, the former from the army as a whole. In other words it formed a "CENTRAL POOL OF ARTISTES".

Colonel Brown was already involved in the Army Welfare Department, and his organising ability was to prove the dominant factor with Stars in Battledress. Brown formed a partnership with a Major Bill Alexander and a Captain George Black, and these three were a formidable trio: Brown with his knowledge of the service men's relaxation needs through his work with Army Welfare; Alexander was an actor, so would know the minds of the entertainers with all their foibles and eccentricities; George Black, who knew the production side of show business, being the son of the "great" George Black, the man who had turned the London Palladium into a profitable theatre in the late 1920s and early 30s and had also created the world-famous Crazy Gang led by Bud Flanagan and Chesney Allen. His two sons George junior and Alfred had followed in his footsteps.

In order to avoid criticism from the War Office top brass as to the undesirability of withdrawing soldiers from the fighting strength of the army, they ensured that every member of a show unit was a trained soldier who, in a period of emergency, could revert to his or her service duties. In this way Brown, Alexander and Black felt they had a good chance of obtaining the co-operation of the War Office which was necessary if their scheme was to work. Very early in 1942 the organisation was in place and had had the blessing of the top brass when a show was presented for their approval.

The title came about after a walk through Trafalgar Square by the principal organisers discussing the relative merits of Entertainers in Khaki and Stars in the Army, etc. No one is quite sure who came up with the eventual title but before they had reached the other side of the square, Brown, Alexander and Black were the bosses of Stars in Battledress.

Early performers and technicians who joined the organisation included George Melachrino, Syd Millward, Charlie Chester, Nat Gonella, Ken Morris and Stan Hall.

Stan Hall

I started my career in the film industry at the age of seventeen, in the make-up and hairdressing department of Beaconsfield Studios in Buckinghamshire. Beaconsfield Studios, now no longer in existence, were the only film studios to be non-union. It was the old, old story – you couldn't become a member of the union unless you were working in a film studio, and you couldn't get into films unless you were a member of the union! Beaconsfield was the exception.

When Denham Film Studios opened in 1937 I got a contract with Alexander Korda to do make-up, and stayed there until war started, when I went into the army. On my way to London by road to join my unit at one of London's main-line stations, a woman stepped in front of my car at some traffic lights, and although fortunately she wasn't hurt, by the time we had waited for an ambulance and the police I arrived too late, and consequently missed my train to Crewe.

The military then sent me off to another destination instead, and this time it turned out to be Clacton-on-Sea. Butlin's Holiday Camp, no less. So I did my basic training there, and lived comfortably, by army standards, in chalet-type housing. Then the whole unit moved back to their Royal Ordnance Corps depot at Greenford in Middlesex, which luckily was only six miles from my home.

I was in the Royal Ordnance Corps, and the regiment had its own concert party called *Bits and Pieces*, and as they knew that I had done make-up for films I was roped in to help them with their make-up and wigs.

Colonel Basil Brown (later to become Billy Butlin's right-hand man in the expansion of the post-war Butlin's Holiday Camp empire) and George Black junior had already organised a small central pool of artistes, made up of entertainers who had enlisted in the services. Brown and Black were also stationed at the Greenford depot and one night came to see one of our Ordnance Corps shows. The outcome was that I was asked to help form the larger Stars in Battledress unit.

So I was in at the beginning of an organisation that was to become a familiar name to service men all over the world during the Second World War. Gradually the word spread and the boys rolled in. Now if that woman hadn't stepped in front of my car I'd have caught the train to Crewe, and who knows? I certainly wouldn't have been in Stars in Battledress.

At Greenford life was primitive, with quarters in a freezing cold Nissen hut. It was always a bit of a shock for the new recruits arriving from fairly comfortable lives as professional entertainers.

Nat Gonella, the famous trumpet player and band leader, always arrived in suede shoes, and drove a big car, which he parked just at the end of the parade ground.

Syd Millward, who later led a hugely successful band called the Nitwits, was another new arrival, and when asked by an officer, "Soldier, what's your number?" meaning his army number, Syd gave them his telephone number, Sloane 3429!

The performers who came to Greenford were all from different army units, and I feel many of their commanding officers were probably quite pleased to get rid of them, as a lot of those entertainers were generally hard to discipline. We put an advertisement in the *Stage* newspaper, asking for anybody in the army who might be interested in joining our unit to write to us. We got masses of letters and telephone calls. Some couldn't be transferred to us because they were in valued units like the commandos and couldn't be spared. Some even cried down the phone, begging us to get them transferred to SIB so they could do their own thing and perform again. But the order for transfer had to come from their own unit.

By this time I was the unit quartermaster-sergeant doing the pay, ordering rations and things like that, so I was ideally suited for helping to organise the unit, and doing the wigs and make-up as required.

Enter Sergeant Charlie Chester

The millions of listeners who tune in regularly to *Sunday Soapbox*, the popular radio programme hosted by that irrepressible character Charlie Chester, would find it hard to believe that during the war Charlie was once offered a post in counter-espionage, or that during the liberation of France and Holland he was up at the front line with one of his concert parties!

His long and varied careers in the entertainment business both pre- and post-war are quite fascinating. He was born in East-bourne in Sussex and at about the age of fourteen he entered various talent contests, playing guitar, singing and yodelling! Later on, when his family had moved to London, he realised comedy was in short supply and changed his act, putting on a funny hat, playing a ukelele and telling some jokes, and won the All South London Talent final.

By the time he was seventeen he had his own accordion band, but eventually he reverted to his solo act, and he started playing working men's clubs, gradually getting better dates and better money. Once he hired a Daimler for 12/6 (60p) and dressed a friend up as a chauffeur to arrive in style at a hotel in Holborn. The management were so impressed they doubled his fee and offered him a return engagement!

Although Charlie was born in Sussex his style has always been that of the cheeky Cockney comedian. Once, in a mood of desperation, he rang up the boss of Moss Empires, the all-powerful Val Parnell, and said, "Mr Parnell, I'm a young lad, and I want to work." Parnell replied, "Buy yourself a pick and shovel," and put the phone down! Yes, times could be hard!

But by this time, in the 1930s, Charlie had started doing radio work for the BBC, shows like *The Pig and Whistle* as Percy the van boy, with Syd Walker the famous "Rag and Bone Man".

In 1938 when he was at the Prince of Wales Theatre, in a show called *Frivolities of France*, the advent of war was casting its shadows and Charlie remembers the atmosphere as very tense. Called up into the army, he joined the Irish Fusiliers and was posted to Newtown in Montgomeryshire, where he wrote his hit song "Forget-me-not Lane". This was taken up by the regiment as their marching song and was later a big hit for Flanagan and Allen. Charlie remembers:

The day we marched out of Newtown the town turned out to see us off, and they were all singing the song. A very moving moment, I can tell you! I had a great big lump in my throat as we marched away!

His next posting was in the North Wales University town of Bangor and he recalls an incident that happened one wintry night in 1940.

27

It's two feet of snow, thirteen minutes past seven in the evening, and it's black as midnight, really black. The Jerry bombers are going over to clobber somewhere, and I'm in my greatcoat, shivering. I'm just going down into the town when I see a pinpoint of light flashing out from the hillside across the other side of the valley. It was signalling a message in code. Now I can't read Morse Code, but I had a matchbox in my pocket and a stub of pencil, so I jotted down the dots and dashes as I saw them. I then tore down to the Officers' Mess, and got hold of a Major Fluett, our intelligence officer. He was having his dinner at the time so he was not very pleased! However, I explained about the flashing lights, but that I couldn't read Morse Code. "Well, tap it out, man, tap it out," he said, so I started tapping out the dots and dashes I'd written on my matchbox, and as I was doing this he was writing NWU, NWU, then he said, "My God! It's North Wales University!" So we put a night compass on it, and I understand they caught two men signalling to the German bombers, to give them a landmark on their way to bomb Liverpool.

The next day I was sent for by the colonel, and was made a corporal! Then he said to me, "You were an actor, weren't you?"

I said, "Yes, sir!"

"Good," he said, "so you're used to disguises – how would you like to volunteer for special duties?"

Well, anything to get out of marching with a pack on your back and with a rifle slung over your shoulder. So (foolhardy Chester!) I found myself deep in the middle of darkest Wales, getting involved in counter-espionage!

Charlie was entertaining within his division when he received a message to report to Greenford Barracks in Middlesex to see Captain George Black and Colonel Basil Brown of the Central Pool of Artistes. Charlie found himself in good company:

Some good men, marvellous performers, but their soldiering wasn't too hot. I mean, could you imagine Terry-Thomas bayoneting anybody? Nat Gonella, a wonderful trumpet player, but he couldn't take an order if you gave him one. So Gonella, Terry-Thomas, George Cosford, a great composer who used to turn up on parade with his umbrella up if it was raining, and Ken Morris and Arthur Haynes were all destined for the "Pool". There was Willie Solomons, the famous pianist with a big fat belly and a uniform that fitted where it touched, we had Eugene Pini the famous violinist, with a very delicate approach to it all, and I was now, with the rank of sergeant, put in charge of them!

From its shaky start the Central Pool of Artistes finally got its official recognition when Sir James Grigg, the then War Minister, sat in the audience to vet one of Charlie's shows. Chester was very careful to make the show entertaining, bright, and above all clean. Sir James thoroughly enjoyed it and was the first to go backstage afterwards to tell them, "This show will be worth its weight in gold to the men at the front." Stars in Battledress had arrived!

Geoffrey Keen

A straight actor who was to star in many films, television drama series and in the theatre after the war, Geoffrey Keen was an active member of SIB.

I was a corporal in the RAMC at Netley Military Hospital near Southampton when in 1941 I received a letter from Captain George Black, commanding officer of the SIB unit saying he was looking for professional actors to take part in a play to be produced to tour service bases in this country. I was working as an actor before enlisting in the army and Black said he could arrange for me to be posted to Chelsea Barracks. This was so that I could be available for rehearsals in London. The play, *Men in Shadow*, had been written by Mary Hayley Bell, the wife of John Mills and mother of Hayley and Juliet. The actors in the play included Robert Webber, William Kendall and John Longdon; also in the cast was actor Len Marten, who was to become the associate producer of television's *Opportunity Knocks* for many years.

The play had a marvellous set, with professional lighting, and took about four hours to put up, which was a miracle as it was very complicated in its structure. It filled a very large army lorry when being transported. At one camp we played, the commanding officer asked us whether we built a new set at each camp. As the original had taken seven weeks to complete and we only arrived at a camp a few hours before the first performance began you can imagine the officer's theatrical IQ was pretty low.

We toured all over the UK doing one-night stands. Then after the Normandy landings we rehearsed a farce, *Someone at the Door*, with which we were told we would be touring Italy. The cast of this piece included Kenneth Connor and Faith Brook, screen actor Clive Brook's daughter. Kenneth and Faith have of course achieved great things in all branches of the entertainment business since those service days.

After three weeks on a troopship in a large convoy we arrived in Naples. Colonel Nigel Patrick (a fine post-war actor until his death a few years ago) was in charge of routing service companies in Naples and told us we were to take the play to Rome for a tour of venues there. We were all loaded on to an open lorry which made the journey terribly cold as we started to climb over the mountain ranges in freezing snow. With meagre rations it was to say the least a memorable experience.

This experience is explained more fully later by Faith Brook!

In Britain shows were taken out to gun sites and places like that, and it was really hard work. It was certainly no joy-ride and the units seldom got back to Greenford before three in the morning, and often without anything to eat, and then had to be smart on parade as usual in the morning. "The powers that be" were very hot on maintaining discipline, morning parades and suchlike. There was some criticism because everyone thought they were all having a good time. Even the national press was beginning to ask questions at the War Office. They had to watch their step because they were soldiers first, entertainers second.

Because some gun sites were secret, only military personnel were allowed there, which is why Stars in Battledress could go, and ENSA weren't allowed.

Stan Hall

I remember the first girl we had posted to us was Janet Brown. She was very young and had just joined the ATS [the Auxiliary Territorial Service]. I was a sergeant-major by then, and as the unit had very little transport, we used to hire trucks or removal vans. The boys would be in the back of the van with the scenery and the props, and I would sit up front with Janet; she was very adorable, still is of course, and the boys loved having her in the show.

There was now quite a collection of talent to draw on: Charlie Chester, Syd Millward and his Nitwits, classical musicians such as Edmund Rockler, Eugene Pini and Vic Byfield and, quite apart from Janet Brown, quite a number of girls came into the pool of artistes from the ATS. They included Stella Moray, Sally Rogers and Frances Tanner from the musical side of the business and Faith Brook and Margaret Courtenay from the straight theatre. This enabled plays to be produced as well as variety shows and they were much appreciated by the boys.

Many straight actors were now being released by the service units and drafted into Stars in Battledress and one such play produced was *Men in Shadow*.

Murray MacDonald, who was then called Captain Honeyman, was stationed at Salisbury and was a great champion of ours. Consequently a lot of shows started their tour at the Salisbury Theatre in Wiltshire. Sometimes we would do special shows with guest artistes like Laurence Olivier, who would do a speech from *Henry V*, all very patriotic.

During the war Queen Mary was staying at Badminton in Gloucestershire with her cousin the Duke of Beaufort and had a company of soldiers there to protect her. A Stars in Battledress unit went down to entertain them and Queen Mary asked if she could be present too. The show was put on in the village hall, and the Queen's own special chair of red leather and gold was brought in for her. I tried it for size, and it fitted like a corset! There was only one way to sit in it and that was upright. No wonder the chair went everywhere she did! She was a great champion of the variety stage, and was a wonderful audience for us. I managed to peep through a hole in the curtain during Boy Foy, the unicyclist's act, and there she was sitting like a ramrod but smiling, beating time to the music, and enjoying every minute of it.

In a little while the headquarters of the group was moved from Greenford to the Duke of York's Barracks in Chelsea, but when that was unfortunately bombed twice they moved again to offices in South Eaton Place. As the unit grew they had to move yet again, to premises at 10 Upper Grosvenor Street.

Re-enter No 2077946 Sapper Norman James Macleod

Norman and his brother John, senior by two years, joined the Territorial Army in May 1939. The TA was a first reserve of the regular army. Its personnel consisted of men who wished to continue their own particular trade in a service unit, or who felt that with a war looming they should gain some experience of service life to be prepared for a different lifestyle as regulars. There were also those who may have been bored with their peace-time job or, in some cases, not have a job at all. Joining the Territorial Army consisted of part-time training, mostly at week-ends, and two-week camps once a year spent under army con-ditions. It also brought a comradeship into men's lives that some of them had not experienced in peacetime. Norman and John Macleod joined the TA so they would be prepared for army life in a war which they thought was inevitable. The thought that they would eventually play a dual role of soldier/entertainer certainly hadn't crossed their minds. As Norman says:

John and I joined the TA in May 1939 attached to the Royal Engineers Regiment at the Duke of York's Barracks, and a few weeks before the outbreak of war we were called up into the army proper. Our first few months after call-up were spent under canvas on a hillside in Wales. This was the period of the phoney war, when only the occasional shot was fired in anger and the German air force killed a rabbit in Scotland. As Sappers (REs) we were mostly building tank traps and pill boxes. It was during this period that my brother and I started a little concert party within the unit with two or three other fellows. You may ask why should we think we had any knowledge to form an entertainments group in the army. Well I'm going to jump ahead thirty years to the year 1969, and this may give you a clue.

In 1969 I had the great pleasure of playing at the Theatre Royal, Drury Lane, in *Mame* with Ginger Rogers, and I took my mother backstage after the show and up to my dressing-room, only to be told by her that the backstage as far as the actors were concerned hadn't changed much since her day! You see, my father and mother had worked at Drury Lane, and also at the nearby Royal Opera House, Covent Garden. My mother, as a young girl, played on stage there with the great Caruso, and my father at the "Lane" in *The Whip* where they had a horse race and train crash on stage. It was probably taken for granted that my brother, sister and I would at some time follow our parents into the theatre.

In the first army concert party we organised, brother John and I did a double act called "Mack and Tosh". We had, through our family connection in entertainment, been brought up hearing gags and sketches. John also played the piano well, and I played the guitar and sang. The other fellows in the concert party consisted of a chap who played the spoons and whistled, another did farmyard impressions and another ex-Cockney barrow boy had a fund of funny stories. This was with 504 company which was now stationed at Billingshurst in Sussex.

My brother and I stayed with the unit for about two years, but were then separated when I went into hospital for a few weeks. After that I was despatched to a holding battalion to await overseas posting. We were billeted in a disused mill in Halifax, Yorkshire. Almost as soon as I had arrived a corporal came up to me and said, "I hear you've been entertaining in 504 company. I'd like you to report to the company office because the regimental sergeant-major is looking for entertainers and musicians who get posted here." There was a huge amount of service personnel in Halifax and apparently entertainment was in very short supply within the units and in civilian establishments. When I reported to the RSM I suggested to him that my brother, who was in another unit, would be very useful in forming a dance band. He was very enthusiastic about this, and said there would be no trouble in getting him posted to Halifax. Brother John duly arrived, and we were back in the old routine.

We gradually organised a dance band, with John doing the musical arrangements, and soon had a good concert party going. During the day we of course had to carry on with our regular service duties. We started doing concerts all over Halifax and, much to the RSM's delight (after all, it was all his idea in the first place), we also did some radio broadcasts for the

BBC in Leeds. Another band had been got together by the Royal Army Service Corps under the leadership of Ken Mackintosh. Post-war, Ken started on one of the most successful careers in the band business.

It was during one of our concerts that we had a visit from Captain George Black of the Stars in Battledress unit. By this time we had enlisted the help of a great tap dancer/comedian/singer called Joe Melia and he, John and I formed a three-handed act calling ourselves the Ross Brothers. Captain Black said our act, plus other things we could do, would be useful to SIB, and said he would be in touch with us. Before he could we were all posted to different units around the country.

Several months went by, and then I was contacted at my new unit and told I was being transferred to the Central Pool of Artistes (the origination of Stars in Battledress) in London. The next day I was on the train to London. Once there I took the Underground from Euston to Sloane Square. I stepped out on to the platform and there getting out of the next carriage was my brother John, and further up the platform was Joe Melia. We'd all arrived from different parts of the country after a call from the Central Pool of Artistes.

We reported to the company office of the unit, and were informed that they would like us to get together our own travelling variety show. We were now free from normal service duties while doing this. We rehearsed during the day and had our evenings free.

During this period in London there was some great service entertainment and we were very fortunate to see and hear it. The London Casino (now the Prince Edward Theatre) then had the famous Glenn Miller Orchestra, Robert Farnon and the Canadian Forces Orchestra, with vocalist Paul Carpenter, who stayed over here after the war and appeared in many films, and also the Squadronaires Orchestra at the Lyceum.

We soon had a full complement for our show, including a stage manager, Pete Warren, and under the heading "Stars in Battledress", we toured mainly in the south and west of England, playing at garrison theatres, and anywhere there was a large number of service men and women.

We toured for quite a while, in fact until Japan surrendered. At last the world was at peace, or so we thought. Suddenly we were recalled to the SIB London HQ which was now in Upper Grosvenor Street, and told we were to take the show to India as soon as possible. We had to travel light as we would be flying out there, and any stage equipment we required would be available on reaching our destination. We carried no stage manager on this trip so my brother John was put in charge of the unit and was promoted to sergeant . . . I always reckoned the army had a sense of humour!

We reckoned we'd had a fairly comfortable war, but little did we know the hazards we would come across in India, which was already showing signs of turmoil before eventual independence. When we were preparing to leave for India other units of SIB were already back in the UK after several months of slogging it around Europe which had begun very soon after D-Day in 1944.

We will hear later how Norman (and Little Johnny) fared in India

Bryan Forbes

Bryan Forbes's army service was, like most other infantry soldiers', a mixture of discipline and regimental orders, some of which were probably not even understood by those who gave them, and gave rise to a certain amount of disbelief as to why you were carrying them out. Later, during a spell in France after the Normandy landings, his service was interrupted when he contracted pneumonia and was sent back to an army hospital on the Isle of Anglesey.

The following extract from his autobiography, *Notes For a Life*, published by Everest Books, is reproduced by kind permission of Bryan Forbes.

The medical officer of the day waved the telegram at me accusingly.

"What's all this about, Forbes?"

"No idea, sir."

"Says here you're to report immediately to War Office Section 6 Upper Grosvenor Street, and you say you don't know anything about it?"

"No, sir."

"Well, it's bloody rum. How sick are you?"

"I don't know, sir."

"Well, I mean, do you feel well enough to travel? What're you supposed to have had?"

"Pneumonia, sir."

The MO took my chart from the foot of the bed and stared at it. Then read the telegram again. "Report immediately," he muttered to himself. "God, I don't know. Is it something hush hush? You're intelligence, aren't you?"

"Yes, sir."

"Well, you'd better go, hadn't you? Can't ignore this. No telling what it is." He put a hand on my forehead. "Coughing, are you?"

34

"Not much, sir."

"Feel fit enough to travel then?"

"Yes, sir."

"Yes, well, I'll arrange a railway warrant. Only for Christ-sake don't pass out before you get to wherever you're going. You'll have to sign a form saying you're A1, then, you know, it's somebody else's pigeon."

He wandered off down the ward as confused as I was. The other inmates immediately started to question and congratulate me. I got out of bed and started to get my kit together. It was an army rule that one travelled in best battledress and boots, fully Blancoed-up, and it was two hours before I was passed presentable and had been issued with the necessary papers. I got a lift in the back of a five-hundredweight truck to the station and caught the next London train.

As I recall it was about six o'clock in the evening when I finally staggered out of the train, having been forced to sit on my kit-bag in the corridor the entire journey. By now I was feeling distinctly under the weather and sweating profusely, since traces of the disease still lingered. I made my way across London to Oxford Street and then humped my kit to Upper Grosvenor Street. The house had obviously been a private residence of some quality before the war, but now it bore all the signs of commandeered army property. The impressive entrance hall and staircase were deserted and bare of furniture except for a trestle table and the inevitable notice-board for standing orders.

I stood there for a few minutes and eventually a captain came down the stairs, looked at me and then disappeared into a side room. I had naturally come to attention as he approached and I found it a little odd that he failed to return my salute, but merely gave a somewhat enigmatic smile. I remained there at attention.

The captain returned, started up the stairs again and then retraced his steps.

"What can I do for you, young man?" he said.

"Sir!"

I threw him up another salute and handed him the telegram. He read it.

"You're not what it says here, are you?"

"Sir?"

"I mean, this isn't your stage name, is it? You're Bryan Forbes, aren't you? Do stand easy."

I relaxed slightly.

"Are you Bryan Forbes?"

"Yes, sir."

"We've been so looking forward to you getting here. My name's Brandon-Thomas, by the way."

He held out his hand. I shook it, then dropped my hands to my sides again. I realised I was being put to some sinister test. I calculated that I had been posted to some strange intelligence unit and that my future would be determined by my reactions to a series of trick questions. I tried to take a grip of myself. I was exhausted and hungry and somewhat obviously running a temperature.

"Have a good journey?"

"Not bad, sir."

"Where've you come from?"

"Anglesey, sir."

"No, I mean, what unit were you in?"

"I was in hospital, sir."

"When?"

"This morning, sir."

He took a step back and looked genuinely shocked.

"*This morning!* But that's dreadful. What were you in hospital with?"

"Pneumonia, sir."

"And they let you travel like this, all that way? Well, it's perfectly disgraceful. You don't look well."

"No, I don't feel too good, sir, as a matter of fact."

"Jevan. My name's Jevan. You don't have to call me sir. Here, let me help you off with your pack."

I was now convinced there was a catch in it. Full captains did not help privates remove their heavy packs, but I was a little light-headed and allowed him to loosen my shoulder-straps and remove the pack.

"You've got a ghastly rifle too, haven't you? You had to carry that, I expect. They've no right to send people out of hospital like that. Have you had anything to eat?"

"They gave me some rations for the train, sir."

"Jevan. Please call me Jevan, we don't have much formality here. Look, we must fix you up with something to eat. Come and meet the CO. We knew you were coming, of course, but we'd no idea you were in hospital. You should have let us know and travelled when you felt really well."

He carried my pack and rifle upstairs and I followed him, by now utterly convinced that I was on a lunatic collision course. We went up to the first floor, which was ornate, with a lot of marble and gilt scuffed by army boots and army disregard, and he led me towards large double doors. Pinned to one side of the door was a notice which said: Commanding Officer. Instinctively I braced myself.

"Noel," the captain said as he entered the room, "you'll never guess what they've done to Bryan Forbes. He's had pneumonia in some hospital and they let him travel!"

I found myself face to face with a dapper major who got up from behind his desk as we came in and advanced to meet us.

"This is Major McGregor," the captain said.

"Noel McGregor," the commanding officer said. I had never known a more matey set of officers. "Get him a chair, Jevan."

"He hasn't had anything to eat, of course."

A chair was produced. I sat down on it, but managed to sit down at attention. Whatever game they were playing they weren't going to catch me out on discipline. The commanding officer offered me a cigarette from a rather elegant case. I was just about to take it when he withdrew the case.

"D'you think you ought to smoke?"

"Well, I wouldn't mind one, sir. Thank you."

"Would you like a cup of tea? We can't offer much in the way of a meal, I'm afraid."

"Well, if it wouldn't be too much trouble, sir, yes, I'd like a cup of tea."

"No trouble." He turned and shouted towards an open door.

"Sergeant-Major! Would you get Bryan Forbes a cup of tea?"

I stiffened in my seat. This was the crunch. However eccentric officers might be, there was no question of senior NCOs making cups of tea for private soldiers. I tensed myself for the rabbit punch on the back of my neck. Sweat dripped down into my eyes. My steel helmet sat like a ton of lead on my throbbing head.

The blow never came. Instead a slim and youthful sergeant-major, sporting non-regulation-length hair and carefully tailored battledress, put his head round the door and said: "How many sugars?"

I was on my feet standing to attention by reflex action. "Two, sir."

"That's Sergeant-Major Hall," the commanding officer said with pride. "And do take your helmet off."

I sat down again and removed it. Sweat poured down my face. The commanding officer showed great concern.

"You look as though you've got a temperature, you know. Where're you going to spend the night?"

"Sir?"

"Have you got somewhere to go to?"

"How d'you mean, sir?"

"Somewhere to sleep?"

"I've got room in my place if you're stuck," the captain said.

"You mean I shan't be staying here, sir?"

"Oh, good lord, no. Nobody sleeps here. You get a London pass, you see. You merely have to report here."

"Well, I could go home, sir. Newbury Park."

"I think you ought to take leave," the commanding officer said.

"Not entitled to leave, sir."

The elegant Sergeant-Major Hall returned with a cup of tea and a biscuit in the saucer. "Hope you like it weak," he said.

"I was saying, Sergeant-Major, he ought to take leave. He's just come out of hospital."

"Disgraceful," the sergeant-major said. "They just don't care, do they?"

"Can we fix him up?"

"Course. Just on medical grounds alone."

"Now look here," the commanding officer said. "When you've had your tea we'll get you a taxi . . ."

"I can get him a taxi," the captain said.

"Take you to the station, you go home, get a good night's rest, and in the meantime the sergeant-major'll fix you up with some leave papers and a railway warrant. Where would you like to go?"

I said the first thing that came into my stunned mind. "Helston, Cornwall, sir."

"Right, well, we'll arrange that. You take a fortnight's leave, and if you don't feel well enough at the end of that, just ring in and we'll extend it. We've got nothing for you at the moment, so you won't be missing anything."

I thought: this is how the Gestapo work. They give you a cup of tea and a cigarette and tell you you're going home, and then they slam you in the kidneys. Either that or they were all three mad. The rest of the building appeared to be deserted. I was alone with three uniformed lunatics. I sipped my hot tea and kept my head down.

"Going to be great fun working with you," the captain said. "I'll nip downstairs and see if I can bribe a taxi." He disappeared.

"There are one or two interesting things coming up," the commanding officer said. "But you just take your time, get yourself fit, and then we'll talk about them."

"Yes. Thank you, sir."

A voice shouted from down below. "Got a taxi."

Sergeant-Major Hall came back and thrust some papers at me. "They're all in order," he said. "And I've put this phone number on the back of your warrant. Don't lose it." He picked up my pack and rifle and helmet and started for the staircase. The commanding officer gave me a paternal smile.

"Have a nice leave."

"Thank you, sir." I couldn't salute without a helmet or cap, but I brought my heels together, did a smart about-turn and followed the sergeant-major.

The captain was waiting at the kerbside with the taxi. My kit was deposited inside and the door held open for me.

"I'll wait for you to phone," the sergeant-major said.

I hesitated. "Sir. Could you tell me what unit it is I've joined?"

38

"Oh, didn't you know? Army Theatre Unit. Stars in Battledress."

He closed the taxi door and I travelled into the night feeling better every second of the way.

Once I had recovered from the initial amazement at being posted to No 10 Upper Grosvenor Street, I quickly became bored and querulous. I was in uniform, denied some freedoms, but not a captive and not quite a soldier. The basic lunacy belonged to the War Office, for only officialdom could have brought into being an outfit run on army rules but with all the reasons for those rules removed. It was joke stuff, of course, and we quickly ensured that nothing went according to plan. The War Office instructions were that serving actors, properly administered, could and would provide entertainment of a suitable nature for the troops. The result was an absurdity.

In the first place it had been decided at top level that acting was not a suitable occupation for officers. Commissioned ranks could produce plays but not appear in them. Further, it was laid down that there should never be more than twelve personnel in any one production, such complement to include the stage management staff as well. This naturally limited the choice of material. All female roles had to be played by serving members of the ATS, and since there was only a handful of professional actresses in khaki, a recruiting drive was launched. The War Office held auditions. I am only sorry that I didn't get an opportunity to witness any of these sessions, for the idea of a group of desk-bound brass hats solemnly sifting through possible female candidates for an army theatre unit is in the best traditions of British farce.

We were allowed enormous freedom, which we cheerfully abused. Additional premises were commandeered for our rehearsals and before long there were a number of flourishing rackets in progress. We had the run of an enormous house on the corner of Grosvenor Square and another in Lower Sloane Street. Once the ball had been set in motion it rapidly got out of control. Recruits flooded in. There was a variety section which included Sergeant Harry Secombe, Terry-Thomas, Charlie Chester and many other soon-to-be-famous names. It was an open secret that most of them were appearing, quite illegally, in West End cabaret in the evenings. The legitimate actors, myself included, spent abortive weeks rehearsing unsuitable plays. At a given moment these were deemed to be in a state of readiness, and we would then give a dress rehearsal in front of "referees" from the War Office. In the majority of cases official approval was withheld, the cast read the verdict in standing orders the following morning and started rehearsing a different play.

Since there were so many different regiments represented in our ranks, it was the custom to identify them on pay parades. A truly amazing assortment, we would form up in the street and be called to the pay table on the sidewalk. Poor Sergeant-Major Hall had the unhappy public task of reading out the names. The whole operation was something of a charade and passing spectators would be greeted with the unmilitary spectacle of Sergeant Harry Secombe blowing kisses as he received his money, tripping on his way back to the ranks, where he was given applause and then, when the next man stepped up, letting rip with one of his famed *Goon Show* raspberries. Most of us sported long hair, every battledress had been tailor-made (those in the wardrobe department supplemented their pay with bespoke service) and several were collector's items.

Some hint of what was going on must have percolated through to the War Office because a new adjutant arrived, stiff-necked and glaring, who immediately announced sweeping changes and a general tightening up of discipline. Terry-Thomas had to cancel a few cabarets and actually show his teeth at headquarters, there was a rush to unearth ordinary issue battle-dress and a supply of Blanco was doled out by the scenic section. For a few days the entire unit tried to give their impressions of the regular army. The adjutant established his desk in the front hall so that he could personally check everybody entering and leaving the building, and this ultimately proved his undoing.

By this time, of course, certain productions had been passed fit for human consumption and we had units departing to various theatres of war. These were given special passing out parades by the adjutant and sternly lectured on codes of behaviour. He was determined, he said, to stamp out any criminal activities and there was to be no black-marketeering. It was common knowledge that a tin of coffee could command a small fortune in the recently liberated parts of France and Germany, and the adjutant had somehow deduced that the property baskets were leaving Upper Grosvenor Street laden with high quality beans. "This evil practice will cease forth-with!" he shouted, "as will the various sexual perversions peculiar to your profession. It is an offence under the Army Code for any male serving soldier to cohabit with a female member on active service. It is an even greater offence for two members of the same sex to dirty the King's uniform in the act of buggery. Do I make myself clear?"

By some mischance a certain Sergeant Eric Whittle was absent from parade when these edicts were given out. He was shortly to leave for Germany in charge of a unit and had made his plans accordingly. So one day the adjutant was sitting behind his desk in the lobby when a lorry drew up outside and two very obvious spivs in civilian clothes sauntered into the building.

"Yes? What can I do for you?" the adjutant said.

"You got a Sergeant Whittle 'ere, 'ave you?" one of the spivs said.

"We have such a man in the establishment, yes."

"Right. Sign 'ere then."

A grubby delivery note was put on the desk. "Against number seven. Two hundredweight of coffee. Where d'you want it?"

The adjutant never recovered from this and shortly afterwards vanished as mysteriously as he had appeared. Life quickly went back to normal.

Bryan's early acting career and love of books, followed by post-war film appearances which included *The Wooden Horse* and *The Colditz Story* was just a curtain-raiser for what was to come. It was not long before he turned his hand to screenwriting for such films as *Cockleshell Heroes*, *I Was Monty's Double* and *The League of Gentlemen* in which he also appeared. He directed *Whistle Down the Wind*, *The L-Shaped Room*, *Seance on a Wet Afternoon* and *King Rat* in Hollywood. And who could forget his delightful production of *The Slipper and the Rose*? His writing and directing have been divided between Britain and America and include television and the theatre, and an output of books and contributions to several periodicals of varying substance. His autobiography, as mentioned above, is an interesting and amusing insight into his life, much of which he has shared with his attractive wife, actress Nanette Newman, and two daughters. I wonder if West Ham secondary school knew what immense enthusiasm and talents they were unleashing on the entertainment world when he finished his schooling there?

'Ats off to the ATS

Janet Brown

I toured with Stars in Battledress after the Normandy landings in 1944. Certainly putting on a show over there was a very different business from stage work at home.

The first time I worked to the troops, it felt very strange to appear in the middle of a large field, on two table-tops laid flat for a stage. All the troops sat round on the grass, and we had to make our entrance on to the so-called stage from the back of a truck – it was the truck we travelled in all the time with our kit and our props. And as we did three shows a day, often starting at the odd hour of ten in the morning, you can guess just how many times we got in and out of that truck.

From Normandy we went up into France proper. We gave most of our shows in fields, but sometimes we played in an old hall or a factory, and then there'd usually be plenty of shrapnel lying about the stage, and dust

41

an inch thick. I'd sometimes, when we worked alfresco, have to hang my mirror on the branch of a tree and dress with a blanket round me. It's never exactly easy to wriggle into a costume entangled with a blanket, and it was just a bit harder because there happened to be a tremendous lot of wasps about. I wonder if you can imagine the job I had trying to glamorise myself while coping with the blanket and fending off the wasps. Washing was about as bad – we had nothing to wash in but biscuit tins. I remember the first time I shampooed my hair in one.

Still, we kept moving forward, I with my sheets and blankets under my arm, all prepared to settle down for the night wherever was most convenient.

One day they sent a jeep for me. I thought this was grand, and got in gaily, but I didn't realise I'd fifty miles to go over the roughest, dustiest road I've ever travelled. When we reached our destination my face, my hair, and my clothes were white with dust. There was nothing for it but the biscuit box again. I got clean somehow and stepped on to my tabletop once more. Three thousand lads were waiting for us patiently, and they were such a terrific audience that the dust and the jeep and the journey all seemed well worth while.

And then that night the weather changed – dust became mud. It started to rain. It kept on raining. We watched desperately because if the show went on we'd get soaked – there was no shelter. However, the rain kept pouring down, and the lads kept pouring into the field. So we played to them. They at least had their gas capes to keep parts of them dry.

Next day we simply had to get a place under cover, and we happened to hear of an old factory the Germans had occupied not long before. I'll never forget my first sight of it. I honestly didn't know where on earth the troops were going to sit. But trust the troops! They piled in and planted themselves on the derelict machinery, on the rafters, on sandbags on the floor, and those who couldn't get in stuck their heads through the broken windows. Of course, we'd no lighting or stage settings of any sort at all, but the audience didn't care. They made it pretty plain how much they enjoyed the show. No wonder – it was their first break since D-Day.

We went on through France, we went then through Belgium, and at last into Holland – and winter. The first time we went to give a show in Holland we were travelling in the back of an army three-tonner, and we got lost for several hours. Everyone was by now freezing cold. We got to our destination about nine o'clock at night, and I still don't know how that show went on. My hands were so numb with the cold I could hardly manage to get into my costume. The days of the wasp menace seemed like a lovely dream. No words can give you any idea of that bitter cold in the Netherlands.

I can look back now and remember the dust and mud of Normandy, the thrill of reaching Brussels, and the cold of Holland. Understandably it's something I'll never forget but it was pretty good to come home and see a real fire again and, even better, eat some of my mother's plain well-cooked Scottish food.

This is part of an interview Janet gave on radio when she returned from France.

After her demob from the forces Janet Brown was soon making a name for herself in radio and theatre work, and in more recent years almost became "Mrs Thatcher" with her marvellous impression of the Iron Lady. Janet has worked all over the world doing her immaculate impressions of all the big stars. She was married to the late Peter Butterworth, one of the funniest men I ever worked with. Their two lovely children are a credit to them both.

Margaret Courtenay

When Margaret Courtenay was first called up into the ATS she was sent to a training camp in Wrexham, North Wales, along with three thousand other girls from every walk of life. They slept twenty-six to a hut, and endured tough army discipline from the start. During her initial training there the fifth anniversary of the ATS became imminent, and a volunteer was called for to organise a show to celebrate the event. Margaret volunteered for the rather daunting task and was, along with the Junior Commander, Lucas Tooth, put in charge of producing a big show.

As luck would have it George Black was present during the performance, and Margaret was introduced to him. Another George, Melachrino, the popular conductor and arranger, brought his band along to play for the show, and a very young Janet Brown entertained with her impressions. This was not a case of fools rushing in where angels might fear to tread, as Margaret's early life in Cardiff, South Wales, had trained her for just such an undertaking. Her mother was an actress with the BBC Repertory Company on radio, and was a founder member of Cardiff Little Theatre. She saw to it that her daughter took dancing lessons, and also singing under Madame Clara Novello (Ivor's mother). Small parts with the Little Theatre followed, and Margaret learned every aspect of theatre and radio work at an early age.

After going on several training courses that didn't lead to much, Margaret found herself sent to the War Office to work for the

Overseas Recorded Broadcast Service. The powers that be had finally got the message that being a filing clerk in an office was a waste of talent, and had decided to put previous theatre and radio experience to good use. The posting was more easily achieved because of that first concert she helped organise in Wrexham at the start of her training.

Having obtained a "sleeping-out pass", and being with her aunts in London, reporting for work at the War Office every morning, Margaret would find herself despatched to the Paris Cinema, Lower Regent Street, or the Criterion Theatre, Piccadilly Circus, to compère with the Melachrino Orchestra and do the links for the programmes. These were recorded broadcasts for the forces, and the audience too was made up of serving men and women.

The Army Education Department decided to form a drama company under the auspices of the Army Bureau of Current Affairs, to present in the form of playlets the news of the day. It was an old idea brought up to date. What better way to impart news and information than in dramatic form? The scriptwriters worked alongside the actors and, with a basic plot, changed the dialogue according to what was happening in the news.

The unit took the playlets around to various camps and barracks with all the necessary gear for staging a show packed into a two-ton lorry: lights, costumes, rostra, tabs, make-up and so on, using the Duke of York's Barracks, Chelsea, as their base.

When this unit split up later to go to Germany, Italy and the Middle East, Margaret was transferred to a drama unit of Stars in Battledress doing *The Wind and the Rain*, first in Gibraltar, then on to Naples, and up and down the length and breadth of Italy, playing in opera houses, now designated "garrison theatres".

In Venice on one occasion they had to wait for the tide to rise in order to get the scenery to the theatre by gondola! Following on into Austria, to the lovely city of Vienna, which had been very badly bombed. There the company met an old wigmaker who had been with the State Opera and had managed to survive in the ruins for five years, just living on scraps. He offered to make all the artistes' wigs, moustaches and beards, all for a bar of soap!

After touring Europe with *The Wind and the Rain* (Richard Pascoe played one of the leads) Margaret returned to England to be demobbed. It was now 1946, and the few clothing coupons that were issued to the women leaving the army in lieu of a "demob suit" were rather inadequate to provide for the cruel winter of early 1947, one of the coldest on record.

Fortunately, Margaret was soon engaged by a repertory company at Bexhill-on-Sea, and it was while she was there that she came up to town to audition for Stratford-upon-Avon. She was in company with, among others, John Warner, Donald Sinden and John Schofield, and as she recalls, "We got paid the astronomical sum of £8 per week, and I played four small parts and understudied thirteen others. We had a 'forty years on' party recently and we all got together, and I must say, on the whole, we didn't look too bad!"

Stella Moray

Stella Moray, or as she was born, Stella Morris, joined the Stars in Battledress unit when she came to the notice of the Black brothers, Captain George and Alfred, while singing with a divisional band in Chester. She had, prior to that, been performing with the Royal Ordnance Corps band in Donnington in Derbyshire where she was based for a time after her call-up into the ATS in August 1941.

It was very tiring at Donnington singing with the band because we had late nights but I still had to be early on parade next morning with the other girls.

By the time Stella had been told to report to the Stars in Battledress unit in London she had reached the rank of sergeant, but promotion didn't last long.

An officious officer stripped me of my stripes because he had seen me taking photographs with my little old-fashioned camera of one of the girls I was friendly with, in front of a tank. You would have thought I was photographing something highly secret the way he carried on. I just didn't think.

However, stripeless, I came to London and at the Stars in Battledress headquarters in Upper Grosvenor Street I was interviewed by Captain Alexander, and I also met his assistant Phyl Rounce for the first time.

Stella passed the audition and was posted to Battersea to await instructions. Her reputation as a singer had gone before her, so in the meantime she was asked to join the George Melachrino Orchestra which included Frank Chatsfield, another musician whose career took off after the war. Stella sang with the Mela-chrino Orchestra in a radio programme designed for the forces called *Merry-Go-Round** and broadcast weekly. This title was used later to introduce the three service radio comedy pro-grammes directly post-war, *Stand Easy* (the army), *Waterlogged Spa* (the navy), and *Much Binding in the Marsh* (the air force).

Almost my first assignment on active service with Stars in Battledress was a posting to the Middle East, first based in Cairo and Alexandria and then following up after Montgomery's Eighth Army clear-up of Rommel's forces, with shows in Mersa Matruh, Benghazi and Tripoli. I'll never forget sitting in a broken-down old house in Benghazi watching Laurence Olivier's film of *Henry V*: it all seemed quite bizarre.

Stella then came home for some leave before being sent to the Far East in a unit headed by comedian Reg Varney. Their SIB show was called *Jamboree*. They had played various military venues in the UK before going abroad, including some theatre dates, and I have seen a newspaper crit of that show which is excellent, and in particular it says, "It was Stella 'Morris' who really took the honours of the evening. Her full-blooded flam-boyance and engaging personality took the house by storm!" Well, you can't do better than that!

The beginning of the tour of the Far East in 1945 started with a very long air flight to Singapore lasting a whole week, huddled up in an Avro York aircraft, but all very exciting.

At one point on the tour Stella and the two other girls in the show were separated from the men and billeted in the infamous Changi Barracks, part of the notorious Changi Jail where the British soldiers had been held by the Japanese. "Those were pretty rough 'digs'." The unit also played in Hong Kong, Sumatra, and Java. "We finally finished the tour and were homeward-bound and demob."

After seeing her parents in her home town of Birmingham, Stella came back to London with her £55 demob gratuity and a determination to make the professional theatre her career. The first thing she did on arrival in London (after finding digs) was to enrol in the Lucy Clayton model agency.

* Called *Mediterranean Merry-Go-Round* later in the book.

I felt I needed a few deportment lessons after all the square-bashing in the army. It didn't last long. Balancing a book on my head I fell down some stairs.

One day, Stella was walking down Charing Cross Road with a friend when they saw a big sign on some offices saying "Dean Moray – Theatrical Agent". "My friend said, 'That would be a good stage name for you – Moray,'" so from that moment on Stella Morris became Stella Moray.

She fairly quickly obtained her first job in *Belinda Fair* at the Casino, then followed that with *Wild Violets* at the Stoll Theatre in the company of Ian Carmichael, Allen Christie, and David Croft (he gets everywhere – not to mention being producer/director of TV's *Dad's Army*, *It Ain't Half Hot, Mum*, *Hi-de-Hi*, *'Allo 'Allo* and *You Rang, M'Lord?*).

In recent years her big West End successes have included *Funny Girl* with Barbra Streisand at the Prince of Wales Theatre and starring in *Annie* at the Victoria Palace.

Phyllis Rounce

Phyllis Rounce was a bit of a rebel at school, preferring the playing fields to the classroom, and when the time came for her to leave it was difficult to tell who was the most relieved, she or the school! However, her mother insisted she take a secretarial course, and that stood her in good stead for her first job, which was for the BBC. She was put to work, much to her horror, in the Engineering Department, but soon managed to get posted to the variety section at St George's Hall, then opposite Broadcasting House, which was more her cup of tea. With her keen flair for spotting talent (that was to prove so useful later on) she soon found herself helping with variety shows and booking the artistes.

When the blitz came in 1940 the whole department, having been bombed out in the capital, were moved to new headquarters in Bristol, where shows such as *ITMA* and *Palace of Varieties* kept the nation laughing in spite of the harrowing times. The blitz followed them to Bristol and once more the department was on the move. This time to Bangor in North Wales.

It was while she was in Bangor that she decided to join up. Although her job in broadcasting was a reserved occupation she was determined to see some action, and went along to the ATS camp at Wrexham and signed up. Because of her radio background she was soon posted to London and the Guards at Knightsbridge Barracks. As Phyllis recalls, "They moved the horses out and the ATS in!"

Soon she was working in the Army Centre of Music, just behind the Albert Hall, and her CO gave her the job of organising a show to take to civilian audiences to raise money for army charities. They played all over the country and raised a lot of money. On one occasion the unit was playing in and around Newcastle for a time, and it was there a very high-ranking officer in the ATS mentioned that Army Welfare at the War Office were looking for more staff. In Phyllis's words:

I rang up the War Office and got through to the captain in charge. I said, "I've heard you've a vacancy for an officer, and I would like to be considered for the job. I've been doing this and that, etc."

His reply was, and very loud I might add, "I'm not having any bloody women on my staff, I've had enough trouble with women in the army, so don't come anywhere near me!"

So I put on my best officer voice and explained that I'd had a lot of experience putting on shows, and his reply was, "I don't care what experience you've had, I've had enough, I'm up to here with women! And don't think you'll do any good coming down to London, because I won't see you!"

However, I caught the night train to London from Newcastle and went straight to the War Office, and found the right department and sat on a chair outside his door. In comes the captain and practically trips over me and asks rather rudely what I wanted.

"I've come for the job, sir," I replied.

"My God! You're not that bloody woman who phoned me, are you? Oh well, you'd better come in then!"

This was Captain Bill Alexander, later colonel, and I went into the office and gradually wore him down. He took me to lunch and told me I'd got the job for having the nerve to do all this.

Bill Alexander had served in the First World War in the Horse Artillery and went all through Ypres and the Somme, and in the Second World War found himself, after a stint of training new recruits in the intricacies of artillery, at the War Office in Army Welfare.

Phyllis's first job as assistant to Alexander was to work out the routes the shows would take in France, Italy or North Africa for the Stars in Battledress units who were following our liberating forces. Later on Alexander took over from George Black and was running the production side as well as administration from the offices in Upper Grosvenor Street.

On their demobilisation both Bill and Phyllis decided that the only thing they knew anything about was the entertainment business, so they decided to set up an office together as an agency. They met up with an American who was in the film business and he suggested that he would look after the American side. That is how International Artistes was born.

Having no capital or assets, except an American forces type-writer with a label on the back stating "**Not to be removed from American Air Force Base**", they rented the first floor of a bombed-out building in Irving Street, near Leicester Square. It had no windows in, no floor covering and no furniture.

So I sat on the floor with my typewriter and said to Bill, "What do we do now?"

He said, "I'm buggered if I know!"

And that was how we started.

Soon some of the Stars in Battledress boys and girls who had been demobbed went to see them, and bit by bit work was found for them in what shows could be got together, with little or no resources. Television was just starting up again at Alexandra Palace, so Phyllis got together an album of photographs of the artistes on their books and trundled it up to "Ally Pally" and knocked on the doors of the TV producers, trying to get work for her artistes.

One such young hopeful was Terry-Thomas. He lived in a small wooden hut in South Kensington called the Cowshed and it was crammed full of souvenirs and stuff brought back from his trips abroad in Stars in Battledress. Terry's accent, "frightfully frightfully", was used to good advantage, and got him in anywhere. He was the first artiste handled by International Artistes to get into television, and his first big break came in *Piccadilly Hayride* at the Prince of Wales Theatre, the show that catapulted comedian Sid Field to fame.

Terry was doing his radio DJ spot about the announcer who goes into the studio to do his record programme only to find there are no records to play. He then proceeded to impersonate all the well-known artistes of the day, with the tag of the act trying to impersonate the Luton Girls' Choir!

"*Right-o, I'll tell you what I'll do: I'll swap our second piano-tuner for one of your six comedians if you'll give me a written guarantee that he isn't a female impersonator.*"

Punch Publications Ltd

Phyllis also used to book acts to appear at the Nuffield Centre, just off the Strand, that wonderful service men's rest and recreation centre, complete with a small stage for shows. Many future comedians and TV personalities got their first break there in the weekly showcases: Frankie Howerd, Benny Hill, Charlie Drake, Ronnie Corbett, Steve Race, even Bill Pertwee!

Phyl is still in business with International Artistes, giving her immense experience to today's entertainers.

Faith Brook

If someone is successful in their chosen profession it is often the case that their offspring are criticised for daring to follow in their footsteps.

In the case of actress Faith Brook it was rather the reverse, and criticism of another kind. Her father, Clive Brook, a very successful screen and stage actor on both sides of the Atlantic from the 1930s onwards, was taken to task for daring to send his daughter to America, where she had been brought up, to avoid the bombing of London during the Battle of Britain in 1940.

Faith, who was actually born in England, had begun her stage career at an early age and eventually enrolled as a student at the Royal Academy of Dramatic Art. It was just after this that her father made the decision to send her back to California.

Many children were being sent away to the countryside from our major cities at that time to avoid the bombing but because Faith was sent to America it was considered some sort of crime on her father's part. She did come back here in 1942 and immediately got a job in the theatre in a play called *Aren't Men Beasts?* with those two great farceurs Robertson Hare and Alfred Drayton. They opened at the Brixton Theatre in south London and almost at once the press started a campaign of almost libellous proportions against her father, which naturally also affected Faith herself. One paper stated, "Faith Brook deserted the country in 1940 and has now come back into the good life of the theatre without first paying her dues." The matter even reached the Palace of Westminster where, would you believe, questions were asked in the House of Commons at great length about her father's actions. Needless to say Clive Brook was not too happy about it all. Faith talked to me about that period.

After *Aren't Men Beasts?* had finished I applied to join ENSA. However, on the same day I received my acceptance there my call-up papers for the army arrived. Incidentally, I had earlier tried to join the Wrens but was told it could be difficult without some influence in certain places, whatever that meant. Had the past events had some bearing on this? I asked myself. Anyway, now I was in the army, the ATS, which didn't appeal to me greatly, and the ironic thing was that shortly after joining up I was asked to take part in a publicity campaign for the War Office to enlist more recruits for the ATS.

I was then sent for training to a motorised unit and I had to take tests for driving heavy vehicles. I passed all the tests and once I was proficient it appeared I was to be on the move again, this time to the Central Pool of Artistes' Stars in Battledress company.

Faith Brook was certainly becoming a versatile soldier, to say

51

the least. It was not long after this that Major Murray MacDonald began running a garrison theatre at Salisbury in Wiltshire and subsequently picked a group of SIB personnel, including Faith, Wilfrid Hyde White and Kenneth Connor, to appear in a production he intended to do of Terence Rattigan's *Flare Path*, with Wilfrid playing the group captain.

We toured for a year with the play all over Southern Command doing one-night stands and whole weeks, and as Stan Hall has mentioned, we also did a performance for Queen Mary and members of the RAF Regiment at the Duke of Beaufort's country home, Badminton in Gloucestershire, where the regiment was stationed. I remember we had a very good meal after the performance.

It was all a very strange time really, because the army was keeping an eye on us, insisting that we be on parade at seven in the morning, with our hair two inches above the collar and no nail varnish, and we'd probably got in to the barracks where we were stationed at six after a performance somewhere. So we'd scrub our nails, pin up the hair and dash on parade. Eventually we sorted things out and the army became more lenient.

Our first overseas tour started in Italy and we were there and later in Greece for about eight months in the latter part of 1943 and part of 1944. The problem in Italy was the complete lack of co-ordination between ENSA, who were routing our company, and the army. Confusion seemed to mount because the venues weren't sure who was coming or when. We would arrive somewhere and they would say, "Oh, we thought you were coming last week", or "We didn't expect you for another couple of weeks." I must say it was a bit frustrating because to do the shows we sometimes had to travel very long distances.

We had one horrifying journey when we were stationed in Naples. The word got around that Basil Dean, who was the boss of ENSA back in Britain, was coming out to Naples to check on how all the trips were going.

There were about sixty ENSA companies in Naples in 1943 and 1944 not doing anything at all, and Basil Dean was going to be arriving any minute. All hell broke loose, and Colonel Patrick sent companies of ENSA and SIB units out with little or no organised intent, just to get them out of the way. Our unit was sent to Rome for a while although we didn't do any work and then we were rushed up to Florence, spent the day there, did a U-turn and went all the way back to Naples again. Twenty-four hours later we were on a lorry bound for Bari, a journey right across to the Adriatic coast where there were enormous concentrations of troops.

We set off in a convoy, and eventually got to a place called Puglia and it was completely snowed under and we realised we were stranded. We sat in the back of the lorry for thirteen hours with no food, freezing to death and unable to move because the snow chains we had with us wouldn't fit the lorry's tyres. Finally they got another truck and drove us back to Naples where the sergeant in charge of the unit was Terence de Marney; he and his brother Derek were both well-known stage actors.

When we got back to Naples we were deposited in a fine building that Nigel Patrick, the Lt.-Colonel in charge of ENSA in Italy, had as his headquarters and I remember we were standing at the bottom of this grand staircase waiting for him. He came out on to the top of the stairs and we could see the glow of a lovely fire coming from his room in the background, and we were freezing cold from our journey. Nigel stood there very nonchalantly as though he was playing in a Noël Coward comedy. He said, "Oh, you're back, are you?" and I blew my top, telling him in no uncertain manner how we felt about our dreadful trip. I was really pretty rude about his stupid organisation, so much so he put me on a charge. I suppose as a private in the army it was a crime to talk to an officer like that, but I was really upset at the time. In the end I apologised and he forgave me, but I did say I'd been provoked because of sheer exhaustion.

We eventually got back to Bari when the weather changed, but we were stuck there for weeks and weeks. It did give us time to visit a lot of lovely places such as Rimini, Riccione and Termoli, all down the Adriatic coast. This area of the Adriatic had housed thousands of British prisoners from the North African campaign until the Italian surrender. The places were empty of people and the only sign of war I saw was the remains of the bombardment of Monte Cassino, and that was awful.

When we were in Greece our entertainments officers were Hugh Hunt and William Devlin who were most helpful in making our stay a comfortable one. We were made temporary officers while we were there, enabling us to use the Officers' Mess, which was very nice. Hugh and William seemed to take a liking to me, and when the war was over we met up again when they formed the first season at the Bristol Old Vic in 1946. While I was there I joined up once more with Kenneth Connor.

After this I was invited to go to New York with Bill Devlin to do a Bernard Shaw play called *You Never Can Tell*. I stayed there until 1947 and came back to London to do a season at the Old Vic. Shortly after that I met an American in London, married him and went back with him to America. I worked for four years in New York doing stage work and live television, and then came back once again to London. I've been back to America on the odd trip or two to see friends since then, but that's all.

I can really say I've enjoyed all the various things I've done, the theatre, television and films. Productions like *Irish RM*, *Sea Wolves*, *All Passions Spent*, *I Thought They Died Years Ago* and *North Sea Hijack* with Roger Moore and James Mason in which I played a lady Prime Minister. I loved playing Gertrude in *Hamlet* with Ian McKellen and recently I did a Margaret Dewheart play for the Fringe and I enjoyed that. I'm not too keen on doing revivals of plays now, there doesn't seem much point. I like trying out new pieces. Mind you, I'd love to do more Shakespeare, and I think I can still enjoy most things, as long as it is done professionally.

It was a pleasure to talk to Faith in her very pretty house in south London. She obviously loves plants, and her small but originally designed back garden is packed with flowers and shrubs of every description. She herself is a most engaging person with an amusing and quite delightful smile; a smile that I am sure has captivated and will continue to captivate her audiences.

Frances Tanner

The wartime experiences of Frances Tanner laid the foundation for the success she enjoyed with her sister Stella in the post-war years. As youngsters the girls were always entering talent contests, doing the American "Andrews Sisters"-type songs, sometimes at the very large State Theatre in Kilburn, north London. Frances then decided to join the ATS, while Stella went to work at the Air Ministry, so the budding duo was temporarily disbanded.

Frances spent her first few weeks at a training camp near Aldershot and on her first night in the army she was in a hut with about twenty-five other girls.

One of the girls in the hut recognised me from one of the shows Stella and I had done at the State, Kilburn, and told the other girls. She even remembered my name, because Tanner is my real name and there we were, all in bed with the lights out, and she said, "Will you sing us a song?" and I said, "Oh, no, I'd feel silly," but they all started saying, "Go on, give us a song," so I did. I sang "I'll Be Seeing You", and at the end of it they were all crying, it was their first night away from home. Lots of them had never been away from home before, including myself.

I did all sorts of different courses in the army and it was very good for me because I went all over England learning different things. I went to Command Headquarters at Chester and when I was there I went in for a talent contest on my own at the Odeon Cinema and I won it.

When I was in Chester I met a bloke called Ronnie Hanbury. He was a scriptwriter, and together we put on quite a few shows. He was in the Royal Corps of Signals, and he was terribly ambitious and he fired me with ambition. Then somebody suggested that I go into Stars in Battledress and said that if I applied to Captain George Black I might stand a chance of getting in. I thought, Why not have a go? so I did. Before I was accepted into Stars in Battledress I was to become a Corporal Physical Training Instructor (PTI) and was sent to Donnington. I didn't do any shows while I was there but eventually I got a call to go down to Chelsea Barracks to meet Captain George Black and he sent me to a lady for costume fittings. After that he sent me to meet Arthur Young, who was a very famous pianist and band leader in the West End.. I went up to his flat in Knightsbridge, and he was in civilian clothes, although he was in the army with the rank of corporal or sergeant, I'm not sure which. He was living in Knightsbridge with this lady right at the top of a lovely block of flats and it was beautiful with a piano and all the trimmings. I'd never been in a place like that before. He played Gershwin's "Summertime" and asked me to sing it, which I did. I remember it was very, very high, and he was really impressed.

The next thing that happened was we're back at the Duke of York's Barracks, Chelsea, and I'm being introduced to Biff Byfield who was a terribly debonair musician. He and Arthur Young were both playing in the West End at the time. Although they were both in the army nothing interfered with their "outside" job. Others I met at the Duke of York's were Peter Cavanagh, the radio impersonator (one of his superb impressions was General Montgomery, brilliant) and Wilfrid Hyde White, and we were all to get together and do a show, create a little unit with the band and a compère. I was very impressed with Wilfrid Hyde White, whom I'd never met or even heard of before, and there he was, a private dressed as an officer. He had a silk shirt on that he had had made in Savile Row, and an army officer's uniform made with special material by his tailor, and he was just an ordinary private. He looked so elegant, and he was "old boying" it all over the place. He was more like an officer than an officer. He never seems to have been any different. Wilfrid was quite a young man then, but no different than you see him in the movies, maybe a little greyer, that's all.

The great thing was we were a completely different bunch of people but we all got on like a house on fire. I suppose really they were all delighted not to be handling guns and things. We started off by entertaining ack-ack batteries around the London area, but I didn't stay with them very long. I was to be sent abroad to Normandy with Biff Byfield, a pianist who was one of the most original fellows I'd met. He was a sergeant and terribly charming. We had a little dance band and had Wally Stewart, later with the Nitwits Crazy Band, as the comedian, a magician, and an Italian who was to sing romantic songs with me. He was always looking for a *chambre*, with a female of course, and a weird pianist called Tony Spurgeon who really needed looking after. I was the only girl and I was to sing all the standard songs, and I remember when I went to join this company, just before we left for France Captain George Black gave me a word of advice. "Always carry a 'housewife' with you, because you never know when one of the fellows wants a button sewing on his shirt." Very good advice, but not much help to my career.

One of the things that I had to do before leaving for France was to go to the Theatre Royal, Drury Lane, and meet George Melachrino who had an enormous orchestra which he conducted, and they were all musicians who were in the army or air force. I recognised George Melachrino who was awfully nice to me, and it was there that I met Janet Brown and a girl called Sally Rogers who was a real beauty, an actress and a real pin-up girl. I'd never met Sally before, but I knew Janet who was terribly talented and did impressions.

I was sent to Drury Lane to get together with the orchestra, because George Melachrino was putting together some special recordings to be sent to the British troops in the UK and overseas. I did a couple of songs with the orchestra. I'd only brought two orchestrations with me, and George asked me if there was anything else I could do, so I said I had done some harmony singing with my sister Stella, but she wasn't in the army, she was working at the Air Ministry in the typing pool. He said get her along, so I phoned her up and she tore down to Drury Lane in her lunch-hour. They had a recording studio in what used to be one of the theatre's bars so we rehearsed very quickly with a small rhythm group and we did about four routines, "Alexander's Ragtime Band" and "St Louis Blues" among them, and they were very pleased with the recordings. My sister was pretty surprised by the whole episode because it was all so unexpected and she wasn't prepared, but it didn't take long to get the old vocal harmony blend going again. We'd never worked with a microphone in a studio before, and it was quite an experience.

After this I was off to France where I joined the show just behind the front line in Normandy, and I can remember the experience of driving in an army truck over those roads, full of potholes, and clutching a handful of letters I'd been given for the boys. It was very important this, I felt like a postman for the fighting lads. They were delighted to see me because of the letters. It was all new to me in France, it really opened my eyes.

I remember being approached by a French lesbian in the street and I didn't know what she was talking about. I saw shops selling brassières that I'd never seen before, with a sort of bottom bit with tape over the top so that the breasts could poke through.

We had to think for ourselves because the SIB units were allowed to go up to the front line if there was a garrison or fighting unit who needed entertaining. This was the difference between us and ENSA shows because if they had been near the front and happened to be captured, being civilians they could have been shot as spies. I think a few solo artistes did get near to the fighting areas but I think that was their personal decision.

Not long after this we went to Holland, and being the only girl in the unit I couldn't be billeted at an army camp with the men, so I was sent to a civilian home. There were a lot of people in the family and the only one who could converse a little in English was a young girl, the daughter aged about eleven. The idea was for me to eat with the troops and just sleep in this house. When I arrived at their home they were all huddled around the radio listening to the BBC. It was *ITMA* in English and they couldn't understand it but they all laughed when the studio audience laughed.

The young daughter of the house used to follow me everywhere, and I asked her, "What did you have for breakfast this morning?" and she said, "Some bread and some tea," so I said, "And what do you have for your lunch?" and she said, "Some bread and some tea." "And what are you going to have tonight?" I asked and she burst into tears. They had no food left. It was a big family of people and even now just thinking about it I feel awful. So I went to our army cookhouse and said to the cook there, "Look, you've got to give me some food, whatever you can, there are a lot of people starving where I'm staying." I know we weren't supposed to do this as it was against the law to take food out of the camp but I just bunged it all inside my battledress and put on my greatcoat, filling that as well, and went back to the house. I put it all on the table and they were all crying and they ate the food immediately.

Many years later, after the war, Stella and I went to Holland to do some broadcasts for Radio Hilversum and these people in the family remembered my name, Frances Tanner of the Tanner Sisters, and they came to see us at Hilversum. They had remembered me and brought me presents of Delft pottery and said they'd never forgotten me. It was quite a moment, I can tell you.

After we left France, Belgium and Holland our unit went on to Gibraltar, Italy and North Africa and then it was back to England. Back in the UK I toured with Terry-Thomas and we went all over Scotland and the Orkneys, playing to army units. Terry was a corporal then and he already had his cigarette-holder, his eventual trade mark, and was doing his first act which was a very funny parody of a BBC disc jockey with everything going wrong where he had to ad lib his way through the programme. The troops loved him. We had done a tremendous amount of travelling with the SIB company, all of it in just over a year, and the majority of shows that we had done were one-night stands.

When I was demobbed I did some auditions for the BBC Light Programme at the Aeolian Hall, Bond Street, and the first show I did was called *Breakfast Club*, which was an early morning show, a sort of magazine programme with music. Because of this I got some dates in the theatre in variety. Then my sister Stella and I started working together again and we got into a hillbilly-type show with the BBC produced by David Miller, a Canadian. We did quite a few programmes for him and then did some variety in the theatres as a duo and we were kept really busy. I must say I never did sit down and wait for something to happen, even in the army.

I've always thought you should help yourself as much as you can, and if the opportunities are there you should try and make the most of them.

The Tanner Sisters became a popular top line act not only in the theatre but also on radio and records.

Charlie Chester

By 1942 the title Stars in Battledress was being generally quoted, even though service men and women were still inclined to think of the entertainment units as from the Central Pool of Artistes, which of course they were, but it was agreed by pretty well everyone that SIB was a more appropriate and explanatory name.

By 1944 our own show was in France on D-Day plus six. We had originally landed at Luc-sur-Mer, a seaside resort in Normandy. All the houses in the area seemed empty so we took over one or two and made ourselves comfortable while awaiting orders. We hadn't been there long before a provost-sergeant came along and said, "Some of these houses may have been mined and booby-trapped by the Germans before they left." We didn't wait to find out, we packed up and were out of there pretty quick. We found out later the sergeant was right – weren't we lucky?

Our unit worked its way through northern France making for the Dutch border. Although the German army was in retreat there was still plenty of fighting going on, and it was all too easy to get behind enemy lines and not know it.

There were a lot of near misses during the confusion of the liberation of France. At times it was very difficult to tell friend from foe. Once when I was guarding all the theatrical props and mini piano a bullet whizzed past my ear and embedded itself in the door inches from where I'd been standing. Whether it was a German left behind the British lines or Free French doing a bit of private liberating I never knew, but I treasure the bullet to this day, now used as a paperweight, as "the one that wasn't meant for me".

Towards the end of the war we were entertaining in Holland and I remember one show in a Nissen hut with the lads sitting there all ready for action, blackened faces and bits of greenery in their helmets. While the show was going on a sergeant-major crept in and very quietly said, "You, you and you", and he repeated this two or three times, and each time another few soldiers got up and left. They were going out to one of the scores of little islands near where we were working to engage the German raiding parties. The Germans used to land on these islands and take a few prisoners after a brief encounter, and our lads had to go and sort them out and bring back a few German prisoners. After an hour or so you would see our lads coming back into the Nissen hut, and although we were performing we started counting them mentally and we saw there were eventually two or three empty places, and you feel "Oh hell, some haven't come back." It was a strange feeling, here we are cracking jokes and all that, and the lads laughing, and we realised this wasn't a party, it was still war.

In a few weeks Germany had practically collapsed; although peace had not been declared, it was just a matter of a cleaning-up operation. My unit had by now gone right up into Germany and then I was called home because all the armies of occupation would eventually need entertaining, and I was needed to help with getting more units together to go to all the fighting areas that would soon be liberated. I was put in charge of the scriptwriting section (I was always jotting down ideas even when we were moving about on the Continent) and they said, "Get cracking as quickly as you can because we're going to need material for the shows."

At the SIB HQ I started writing: gags, sketches and songs so I would be in advance of demands, as it were. At the same time I was working on the idea of a radio show I'd had when we were in Normandy and one day the BBC visited our HQ and said they were worried about the lack of an army version of their weekly service show *Mediterranean Merry-Go-Round*. They had an air force show, later to become *Much Binding in the Marsh* starring Kenneth Horne and Richard Murdoch and a navy production starring Eric Barker, his wife Pearl Hackney and Jon Pertwee, but the only army contribution at that time was the George Melachrino Orchestra. So up I get and say. "I've got an idea for a show, sir." Well, the BBC took up my idea and away they went. Then our colonel jumped in and said, "Any payment for the show must go to regimental funds and you, Chester, will have £2 a week for your expenses, food, taxis and so on."

Well, I knew the type of show I wanted and the people who I wanted in it so I thought if I'm going to do all the work I want to be the top man in it, and I don't want the army to take the money for it for ever more, so I thought of an idea. I did originally think of the title being *Panchinello on Parade* so I go and see the colonel [Alexander], later to become one of the best-known theatrical agents in London, and I said to him, "I will have a contract drawn up by a music publishing company, Victory Music, assigning all rights of the show to the War Office." The colonel was quite satisfied. I then rushed round to the BBC and said, "I've thought of a very good title for the show we discussed at the SIB HQ. I'd like to call it *Stand Easy*." The powers that be at the BBC thought it was a very good title so the outcome was that Colonel Alexander and the War Office now owned the rights to a show, *Panchinello on Parade*, that didn't exist but *Stand Easy* did.

I went on writing material for the Stars in Battledress shows until I was demobbed and then the BBC asked me whether I could do a civilian edition of *Stand Easy* to alternate with *Much Binding in the Marsh* and *Waterlogged Spa* (the naval show) and I said yes. We kept the same title for mine, *Stand*

Easy, and the lads who had done the army version, so we were soon up and running, and it quickly became as successful as the other two.

I was all for using publicity gimmicks in those days (well, if you've got a good product let people know about it!) so when I was demobbed I persuaded the demob centre assistant to let me take my time selecting my demob outfit, suit, hat, socks, tie, shirts, shoes, etc. While I was going round having a look at all the gear I dropped little cards into the pockets of all the suits. On one side it said, "Don't forget to listen to the Charlie Chester radio show *Stand Easy*," and on the other side, with a big printed thumb mark it said, "Beware the mark of Whippet Quick" (one of the regular characters I had created for the show). I also had handbills stuck up on the Underground railway saying, "Beware, Whippet Quick intends to enter your home." Some people took it seriously and were asking, "How can we protect our property from this Whippet Quick?"

Len Marten was the crime reporter who was "investigating" Whippet Quick, Ken Morris "murdering a song at the piano", and of course we had Arthur Haynes, and he introduced among other things a newcomer who I had actually met in SIB, "the voice of Frederick Ferrari". Fred Ferrari was an immediate sensation to the listening public along with the whole gang. We had our own noisy signature tune which also caught on. It went:

Ring that bell [ding ding], beat the drum [boom boom]
Sound that horn [toot toot], shoot that gun [bang bang],
Stand Easy and this you will know,
Is the Charlie Chester Show.

The show went from strength to strength, and we also took it into the theatre. We did a tour for Moss Empires (the biggest variety theatre chain in the country). We also did two very successful seasons at Blackpool, the first called *Sky High* and the second year *Mid-Summer Madness*. Both these shows were brought to the Palladium Theatre in London. They really were lavish shows, with twenty-four Tiller girls, eight ballet dancers, six show girls, several speciality acts, and of course the gang and me. I always felt a good gang show can go places. There was Bud Flanagan and the Crazy Gang, Ralph Reader with his crazy lot, Doctor Crock and his mad band of "Crackpots"!

Eventually the lads said they wanted to go their separate ways, which is understandable. Ken Morris, Arthur Haynes and Len Marten went on the variety circuits doing their own thing. Frederick Ferrari left the business entirely, and I went almost immediately into television doing a six-part half-hour series based on the character Educated Evans, the racetrack character. This went on for two years and then, after a lot of persuasion, the BBC agreed to let me do a give-away show on television which I called *Pot Luck*. The top prize then was an electric blanket, a good prize in the 1950s. It lasted five years and then I took it on a tour of the theatres.

It has been quite an extraordinary life when I look back: performing, writing music, and painting. Do you know I had a phone-call from the Chinese Ambassador once, who said he'd heard about my painting and would you believe he bought two of my horse paintings? It all seems a long time since my boy soprano yodelling days, but my goodness it has been fun!

Nick Nissen

Belfast-born Nick Nissen – though now into his eighties – has a very clear memory of his SIB service days. A comedy musician, and a very good one at that, Nick had spent several years touring the UK in variety shows with George Formby, Wee Georgie Wood and Tommy Trinder in *Laugh It Off.*

His calling-up papers caught up with him in 1942 when he was posted to the Royal Army Medical Corps depot at Crookham near Aldershot. Members of the Medical Corps also had to undergo conventional military training, and Nick Nissen became the best shot in the regiment. He was able to produce some entertainment once a week at Crookham and later his old friend Tommy Trinder contacted Captain George Black at SIB headquarters telling him he should get Nick into the new organisation that he (Black) had set up. When enquiries were made at Crookham, Black was told that Nissen had a very responsible job and couldn't be released. After further enquiries it came to light that the "important job" was in fact Inspector of Latrines!

When Black heard about this he contacted the War Office and had Nick transferred to SIB headquarters at the Duke of York's Barracks, Chelsea. He left Crookham with a full pack, and when he arrived in London he was greeted by Sergeant Stan Hall who said, "You can take all that heavy stuff off, and your boots, and put on a comfortable pair of shoes. There's no sleeping accommodation in the barracks so you'll have to sleep at home for the time being, if that's all right. We'll start getting organised in the morning. If you could be here at about ten o'clock; that's not too early, is it?"

I couldn't believe my ears. All of a sudden it seemed I was in a different world after the rigid service routines at Crookham. I was put into an entertainment unit with Arthur Haynes; he was the principal comedian, and there were six other chaps besides ourselves. One of them was a brilliant accordionist who came from Scarborough, and I remember on one occasion, when our pianist wasn't well, this fellow played for the whole show on his accordion.

Eventually, in 1944, we were put on a train and went all along the coast to Portsmouth. There were about eight SIB units waiting to go across to France and we eventually left on D-Day plus five. We were accompanied by Captain Richard Stone who was going to liaise with the various units in France. It was a horrendous journey across the Channel, in flat-bottomed landing crafts, and to a man everyone was seasick. We moored off the French coast within sight of Arromanches, and that night there was a terrific barrage going on from warships and German guns and a few planes machine-gunning the area. The sight that greeted our eyes at first light was amazing, just hundreds of ships, large and small, everywhere.

The landing craft put us ashore and I remember one member of our unit throwing his rifle in the sea, saying, "I won't need that any more." Did he get into trouble! You see, although we were entertainers, members of SIB were trained soldiers. We had to make for the outskirts of Bayeux where we would be based for a while. It was quite a long march before we got to our destination, a recently evacuated German headquarters. It had been stripped of everything, we just had our palliasses to sleep on. We immediately had to set about digging slit trenches all round the building because the German planes were strafing the area at intervals.

We gave our first show on D-Day plus eight. It was Monty's idea, he said it would be good for the lads who had come back from the battle area for a short rest to have some entertainment. We were then about a mile from the fighting lines. We had our mini piano on the back of a lorry and a platform sort of stage was extended from the back. There were fields all round, and we had lookouts posted in nearby barns to look out for stray enemy snipers. We were able to do a full show for the lads, we had great props, and smart dresses for the female impersonator.

During one show the Germans started shelling the area, and everyone disappeared in minutes: audience and artistes all dived for cover. I remember Arthur Haynes saying, "I wouldn't get in those trenches no matter what happens, they're full of water and frogs." When the shelling did start Arthur was in the trench before anybody, and I was in there just as quickly on top of him!

There was a theatre in Bayeux that was still intact, with all the necessary equipment, so we did a week of shows there. Soon after this I was taken ill, and had to return to the UK for an operation. I was sent to a hospital in Bradford in Yorkshire, the main maternity hospital for the area (I told the doctors there I wasn't pregnant!) and apparently part of it had been commandeered by the army.

About six weeks after the operation I was sent back to the Continent, this time to Belgium, where I was met at Ostend by Terry-Thomas who was leading an SIB unit there. I stayed with Terry for a while doing my single musical act and performing in sketches in his show in Brussels. We stayed in a big hotel there, where we all seemed to be heroes to the Belgians.

Eventually I went back to my original unit with Arthur Haynes which was now well into Germany. Bill Waddington was also in Arthur's party. Bill has now made a name for himself in *Coronation Street*. By this time there were all sorts of money-making rackets going on within the services, selling chocolates, cigarettes and the like to the German civilians. I remember Arthur Haynes and I, me disguised as a captain, going to a factory that had stocks of parachute silk. Arthur and I told the owner that we had to have some for essential work in the zone. He gave us three huge rolls of it for two hundred cigarettes. When we got back to the Belgian border we sold lengths of it off the back of our lorry for occupation money.

Arthur went back to the UK before I did to join the Charlie Chester radio show *Stand Easy* and from there he went on to be a big stage and television personality. I did my final show in Holland where we stayed in a hotel and the accordionist, who had been with Arthur's show all the way through, and I opened the windows of the hotel the day peace was declared and played the Dutch national anthem. The crowds outside went crazy with delight.

We came back to the UK and were immediately sent out to Gibraltar, Malta and all over Italy – Naples, Rome, Rimini, Venice and Trieste. We then went all over Austria, finishing up in Vienna.

I was demobbed at the end of 1946 and started to pick up the threads of my career over here. Very soon, though, I was back on the Continent and elsewhere working as a civilian entertainer for Combined Services Entertainment. I did this for about two and a half years, and then got into summer shows, pantomime and concert appearances all over the British Isles.

Nick is too modest to say that he is one of the most successful entertainers ever in these varied fields of entertainment. He seemed never to stop working, and I'm not sure that he has now. A very likable man, with a high sense of humour and fun, and to top it all, a brilliant musician.

Where are those entertainers who made our summer resorts such enjoyable places to be in the summer? Come to think of it, where are the resorts?

Don Smoothey

If you wanted to pick a family that has produced performers dedicated to a lifelong career in entertainment you could hardly ignore the Smoothey family from Fulham in south-west London.

The two Smoothey lads, Don and Len, may not be known by present-day television audiences, but I'll bet there are a lot of theatre devotees who, if asked to recall seeing them at some time in their lives, since the 1920s in fact, might say, "Oh yes, I saw Len, and/or Don, at so and so in a revue or a variety bill or a play." We will take Don Smoothey first and catch up with Len (Lowe) Smoothey with the RAF Gang Shows later on.

As youngsters Don and his brother Len attended the famous Italia Conti Stage School.

Mum said she couldn't afford to keep two of us at the school and as Len was getting well established in the West End theatres playing all the juvenile parts, and I didn't like the straight theatre, well not as much as the variety side of the business, and anyway my mother said it was all very precarious and that I should get a proper job, so I did, in a butcher's shop in the North End Road, Fulham. I wasn't afraid to use my voice when we used to start knocking the meat out cheaply on a Saturday night. You know, "Shilling [5p] off this, lady, two bob [10p] off this joint, lady."

One Christmas Eve we ran out of turkeys so they had to send to the cold store for some more. We wanted to keep the customers in the shop while we were waiting so I got up on the chopping table and started singing songs and telling a few gags until the turkeys arrived. I eventually went to the Smithfield School of Butchery so I would always have a trade to fall back on if I was out of work from earning my living as an entertainer, which I was determined to do eventually. When I got called up in to the army in 1939 a friend of mine said, "As soon as you get in let them know what you can do and you won't go far wrong."

In the months before the outbreak of war, men's fashions took on a military look with the trench-coat and the Tyrone Power [American film idol] hat. So I bought a likewise coat and hat and as soon as I had signed on I was sent to the Royal Artillery Depot at Bulford on Salisbury Plain, but it was so early in the war they had no uniforms for us, so we spent our opening night in the NAAFI wearing our own clothes, me in my trench-coat and Tyrone Power hat. They had the Royal Artillery Band on the stage in the NAAFI and they had a little bugle boy doubling as singer with a soprano voice. After he'd finished the bandmaster asked if anybody else would like to come on stage and do a "turn". I thought I'd have a go, full of confidence with my Tyrone Power trilby, and that really started my eventual move into the Stars in Battledress unit.

I did a show at the Playhouse Theatre in Bulford before being sent on a mechanics course to Rhos-on-Sea where I met up with a fellow called Len Marten. From the first meeting we became lifelong friends. Len in fact was soon to go off to join Stars in Battledress. When he got to London he spoke to Captain George Black about me, so on my next leave home I went to see Captain Black. When I arrived back by train in North Wales after my leave, the coach driver who was taking us back to the camp said, "You lucky bastard, you've been posted." I asked where to and he said, "The Stars in Battledress company at the Duke of York's Barracks in London." That was in 1942. In the meantime I had joined a really crack outfit, the '67 Field Regiment.

My first show with the SIB company in London was a tour of a play *Men in Shadow* written by Mary Hayley Bell. It starred Geoffrey Keen, John Wise and Robert Webber. I played the part of a Cockney soldier which my new-found friend Len Marten had just vacated to go on to do other things. We toured all over the place with this play, and in Nottingham I met two people I hadn't seen for ages, a girl called Irene Slater who had been with me in Noël Coward's *Cavalcade* at the Theatre Royal, Drury Lane, in 1931 and the other person was Miss Conti (from the Italia Conti School). They were both in shows in Nottingham. I remember Miss Conti saying to me, "Your brother Len was the finest Crispian ever in *Where the Rainbow Ends*." All this was before the war, of course.

Anyway, to get back to *Men in Shadow*. When that finished I did a Stars in Battledress variety bill with Harold Childs, Boy Foy (unicyclist and juggler), Alan Clare the pianist (wasn't he just great?) and my old friend Len Marten. He and I got a double act together for this show. Afterwards we were told to report to Sergeant Charlie Chester who was then in Winchester getting another production together. We worked together in various shows at camps all round the country, plus a few broadcasts for the BBC forces programme.

Eventually we went across to France with the show, just after D-Day. I remember Len Marten and I wandering around Bayeux and we find this sort of makeshift NAAFI and we go in to get a drink and the place is like a morgue. Len Marten, who always had an eye for the birds, went up to one of the girls who was serving and said couldn't they do something to liven the place up a bit, so she said in her French accent that she could put the radio on for us, which she did. By the greatest coincidence in the world she switched on to the forces programme, and it was one Len and I had done with the Gang at the Fortune Theatre, before we left England, and there we were on the air singing "Goodbye Heartaches". It was a very strange feeling.

We had one of the first ATS Stars in Battledress join us in France: her name was Anne Belski and she called herself Anne Beverly. She was a soprano and she had brothers who were majors and captains in the army. One night we were working in the dock area of Caen and on this occasion we were doing a show for the Combined Operations Group. As this ATS girl had just joined the show Charlie Chester said to her, "What I suggest tonight is that you sit out front, watch the show, and see what it's all about."

Usually at the end of each show the officers would come round, and we would either get invited to the Officers' Mess or the Sergeants' Mess for a few drinks and chat. Now this young RAF officer came round and said, "We are Combined Ops, and we've got no mess, but my sergeant and I and a couple of the lads have got a place over a shop in the dockland area, and if you'd care to come back there I'm sure we'd find some refreshment for your party." So we all go to this place over the shop in the docks and when we get up there this RAF officer says, "What would you like to drink?" All the lads ask for a beer except Len, who's on the gin, and Charlie and the girl say that they will have a cup of tea as they are non-drinkers. Well, very soon we'd drunk all the beer, and then the officer says, "Sorry, chaps, but all I've got left is some Calvados", and he's pouring out this stuff like there's no tomorrow. Well, we were pretty unsteady after the beer and the Calvados, and I fell down the stairs going back to the lorry, then somebody fell off the back of the vehicle, and then props and things for our show started to go the same way.

When we got back to our base it finished up with this poor ATS girl and Charlie Chester trying to get the piano off the back of the lorry, and the rest of us p....d out of our minds, and this was Anne Beverly's introduction to the show. Charlie Chester had said to her when she first met us, "They are a lovely bunch of lads, you'll enjoy working with them"! Nevertheless, she stayed with us for quite a while.

Eventually Charlie took the show on to Brussels, and we appeared in a big production at the ABC Theatre there. The Charlie Chester show did the whole of the second half. We stayed in Brussels for a while, and then I left the show as I had to come back to England with bad knee trouble (was it falling down the stairs in Caen?) but the Chester show went through to Holland across the Rhine and continued right up into Germany. It was during that period that the Charlie Chester Gang Show (the forerunner of his radio show *Stand Easy*) was formed. I've always had the greatest admiration for Charlie, from the word go. He spent all his spare time writing material and getting ideas for the future when Len and I were probably out looking for a drink.

Frederick Ferrari

From a boy singer in the bath to Stars in Battledress, and then eventual national recognition as one of Britain's best-known post-war broadcasting and stage voices, is not bad for someone who might otherwise have followed his family into the confectionery trade.

Fred, the son of an English mother and an Italian father, was a relaxed sort of kid, and just loved singing. He was eventually persuaded to have his voice trained, and this very quickly gained him some recognition and led to his being awarded three gold medals in his home town of Liverpool. Later he was accepted into the Carl Rosa Opera Company, but alas the war came along and Fred found himself in the army. He kept up his singing practice in the barrack room, and also did one or two gigs (one-night stands) in nearby pubs after being persuaded to have a go by his army pals in Birmingham where he had been posted. His CO heard about his singing prowess and asked him to get a concert together to entertain the "lads" who were bored during the early months of the phoney war. Fred agreed to do this and the service audiences were delighted with his concerts, as was the CO, who got in touch with the Stars in Battledress unit in London (then the Central Pool of Artistes). Captain George Black came up to one of the concerts, liked what he saw and told Fred that he'd be in touch as soon as the organisation was up and running.

Meanwhile Fred and three other lads were posted to Worcester and the rigours of strict army discipline, so the entertaining had to stop, but not for long. The four lads got together a bigger and better concert party in their spare time. Again this was successful and they were nicknamed the Norton Follies (Norton was the name of the barracks).

After a while when we got on to the parade ground the orderly sergeant used to shout at the top of his voice, "A Company on parade, B Company on parade, Norton Follies on parade." We used to get a few whistles from the lads, I can tell you. We then started touring other camps with the concert party and this went on for almost a year. The CO at Norton Barracks started getting very angry about this because we hadn't done a show there for some time and quite rightly he pointed out that Norton was our home base and we should be entertaining his boys. When we started doing shows there again the CO was treating us like long-lost cousins, and me still only a lance-corporal. As we had some really late nights I used to miss reveille and I'm still in bed asleep when I get a tap on the shoulder and it's the shouting and screaming orderly sergeant again – only this time he said, "Would you like a cuppa?" It's amazing what a bit of entertaining can do for you!

Following a brief spell in Scotland I was sent back to Western Command as a pay clerk. The CO at Kidderminster had heard about me and suggested there was enough talent in the area to do a full-scale production of *Pagliacci*. I only had two weeks to learn the part (the others had already been rehearsing with the pianist) and we opened with a full orchestra (the Western

Command Symphony Orchestra) in front of a service audience at the Royalty Theatre in Chester. Everything went well and the BBC did a live broadcast of the performance.

We then took the whole production on tour, playing to service audiences, and they all seemed to enjoy it. Sometimes we were doing two shows a day to accommodate all the service men and women and some civilians who wanted to see it. It was getting very hard on the voice, and we had to be careful not to overdo it.

The last date of the tour was at the Prince of Wales Theatre, Cardiff, and that is where I met Charlie Chester for the first time. He arrived on our last Saturday to do a Sunday concert with a big Stars in Battledress show. Charlie said, "I'm doing a radio show for the BBC when the war finishes. It's all set up and I'd like you to join me." I heard no more and I didn't follow it up. In fact when the war did finish and I was demobbed I didn't want to know about singing and got a job as an insurance agent in Liverpool.

However, after Cardiff, a Stars in Battledress unit was going to France after D-Day and I thought I would be with it, but I was told that as my father was Italian and the Germans were their allies I could be treated as a traitor and shot.

While I was working in Liverpool Charlie Chester came up to appear at the Empire Theatre. I popped in to see him and he said he would like me to join the radio show he had mentioned when we first met in Cardiff. It was to be called *Stand Easy*. My wife said I ought to give it a try, and so Charlie and I agreed to try things out for a month. I wasn't going to give up my job with the insurance firm so I used to go down to London on a Saturday night, rehearse on Sunday and Monday and do the show on Monday night and come back to Liverpool.

I decided I would like to stay with Charlie Chester and the Gang so I gave up my insurance job as the popularity of the radio show brought other engagements. We were engaged for the summer season at the Opera House, Blackpool, and followed it with a season at the London Palladium. It was all heady stuff now with Charlie and the Gang, which included Arthur Haynes, Len Marten, the eventual associate producer to TV's *Opportunity Knocks*, and Ken Morris.

When we got to the Palladium the billing outside the theatre was Charlie Chester and John Boles the American singing star, and the rest of us in small print underneath.

Fred omits to say that the newspaper reviews of the show said, "John Boles suffers by comparison with Britain's own Frederick Ferrari." The year was crowned by his being made a member of the Grand Order of Water Rats and the appearance with the Gang in the Royal Variety Performance of that year, 1948. Not a bad career for a lad who just liked singing in the bath!

Very soon after that Fred gave up show business and went back to, as he puts it, "a day job". He now lives with his wife quietly in Surrey.

Spike Milligan

What can one say about Spike Milligan that hasn't been said before? Well I know a few things, from first-hand experience.

I have appeared with Spike in some of his television shows which I found a fairly hilarious experience (some people would perhaps say a slightly dangerous one), but no one could deny working with Spike is "different".

I particularly remember one TV show I did with Spike (either one of the *Beachcomber* shows or *Q 7*) where I played a priest giving communion wine to the congregation, one of whom was Spike. When it came to his turn he was to ask what vintage the wine was, where I obtained it from, and "Did you get a good discount from the wholesalers?" At the last minute Spike proceeded to say, "Do you know what they have down the road at St Mary's?" and "I haven't tried the Methodists yet, I've been told they do a good wine," and "I've heard the Presbyterians get theirs from the supermarket." You can imagine that it was not long before I completely broke up, and in fact I don't think we ever did finish the sketch.

Before someone grabs a pen and paper to say I am being blasphemous repeating the episode, you have to remember that if Spike had been starved of invention the world of comedy would have been robbed of genius. This was even more evident when I did a pantomime with him at Chichester a few years ago. On the opening night the dry ice (which produces the mist behind the ballet) got out of hand and brought visibility on stage and in the auditorium down to about three feet. Spike couldn't resist putting his head out of the OP stage entrance and shouting, "Someone's knickers are on fire." At another point in the pantomime the robbers (the characters we were playing) had to hide from Robin Hood, me behind a screen and Spike in a huge trunk. He opened the lid and, as if taken aback, said, "Oh, Lord Lucan, what are you doing here?" It got a huge laugh. (Lucan being the earl who disappeared after a notorious incident in a London house in 1974.)

Spike, or to give him his proper name, Terence, began his somewhat anarchic career at a very early age, in fact returning to Britain by boat from his birthplace, India.

I remember we did a turn, which I had worked out. It was a monkey gland transplantation. We had a big white sheet put up in the ship's lounge, with a lantern behind it, and we would have a shadow of a body on the screen, and we would prepare to operate and take sausages out of the body which showed on the shadow screen, and bits and pieces like an alarm clock, a big cardboard heart, a cricket bat and things like that, and then put them into a big bag, then suddenly take the sheet away and there would be a little baby there which we had borrowed from one of the passengers, and that was the first comedy performance I ever did.

Early in my teens I played trumpet in a dance band, then entered for a Bing Crosby crooning contest which I won. Suddenly I heard Louis Armstrong singing, and I forgot all about Bing Crosby and went straight for the jazz. The war came and I went into the army, following in my father's footsteps (well, I was called to the colours – khaki). Soon I was playing in a dance band in the services and later we formed a little jazz quartet in the unit I was in. We were stationed at Bexhill in Sussex and used to play at all the dances there and we became very popular; we were like early Beatles in Bexhill, all the young boys playing the music of the day.

My first attempt at concert party entertainment was when I was stationed at Hailsham, also in Sussex, but it was rather ill-fated. As we were getting the concert party together we were given our orders to go overseas. I remember Captain Counsell (John Counsell who owned and ran the Windsor Theatre for years) suddenly drifted in while we were doing rehearsals for the concert party and was very happy with what he saw. Something might have come out of it, all the seeds were there if you wanted to be in show business, but we were being frustrated by Adolf Hitler. He cancelled quite a few shows, did Adolf. Then I was posted to North Africa.

There was very little entertainment available for us in the desert in the early stages, although we did have a visit from a French opera company. As we had no form of platform to act as a stage for their performance we made one up out of trestle tables from the mess tent. It couldn't be called the safest form of staging but it looked okay. Now you may think this is a tall story, but I promise you what happened was true, it happened before my very eyes. They got the piano and the pianist on to the trestle tables without too much trouble, but then this huge soprano from Algiers came out, Tess Vellion I think her name was, and she was every bit of eighteen to twenty stone. She took centre "stage" on the trestles and started to sing an aria from the opera *Carmen*. Everything was going fine and the lads were really starting to enjoy it. Suddenly right in the middle of the aria the whole stage collapsed; the whole middle section just fell through completely and the soprano with it, and the piano slid down the hole on top of her. Terrible screams and shouts were emitted from the debris, the French entourage running about, falling over one another, trying to sort it out. The nearest soldiers were trying to restore order and organise a rescue. It was terrible, trestle tables, piano and pianist and the rather large singer mixed up in it all. It was the greatest spectacle the audience of soldiers had ever seen. When the lady singer finally emerged there was terrific applause, and the typically sadistic British soldiers started shouting out with cries of "Encore, encore". You could hear it ringing through the desert night.

Our unit formed its own concert party out there. We called it *The Jolly Rogers*. It was quite successful and the show went on to better things. One performance we did made some money for the Royal Artillery Benevolent Fund. It kept going well and was getting such a reputation that Captain George Black of SIB came out to see one of our shows, which he liked and wanted to try and get us relieved of active service and back to London for reorganisation into other areas. We couldn't believe him even trying. The War Office of course vetoed the idea, saying these are serving soldiers and they have to stay in their fighting units.

After our skirmishes in the desert with Hitler and ENSA my regiment, 56 Heavy Field Royal Artillery, was engaged in the invasion of Italy, landing first of all in Sicily, and then going on to the mainland at Salerno. This is where I got wounded and that was in January 1944. I was eventually sent to a convalescent depot; it was for the bomb happy, and I was still shell-shocked. While I was there we were visited by an ENSA show which I shall not forget in a hurry for more than one reason.

We lads of the bomb happy "club" were just lying around one day in a field, sitting on our kit bags and enjoying the peace and quiet behind the firing lines, when a sergeant came up to us and said, "There's entertainment tonight, lads, in field G. You will all face the north-eastern direction, sitting on your kit bags, ready for the show." Well, we all congregated in this field with our kit bags and waited. Finally a three-ton lorry drove into the field, turned around, and backed up. It was all very well arranged; the two in the front of the lorry came around to the back, dropped the tail-board and lifted the canvas flaps hanging at the back of the lorry, over the top on to the roof. There was a row of electric lights on the edge of the half-lowered tail-board and this formed a little stage.

Unfortunately it was a bit windy that night and the flaps that had been placed on the roof of the lorry blew down, and although a pianist had obviously started playing all we could see was the bottom half of a lady – we presumed it was a lady – in a yellow gown and she was thumping away hammer and tongs at the keyboard. Then somebody came round from the front of the lorry again and lifted the flaps back on to the roof, and there was this dear old lady of about seventy and she was playing the piano like she was in a wash-tub, massaging the keyboard, going hell for leather. The piano itself was atrocious, every note joined into the next one, like a great volume of gunge coming out, and when she had finished she yelled, "And now, boys, what would you like?" A sadistic British soldier was soon on his feet shouting, "We'd like some music, dear." Then a man came out and said, "And now, boys, we would like you to meet Lawrence Quelch, the well-known baritone from the Wells." I don't know which Wells he was from, Sadler's or Tunbridge, but anyway this huge baritone came out and the first thing he got was somebody in the audience shouting out, "Lend us your ration book." Then he announced, "I would like to sing 'The Yeomen of England'," and he started to sing, "We are the Yeomen, the Yeomen of England," etc.

Suddenly the air-raid siren went and German Stuka bombers came screaming out of the evening sun. Everybody ran like mad, the whole audience dissolved, and the lorry driver put the lorry into gear and drove the baritone with the lady still thundering on the piano out of the field to the strains of "We are the Yeomen, the Yeomen of England". I watched the lorry go like a bat out of hell up the Caserta–Naples road with the tail-board footlights still on. I often wondered where the lorry and the "Yeomen" ended up. [Author's Note: I have tried to trace Lawrence Quelch to find out if he survived the journey to wherever they were going, needless to say, without success.]

While I was at Arno depot there was a colonel there who saw me playing the trumpet and I think he fancied me on the quiet, the naughty colonel. When I went to the place where he was working it was a very big army organisation for all the officers of the 2nd Echelon. There was a very big dance band there and soon I was able to join it. I think the "naughty" colonel put a word in for me.

There was a stage and lighting at this place, and while I was there a Stars in Battledress company came along with a play called *Men in Shadow*. It featured actor Hector Ross, or Captain Hector Ross as he was then. The following week we boys put on a show which was a send-up of it. Then another play called *White Cargo* came to the depot and the following week we did a send-up of that one and called it *Black Baggage*. We thought they were quite funny (ours, I mean) but I think it baffled one half of the audience and sent the other half into raptures.

I was also still playing trumpet in the 2nd Echelon Officers dance orchestra. We played for all occasions, sometimes before visiting generals like Eisenhower and Field-Marshal Alexander, etc. There was a creep of an officer there, Brigadier Wood, who started making complaints about my trumpet playing, saying it was too loud, so I told him to dance further away. He got me transferred and posted to the Central Pool of Artistes (SIB). Anybody who had been wounded and who could play an instrument or do a "turn" was put in the Pool straightaway. I played both the trumpet and the guitar so I was a natural for the dance band. It was about this time that I first met Harry Secombe. He burst on the scene with a high-pitched laugh, blowing raspberries everywhere and talking so fast I thought he was Polish. He was in the depot after being blown up somewhere by a heavy gield gun. Harry started doing some cabaret in front of the band. I couldn't understand what it was, the whole act was frenetic. I still thought he was Polish and I started talking to him in a very loud voice, as one does when speaking to foreigners, "VERY GOOD ACT". He must have thought I was potty.

Other service entertainers in the area at that time were Norman Vaughan and Ken Platt. Another very funny man was Les Henry. He had a high-pitched voice and was also a brilliant harmonica player.

Then came a meeting with a crazy, untidy and undisciplined gunner called Bill Hall. He was a fantastic violinist and he and I and another character called Johnny Mulgrew, who used to play bass in the pre-war Ambrose band, decided to form a trio (the Bill Hall Trio) and that was a turning point for me as far as service entertainment was concerned.

One of the shows being presented at the base was called *Over the Page* and they were short of an act, so in we went and the act really took off – we were playing in the style of the Hot Club de France. I suggested it would be a good idea to change out of our uniform for the act and go on in bits of nondescript clothing, old rags or anything, looking quite mad, so we did. We put some props on stage, a dustbin, a clothes line and stuff like that. We had trick trousers that fell down and we even did a chorus with a blown-up balloon and sometimes we spoke in foreign accents. The act absolutely brought the service audience to their feet. I've never known anything like it in my life since, quite exhilarating and exciting.

When it was time for our demob Central Pool of Artistes came to us and said would we like to stay on and do shows for them, and they would make us officer status. So we stayed on, and became so good we were asked to play in the Victory Night Concert at the Argentina Theatre in Rome. Gracie Fields was the star of the show. There was an ignominious moment when Harry Secombe, who can't see as far as his hand, had to help with the lighting and work the spotlights. Gracie was going to sing "Red Sails in the Sunset" and asked for a red gelatine in the spot, but Secombe was colour blind and when Gracie started to sing she went bright green, and a voice at the back of the theatre shouted, "You've gone all mouldy, dear." That's show business, folks!

We had a few Stars in Battledress shows coming out from England while I was in Italy. Some would-be performers didn't quite make it. One chap, a private, did an act called "The Great Zam". His real name was Dick something, and he had an assistant who came on dressed in a kind of loin-cloth and his skin was covered in brown boot polish, it must have been, because you could smell it, and he had a black wig on. He was supposed to be a brown person. He started by beating a gong which was obviously a dustbin lid painted gold, and it didn't ring, it just went thud when he hit it, then he would announce, "From the mystic Far East, the Great Zam." And the Great Zam would come on with this big turban made out of old putties on his head, and an old football jersey dyed black, football boots painted gold, and things like that, and he would say, "I am the Great Zam, and I come from the middle of the Congo, and I cannot speak a word of English." He did his act speaking like this, with a very strong Lancashire accent, and at the climax of his act he would say, "I will sit in yon chair, and be able to take ten thousand volts through my human body and survive it." He had this chair with a lot of lights on it, he then sat in it and was strapped in, and suddenly there was a smell of burning hair and he started to shout, "Get me out of the chair, switch it off, something has gone wrong," and that was the end of the Great Zam! That was one of the acts we got.

Another was a sergeant who came on stage, did a lot of somersaults, back-flips, press-ups and things like that, and then started to sing "It's a Long Way to Tipperary" looking upwards, and those of us who were manning the fly bars had to drop an egg on cue so as to hit him and break on his forehead, and spill all over his face. He would then say, "I've finished I'll be bound," and that was his funny line to finish his act. One night we got bored with his act so we boiled the egg to the consistency of a bullet and laid him out cold when it hit him on the forehead.

And then we had another show, a pantomime the SIB were touring round, and it had been playing in some of the Italian opera houses with wide stages. In the pantomime they had a soldier dressed as a fairy who used to fly across the stage on a wire. He was a Lance-Bombardier Ken Carter (who after the war produced and directed the Benny Hill shows).

Ken used to fly across the stage on a wire and say, "I am the Fairy Queen, and all your dreams can come true when I wave this magic wand," and then he would disappear on the other side of the stage. Unfortunately our theatre stage was quite narrow but the stage manager gave him the same sort of shove that he had been doing on a big stage, and he went across, out of the wings, and collided with the side wall, swung back, still on the wire, to centre stage, hanging like a wet rag, unconscious, with blood pouring from his forehead. The pantomime carried on with most of the chorus still singing their hearts out while other blokes somehow got the Fairy Queen down, still bleeding. This was greeted by storms of applause from the audience. I think pantomime was the right name for it.

There were a few ENSA shows going around as well as Stars in Battledress. We also had a concert from Gracie Fields, who was living on the island of Capri at that time. This was before the Victory Night Concert we had done with Gracie in Rome. At this point the fighting line had moved north and we were on leave in Naples, and we went to this palace where Lady Hamilton had met Lord Nelson. It had changed somewhat as it was now a NAAFI, full of soldiers drinking tea and eating "wads" (sandwiches) and suddenly in comes Gracie Fields with one or two army officers and an army captain shouted, "Listen, everybody, order please," banging on a teacup with a spoon. "Miss Fields will now sing for you," and from where she was standing she started singing "Sally, Sally" and then went around the tables singing. Well, she sang for over an hour and in between songs she kept saying, "Have a cup of tea, lads, have a nice cuppa tea." Well we'd had enough cups of tea already and we just had to go, if you know what I mean, and soon the place was empty except for a detachment of mystified Gurkha troops who had more control over their bladders than we did.

When we did the Victory Night Concert with Gracie Fields in Rome we were a very big success and we were visited backstage after our performance by A. C. Astor, an actor and entrepreneur who was connected with entertainment in Italy and he said, "I'll book your act that I've seen tonight when you get back to London." When we finally arrived home after the war he did, and the Bill Hall Trio did very well in the night-clubs, like the Coconut Grove for instance. We also started to do the music-halls, and suddenly there was a different attitude with those audiences: they were not used to seeing the crazy sort of act that we were.

We appeared at the Hackney Empire during the dreadful winter of 1947, snow everywhere, and Val Parnell, a very important man in the theatre, then head of Moss Empires circuit, came to the theatre to see us, and sat in a box on a freezing night with hardly anybody in the audience. We did the act, it was miserable, and we never heard from Val Parnell again. Then we started going round and round in circles, sort of getting nowhere. We were booked abroad at one point in Zurich, with a Will Collins show called *Would You Believe It?* during which I had to play on a man's head with ping-pong balls, while he made xylophone noises with his mouth. Then we were asked to tour Italy and going back there was wonderful, we were again a big success and we just kept working; but then we started to be cheated by some of the Italian entrepreneurs, not paying our money and things like that.

Finally we came back to England and we did get some Moss Empire dates, the Sheffield and Leeds Empires, Golders Green Hippodrome, etc. We also did one or two television shows but the other lads wouldn't change the act or experiment which I knew you had to for TV, so I broke away from the trio and started an act on my own. This was in 1949. At the same time I was starting to write some scripts for Harry Secombe, Alfred Marks, Peter Sellers, Bill Kerr and one or two for Frankie Howerd, and I got a job with the Joe Loss Orchestra doing a crazy act in front of the band.

Then Spike started to get the idea of writing a *Goon Show* and that happened, and the rest is radio history. The *Goon Show* turned radio comedy upside down, but I am sure Spike would agree that having to write so many original scripts a year because of its huge success tired him out. Luckily for us all he came through that period of overwork and has continued to be the most "original" Spike Milligan. As a family man and friend he is a most generous person and dining out with him, or being entertained by him and his wife Sheila at their lovely home on the Sussex coast is a very pleasurable experience.

Ken Platt made a terrific name for himself after the war on radio, particularly in programmes like *Variety Bandbox*. He was a tall fellow with a sad-looking face, and he used to begin with, "I won't take me coat off, I'm not stopping" (instant laughter and applause).

Les Henry formed an act with two other lads and they called themselves the Three Monarchs. They played all the big variety houses including several appearances at the London Palladium where they were a huge success. Les now does a solo comedy and musical act.

Sir Harry Secombe, CBE

I have credited Harry with his full title because I suspect not many people know it, and those who do would rarely use it. This isn't through lack of respect but simply because the popularity of the "man" as a human being is, I'm sure, of far greater importance than a title.

His career has been quite extraordinary. How could anyone, except those who have been close to him for many years, be expected to believe that the young man from Swansea with a wide grin and mischievous eyes, began his theatrical career with shaving soap and a brush, and proceeded from there to conquer every aspect of the entertainment business, including starring in the first show at the Sydney Opera House after it was opened by Her Majesty the Queen? A clue to this success lies in his affection for his fellow human beings including his comrades from the 132 Field Regiment Artillery during the bloody wartime battles in North Africa and Italy.

Post-war his early variety theatre days in gloomy digs and even gloomier dressing-rooms, known only too well by many of us,

76

would have made Harry grateful for his God-given talent and for the great capacity and understanding to use it.

Harry's involvement with Stars in Battledress and the Central Pool of Artistes in Italy towards the end of the war followed brief spells in divisional concert parties after he had been hospitalised for several weeks. Even in those days he wanted to please, not just because he had made up his mind by then to become a professional entertainer once the war was over, but because he genuinely believed he could bring some happiness into his audience's lives, if only for a brief moment.

Norman Vaughan told me it was a joy to be with Harry when entertaining the troops, and he was always keen to learn and enquire if he was doing okay. "The boys warmed to his erratic and original style. His infectious good humour went further than a stage performance; it was generally infectious wherever he happened to be. When he came out of the army and started in his career in civvy street it continued."

Harry's ambitions were always tempered by concern for his young family and later, when bringing up those growing children, he was blessed with his wife Myra's understanding of this crazy business of entertainment, even though she had never been associated with it.

After the war, Harry played variety all over the country, making a niche for himself as a solo performer on radio and seasons at the famous Windmill Theatre in London. Within five years of being demobbed he became part of a team that revolutionised radio comedy with the legendary *Goon Shows*, and names like Neddy Seagoon, Min, Eccles, Bluebottle, Grytpype-Thynne entered the English language.

Harry's appetite for unusual and original comedy was certainly whetted when he met Bill Hall and Johnny Mulgrew in Italy, and also through his association with the comic genius of Spike Milligan which manifested itself into the later radio successes.

Before I was in the "business" I saw Harry in variety at the Lewisham Hippodrome in south London and I remember smiling to myself on the way home, not just for what he had done on stage but more because the man made me feel good after I'd seen his act, which was a mixture of logic, madness and joyful singing. His appeal lies in his simplicity, and you can't be more simplistic than blowing a raspberry and hitting a top note, winning a response from an audience of two, or two thousand, who have understood in a few moments that they are in the company of an uncomplicated but rather special person. Someone said to me once, "I think people feel comfortable in Harry's company."

An incident during the 1975 Royal Variety Performance at the London Palladium in the presence of the Queen and the Duke of Edinburgh, which I had the privilege of appearing in along with the cast of *Dad's Army*, provided a moment typical of Harry's good humour.

Just before the finale of the show he came rushing in from his own show, which was running at the Prince of Wales Theatre in Piccadilly, to join Dame Vera Lynn and the Welsh Rhos Male Voice Choir in the last production number of the show. Managements nearly always close their theatres on the night if their artistes are appearing in a royal show. Harry had decided not to do this, and had come hot foot from the Prince of Wales for the last item. We, the other artistes, were all waiting in the wings, and Harry was waiting to join Vera and the choir. He gave a loud cough, shouted out to Vera (not that it would have been heard by the audience), "Show us your knickers, gal," followed by a loud raspberry. This broke the tension that is always around on these occasions and, as you can imagine, made us all chuckle. I often wonder what the royal family think the atmosphere is like backstage at a royal show, particularly when Harry is around.

The tremendous number of concert, television and radio appearances he has made all over the world, not to mention the many books he has written, have culminated in recent years with his *Highway* programmes for Tyne Tees Television. This is a serious programme, but with an underlying feeling of good humour for the subject, presented with great sincerity.

Of all the many great moments he has experienced, I suspect receiving the Honorary Doctorate of Music from Swansea University must be pretty high on the list. Not a bad journey from his shaving bowl and brush in an army tent in Italy in 1943! His "Mam" and Dad would have been proud of him.

You should read *Arias and Raspberries*, part of Harry's autobiography. You will surely finish up smiling, and that is what Harry Secombe is all about – smiling.

Stan Hall with the lovely Evelyn (Boo) Laye.

Stan Hall with Noël Coward.

Play rehearsals for an ENSA tour. Those present include Malcolm Keen, Ronald Howard, Robert Newton, Ursula Jeans and Roger Livesey.

The founders of Stars in Battledress. From the left, Captain George Black, R.A. (who went on to be boss of the London Palladium), Lieutenant-Colonel A. Basil Brown, West Yorks, and Major W. H. Cameron Alexander, R.A. (who after the war founded one of Britain's biggest theatrical agencies).

PROGRAMME

7 p.m. to 8 p.m.
STARS IN BATTLEDRESS

(Produced by Capt. George Black, R.A.)

An Entertainment by the Forces for the Forces

1. It's Grand to meet you
2. Musical Selection
   BLUE ROCKETS, conducted by SGT. GEORGE MELACHRINO
3. Eccentric Dancer
   PTE. WALLY STEWART
4. Clarinet Speciality
   SGT. SID MILLWARD
5. Accordionist
   CPL. KEN MORRIS
6. (1) Blow, blow, thou winter wind
   (2) Down Grade Boogie Woogie
   DRIVER ARTHUR YOUNG AND THE ORCHESTRA
   PLAYING DRIVER YOUNG'S OWN COMPOSITIONS
7. "The Wonder on one Wheel"
   BOY FOY, ROYAL COMMAND PERFORMER
8. Tiger Rag
   PTE. WALLY STEWART, BASS PLAYER
9. Vocalist and Instrumentalist
   SGT. GEORGE MELACHRINO
10. The Three Loose Screws
    SGT. HAROLD CHILDS, GNR. JACK BROWNING AND
    GUNNER BERT SCRASE
11. "Rhapsody in Blue" (Gershwin)
    DVR. ARTHUR YOUNG, SOLO PIANO
    SGT. SID MILLWARD, SOLO CLARINET
12. Till we say "Hello" again

GUEST OF HONOUR:

THE RT. HON. SIR JAMES GRIGG, K.C.B., K.C.S.I., M.P.
Secretary of State for War

An early Stars in Battledress production.

Charlie Chester (with guitar) and his Company Concert Party in 1941, before joining Stars in Battledress.

Stella Moray in concert with Terry-Thomas.

Sergeant Stella Moray.

The Ross Brothers. Left to right: Joe Melia, John Macleod and Norman Macleod.

Frederick Ferrari starring in *Pagliacci*, 1942. Note the full service orchestra.

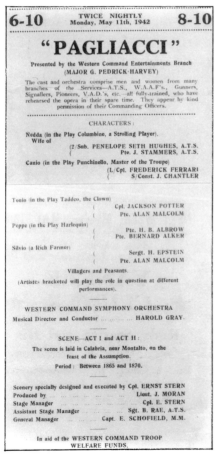

A service audience watching a performance
of *The Marriage of Figaro*.

Pagliacci. Quite an ambitious
service production.

A Stars in Battledress company, 1943. Left to right, standing: Elizabeth Kirkby, Kenneth Connor. Sitting: Wilfrid Hyde White, Faith Brook, John Longden.

Geoffrey Keen and Faith Brook. Italy, 1943.

I'll bet they had a tail (ouch) to tell. Brandon and Pounds' *Out of the Blue* concert party. Mersa Matruh, 1943.

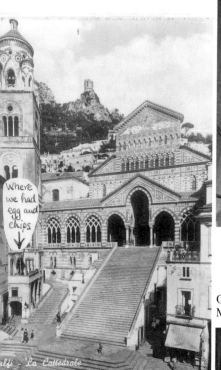

Where we had egg and chips

lfi - La Cattedrale

The Bill Hall Trio. Left to right: Johnny Mulgrew (bass),
Bill Hall (violin) and Spike Milligan (guitar). Italy, 1943.

Obviously a treat in Italy in 1943 for
Milligan and friends.

Spike Milligan second from
right on trumpet. Italy, 1943.

Spike Milligan, Harry Secombe and front centre,
Norman Vaughan. Naples, 1943.

Ralph Reader, founder of the RAF Gang Shows.

Rex Jameson as Mrs Shufflewick.

The No. 4 Gang Show Unit on board a ship bound for the Middle East, 1946, Company includes, extreme left: Peter (Drinkwater) Reagan; next to Reagan: Barry Martin; top right: Rex Jameson (Mrs Shufflewick).

122 Wing RAF Gang Show, Normandy, 1944. Left to right, standing: Jack Healey, Roy Rowlands, Charlie Vickers, Arthur Tolcher, Danny Jarrett, the unit drivers. Middle row: Gerry Leslie, Len Snelling, Joe Smith, Ralph Reader, Al Bush and Dick Emery. Sitting: The Cox twins, Fred and Frank. Two hours after this picture was taken the area was completely flattened by a German air strike.

An RAF Gang Show programme.

Cardew Robinson.

A Gang Show unit in front of their Wellington Bomber Transport on their way round the Persian Gulf after touring Europe and North Africa (1946). Company includes, extreme left: Ken Robertson; fourth and seventh from left: Fred and Frank Cox; front row, fourth from left: Al Bush.

Norman Vaughan

Norman Vaughan, who came from Liverpool with all the sharp humour Merseyside breeds, recounted his early introduction to the world of entertainment and to Stars in Battledress.

I started in show business when I was very young, as a little boy in a boys' troupe (The Silver Songsters). Just before I went into the army I was in a show with a revue producer called Jack Gillam. It was called *Shoulder Arms and Legs* – as you can guess by the title, the war had already started. I was with this act called Wynn, Taylor and Bibbie, and I was Taylor. You had to have a stage name in those days, but of course Norman Taylor was really Norman Vaughan.

Very soon I had to join up. I recently found my old pay book and in it were the words, "What was your occupation before you enlisted?" and it says, "Dancer, professional". When I was called before the major and he looked at my enlistment form he said, "Are you one of those cheeky chappies?" It's funny how their minds worked.

You see, I was a professional dancer, and eighteen when I signed on, and it wasn't Norman Taylor of Wynn, Taylor and Bibbie they called up, it was Norman Vaughan, my real name, and they put me into the infantry.

I was in the King's Regiment stationed at Formby, near Liverpool, and after my training there I was posted to Great Yarmouth, where we did more training, like running around with fixed bayonets and sticking them into sacking dummies, and yelling at the top of your voice. I'd been doing this training for a few days and I thought, If it comes to the real thing I'll never be able to do this to another person. It didn't occur to you then that somebody else might do it to you once you got into battle.

I did six months' training at Great Yarmouth and then was posted to Gibraltar, and I couldn't believe it. The lights were on, you could buy Cadbury's chocolate in the shops. [Much later on in Norman's career Cadbury's chocolates were to grow on him.] After England this was a new world, which was very lucky for me because I was a foot soldier, on active service, and could have easily been posted to North Africa, straight into the line fighting Rommel, but I happened to have been posted to Gibraltar, and the unit I was posted to was run like a peacetime unit. As the unit knew of my connections with entertainment I was asked whether I'd like to join the band, which was marvellous. So I learned to play the clarinet and the cymbals, and it was all great fun, but I was still a soldier on active service. I think that this is what people didn't realise. When they saw an ENSA show the people in it were civilians and had officer status, but if you were in the army and part of the entertainment, it would be back to the barracks perhaps after a late night, and a parade the following morning in full marching order.

I was posted to Egypt to do some more training, all the time thinking I wouldn't be needed because the troops that had been in the North African campaign had now landed in Italy, and our battalion was to be their reinforcements. This is why we had been training in Egypt. All the time we were thinking, We won't be needed to do any fighting, but we were.

However, luck was on my side and it probably saved my life. The great band leader, Harry Roy, who had played for royalty at all the London nightspots before the war, came out from England with his band to entertain the troops in Egypt, and I sat in the audience, like one of the boys, a soldier, but Harry and his dance band were civilians in a sponsored ENSA company. Now I'm sitting there with the rest of the lads watching the show when they started saying, "Vaughany" (that's what they called me in the unit), "get up there and show us what you can do." Now I didn't want to just get up there because, although I am a performer, one is always a bit reticent to do something on the spur of the moment. Anyway they kept saying, "Go on, you'll win a prize," which was three hundred cigarettes. (As I didn't smoke it would have been more for them if I won.)

You see, Harry Roy had an item in his show called "Lead the Band" where someone from the audience would get up on the stage, take hold of the baton and pretend to conduct the band, and the best one at it would win the three hundred cigarettes. So, egged on by the lads, I eventually said okay, got on the stage to lead the band, and being a "pro" said to the boys in the band, "Sheikh of Araby, two choruses, and make the second a stop chorus," which is when the band leave a lot of gaps in their playing when somebody is doing a tap dance. And in my big army boots I did this tap dance in the second chorus and I won the three hundred fags. Three days later, and this was the life-saver, a message arrived telling Private Vaughan to report to headquarters, to join the divisional concert party.

Well it was another world: no square-bashing, or leaping into canals. I couldn't believe my luck, it was wonderful. You see, in the army entertainments, the majority of the performers either did Max Miller's act, played the mouth organ, or sang like Bing Crosby. So when somebody did a tap dance it was something completely different, especially wearing army boots. (Well, I hadn't got my tap shoes with me!)

The division and the concert party did go on to Italy, and we were still on active service and did shows for the boys quite close to the action, much too close for comfort, but we did it because we were soldiers. When I got into the divisional concert party I left the King's Regiment, and all the Liverpool lads I'd got to know. They eventually went to Italy to reinforce the Rapido River crossing. I was then stationed in the headquarters, about twenty miles back from the front line; it was where the top brass were.

I heard about the river crossing while on guard duty when, in the middle of the night, I went to the toilet. Being ordinary soldiers we didn't have a proper toilet, just a pole stretched across a ditch, whereas the general and his top brass had a proper loo, like you would have in a modern caravan. I thought as no one was about I would use his, and while I was sitting there contemplating, there on the wall beside me I saw the battle plans, designated by little coloured flags. My old unit was the 67th and I saw that they were going to have to cross the river tomorrow. It was quite a shock (and I hope the general concerned doesn't read this or I'll be back square-bashing). I remember meeting one of the lads of the 67th. He'd just come back from the front line and he was covered in mud and dust. I said, "How's it going, are they fighting up there?" He said, "Fighting; they're .... killing each other." (I felt like going to the toilet again.)

The majority of shows that we did were for the soldiers coming out of the line for a rest, and that would be in the region of fifteen to twenty miles back from the fighting, which was quite a way in those days. You could still hear the odd crump from exploding shells and things like that, but at that distance we were pretty safe. As we were serving soldiers, however, we were often ordered to do shows right up to the line. There was one show we were ordered to do right up at battle headquarters, but I was told that I wouldn't be needed as I was a tap dancer, and there would be nothing up there for me to dance on, no tables or anything, so I stayed behind. Some of the lads who went in that show were killed by mortar shells, so I was extremely lucky.

We went right through the Italian campaign, and although I wasn't in Stars in Battledress then, I was still with the divisional concert party. Stars in Battledress were based in London and they sent shows out to Italy. All their performers were made up to the rank of sergeant so at the end of their show they could go on to the Sergeants' Mess. When we finished a show, as privates we couldn't enter those sacred portals; the army discipline was very strict.

Meanwhile our division had been pulled out of the line for a rest and moved on to Greece. I was seconded to the Stars in Battledress headquarters in Naples, and made up to the rank of sergeant, and it was in Naples that I met Spike Milligan.

I joined several shows: one was called *Sky High*, another *Ace High*, and that was where I came across Harry Secombe. He was with us in different shows right through Italy, and he used to drive one of those open trucks, with an old white hat on. He looked like an old man, and he kept following us. I kept saying to the boys in our show, and the Italian musicians, "That fellow's a very funny comic with his 'Hello, folks' and raspberry noises." Harry and I finally finished up in Rome.

I mainly stayed in Italy and Austria after that, and it was at one of these shows that Colonel Richard Stone, who was now in charge of Army Welfare productions in Germany and Austria with Ian Carmichael, said to me, "When you get out of the army come up and see me." Richard became a very big agent after the war and I worked for him a lot.

I was finally demobbed in Naples in 1947 and travelled back to Britain by train via Genoa.

Why I'm so grateful for being able to do those army shows is that I joined up as a tap dancer and when I came out I had a string of comedy routines which I had developed from doing army gags, as you did in those days. It certainly was an experience.

After the war Norman played in summer shows and variety all over the country and then in the 1960s he got his big break when he was asked to take over as compère for television's *Sunday Night at the London Palladium* where his "Swinging" and "Dodgy" catchphrases brought him tremendous acclaim.

He later starred in his own TV series for ATV and BBC and was featured in a chocolate commercial where "Roses grow on you". In more recent years he has been partly responsible for the production of *Bullseye*, the very popular television darts game.

Richard Pasco, CBE

For a man who had no inclination to be an actor, Richard Pasco hasn't done too badly in a career that has included radio, television, major film appearances and the theatre.

Richard's first job after leaving school in 1943 was trainee stage manager at the Q Theatre, Kew Green, just outside London. He got paid £2 10s (£2.50) per week while gaining experience. He learned a lot under producer Jack De Leon who ran the Q, and Maggie Dunlop the stage director.

In 1943 a play called *Zero Hour* was tried out at the Q which was transferred to the Lyric Theatre in Shaftesbury Avenue, and Pasco went with it. Unfortunately the flying-bomb blitz of London started and the play only lasted three days. He then got a small part in a play on tour called *Daughter Janie* (the reluctant actor had to eat), but while the play was at Coventry he got called up. That was in 1944.

Although London born, Richard joined the Suffolk Regiment and reported to Bury St Edmunds, a delightful place I know well, at least in peacetime. I'm sure it was the same during the war although probably a little crowded with service men.

Next came a commando course at Skegness in freezing winter conditions which had a lasting effect on Richard who later suffered from pneumonia with complications.

He was then transferred to the Royal Army Service Corps as a clerk. He didn't fancy this, so after some intervention by an uncle who was "in the know" he was presented with an alternative: Stars in Battledress. Because of his experience in the theatre, although limited at that time, he could be useful to the SIB unit.

His posting came through, and he arrived at the Grosvenor Square HQ and was interviewed by Captain Raymond Francis. Raymond was certainly one of the nicest people I ever met, and his portrayal as the police inspector in the highly successful television series *No Hiding Place* in the 1960s became compulsive viewing.

At the time of Richard Pasco joining Stars in Battledress, Raymond was preparing to produce *The Amazing Doctor Clitterhouse* with himself in the leading role. Richard joined the cast and the production went straight out to Germany following the British army of liberation.

The play was presented in opera houses (some without roofs due to the allied bombing campaign), boxing rings and newly set up NAAFI canteens in places such as Essen, Dusseldorf, Bremen and Cologne. All this was within the 21st Army Group. We were mostly billeted with German civilians and the families would be given food for this purpose. One very pretty young girl of about eighteen was so nervous when she was serving the soldiers' food she shook like a leaf, because, one supposes, she was expecting to be raped or shot at any moment. We were also able to give our hosts chocolate and cigarettes which they were most grateful for. It was awful to see people scavenging for food among the wreckage of buildings, which was widespread.

We then produced another play, *The Wind and the Rain*, which we took on to Italy, performing in Naples, Rome and Trieste. We also played Klagenfurt in Austria. This all happened in 1946. Margaret Courtenay was in this production, and Maggie has certainly done well for herself since, and she's a lovely person to work with.

The unit then returned to the UK and it was then back to the RASC for Richard, or the alternative of taking a course in basic radio techniques for the forces broadcasting service. He naturally chose the radio course, which included not only broadcasting, but also scriptwriting and disc-jockeying. When he had finished the course he was offered either BFBS (British Forces Broadcasting Service) in Hamburg or Cairo, or Radio SEAC (South-East Asia Command) based in Ceylon. He plumped for Ceylon and was immediately sent to the Middle East! Well, the army is like that.

I arrived in Cairo and was told I was to go to a radio station in Jerusalem. I travelled on the same single-track railway that Lawrence of Arabia had encountered in his travels, and the most amazing thing was when I told my father about this later on he said he had travelled on the same railway during his service with the Honourable Artillery Company fighting the Turks in the First World War.

Richard's radio station in Jerusalem was in a monastery, and as well as popular music he played some classical pieces which brought an immediate response from the listening service men. He then broadened the programmes he was presenting to include poetry and excerpts from plays which he and his broadcasting colleagues performed between them.

This was in January 1947 and, because of the terrorist activities in Palestine that were prevalent in spite of the British policing the area, we had to be careful about leaving our quarters. This we could only do at certain times. On one occasion a member of our unit got shot, but not fatally, thank goodness. His name was Gordon Rollings.

Many years later Gordon made a big name for himself in television's *Coronation Street* and you may recall his appearances in the John Smith beer advert.

Unfortunately some of my mates were killed by the terrorists, including my great friend Dixie Dean who had been such a help in the radio station.

Around this time I contracted hepatitis and was sent to a military hospital set in an orange grove where I was nursed by a wonderful girl called Sister Duthie. When I had recuperated I was told I would be going home as soon as a ship was available. I had to wait in the Canal Zone with temperatures reaching 106°F while the ships kept passing by on their way back from the Far East, packed to the gunnels with no room left to pick any of us up. Eventually I did get on a boat, the *Samaria*. It was also packed to capacity, but it got us home to Liverpool and dear old Blighty. I was sent straight to Aldershot and demob, so it was all over for me.

By now there was no doubt about what I wanted to do for a living – act – so in 1948 I went to drama school. My idols of that time were John Gielgud, Paul Scofield and Ralph Richardson, particularly John Gielgud. I bought some records he had made and listened intently to his voice and delivery of play readings and poetry. I needed to break down my Cockney accent which was quite pronounced as I was a Londoner born and bred. Later on I had the good fortune to work with all these people I admired, which was just wonderful.

From the early discovery in Jerusalem, at the radio station with Dixie Dean and others, that he would like to earn his living as an actor, Richard has gone on to great things in theatre, film and television. He has toured in major theatrical productions throughout the world, including making his Broadway début in *The Entertainer* in 1958.

Apart from being an Associate of the Royal Shakespeare Company his theatre roles are numerous, including recently *Six Characters in Search of an Author* and *Racing Demon* at the National. Although very much a man of the theatre, he has been just as successful in other media. His films include *Room at the Top*, *Wagner*, and *Yesterday's Enemy*. Television roles include Disraeli in *No 10* and a serial production of *Sorrel and Son* and *Drummonds*. He has also been involved in numerous radio plays and recitals.

Richard lives in the Warwickshire countryside with his very talented actress wife, Barbara Leigh Hunt. He was awarded the CBE in 1977 in recognition of his services to British theatre, which he admires, respects and obviously loves.

Kenneth Connor

I have had the pleasure of working with Ken on several occasions, and not only is he a very professional actor but he is also great fun to be with. In my very early broadcasting efforts I had the good fortune to do some episodes of *Ray's a Laugh* and Ken, Ted Ray and Kitty Bluett showed me the way at that stage in my career. Theatre, films (many of them in the *Carry On* series) and television have had the benefit of Ken's performances.

He started his career with the Open Air Theatre Regent's Park Company.

Early in the war I went into the militia for six months' training, which turned out to be six and a half years of solid soldiering. I was trained in machine-gunnery and signalling, and eventually fought against the foe in 1940 in Europe until I was slung into the sea at Dunkirk. Once back home we started getting ready for the second front, but that was a long time coming, so in the meantime, having been noted down in records as a pre-war actor, I joined Stars in Battledress.

I appeared in this country in a production of Terence Rattigan's *Flare Path* along with Wilfrid Hyde White, Faith Brook and John Longdon. Once the allied armies were into Italy our SIB unit was sent out there to do a tour with *Someone at the Door* (which included Geoffrey Keen).

After that we went to Athens and Cairo and it was there that I received a cable from producer William Devlin saying he wanted me to play Scrut in *Beaux Stratagem* at the Bristol Old Vic as soon as I got home. It took me ages on a troop ship called *Goddisca* to get back to England because there was a strike in Naples on the way home. I remember arriving at Bristol on the morning they were starting to rehearse and I threw my kit bag and equipment down the stairs at the theatre as I walked in. That was early in 1947. That's all, folks!

The pleasure that Kenneth Connor has given to his audiences since then is immeasurable.

Jack Tripp: "Plymouth's Fred Astaire"

That title was bestowed on Jack Tripp at a very early age when, as a youngster, he performed at various venues in that city. His family were unconnected with entertainment, having a bakery business in Plymouth.

When I joined the army I was for three and a half years at the Royal Electrical and Mechanical Engineers depot in Ashton-under-Lyne where I was given the task of issuing spare parts for the trainee drivers' vehicles. The funny thing is I still don't know a big end from a brake drum, but somehow I got by.

In my spare time I helped to organise a few shows at the depot, and I was really in my element doing this. I teamed up with a marvellous pianist called Bill Heywood, and when the whole unit was moved to Aberford in North Yorkshire we were both recommended to join Stars in Battledress. This was a wonderful break, and also an escape from the usual army routine. Of course we had our rules and regulations but there was that feeling of being able to enjoy the moments we spent entertaining, with the added excitement of meeting various theatre people I had heard about. Terry-Thomas was at the SIB HQ, and even as an NCO was still terribly smart ("I say, how do you do?"), with the cigarette-holder and the character he was to become famous for.

Janet Brown, the impressionist, became a great friend, and so later did her husband, that super fellow, the late Peter Butterworth. Janet and I still meet up either at my flat in Brighton or at her lovely farmhouse in the Sussex countryside.

Charlie Chester was always busy with his writing, and helping to organise tours. I also remember seeing one smartly turned out little soldier carrying a briefcase, and when I asked who it was they said, "Oh, he's Bryan Forbes, he does a bit of acting." A bit of acting! Look what he's done since then.

The show Bill Heywood and I arranged was called *Command Performance*, and after auditions and rehearsals the show, which consisted of two ATS girls and six men, was flown to the Middle East, where we did a tour of bases in and around Cairo and then down to Khartoum and back.

The flight out to Cairo was quite memorable. We were issued with RAF flying kit, helmets, etc, because we were flown out in a huge carrier plane. No heating or pressurised cabins then, just makeshift seats and freezing conditions; so to arrive in Cairo with February sunshine and to be billeted in a big hotel for an overnight stay was luxury indeed. This sort of accommodation didn't last as we moved on.

We had a successful formula for the show: comedy, music, a sing-along and dancing, which all went very well.

I remember when we reached Khartoum one of the members of the show was stricken with diarrhoea. He was put into isolation and we could only visit him and make signs through a window. We had to move on to our next date without him, but what worried us was the fact that he was broke at one stage of the tour, and three of us had lent him some money. We knew that he had been paid the day before we were due to leave, so we wanted our few bob back there and then, but owing to him being in isolation we could not get in to collect it. We decided to write a note, which was then pushed through his door, asking him to pour disinfectant (which was beside his bed) over the few notes he owed us and pass them under the door. One of us had to pick up the notes with a handkerchief, wash the notes and distribute them to the "moneylenders". He was out of debt, but best of all he recovered from his illness.

We came back to England on a troopship called *Ascania* on which we did a few impromptu shows. We were fortunate to have been able to do some performances that were not always wonderful but were certainly appreciated on that ship.

We received a certificate from the War Office saying that "10584309 Pte. W. Tripp REME, had been brought to the notice of the Chief of the Imperial General Staff, and I am authorised by him to signify by the award to you of this Certificate, his appreciation of the Good Service which you have rendered." So perhaps the shows had not been too bad.

I've never reached stardom, but have had a long and enjoyable theatrical career, and I feel had it not been for Stars in Battledress I might never have taken up this lovely profession.

Jack certainly has had a marvellous career in the theatre, and also in the late 1950s in his own television series *Take a Tripp*. I first met up with him and his wonderful feed, the late Allen Christie who was also a fine singer, when I was in the famous

Fol-de-Rols concert party with them at Eastbourne in Sussex. The *Fols* as they were known, were the cream of summer show entertainment, thanks to people like Jack Tripp, Allen Christie, Leslie Crowther and David Nixon.

Jack Tripp is one of this country's most brilliant pantomime dame comedians and some would say he has no equal in this field. I wouldn't argue with that as I've had the pleasure of observing his performance at close quarters when I have been in productions with him.

Bruce Trent

The musical theatre in post-war Britain was inhabited by some very talented artistes, and one of them was this fine baritone. A Channel Islander who began his musical career in Jersey, Bruce arrived in England in 1936 and, with the help of a band he had met when they visited the island, he found employment as a singer and double-bass player in West End night-clubs.

In May 1938 I joined the Jack Hylton band in a stage show which was produced on tour and at the London Palladium and in Europe, including the Paris Opera House. They had also appeared in the film *Band Wagon* starring Arthur Askey and Richard Murdoch. In May 1940 I signed up for military service. It was generally accepted that you would be called up in four weeks. In preparation for this I went over to Dublin to see a young lady I had met there (now my wife Mary), then I went home to Jersey to see my family.

While I was in Jersey the German air force was flying over the Channel Islands dropping leaflets telling the islanders they were going to be invaded and not to resist. Several people had decided to leave the islands, and I think I was on one of the last boats to leave, a potato boat. When I got back to England I wasn't called up as I thought I would be, so I was able to join the Jack Payne band. We broadcast almost nightly for the BBC and the team of singers besides myself included Anne Shelton and Carole Carr.

After this I went into a musical stage production of *Dubarry was a Lady* with Arthur Riscoe and Frances Day, both big theatrical names at that time, at His Majesty's Theatre in London. I went back to Jack Payne's band after this, and was then offered the lead in *The Student Prince* opposite Carole Lynne (now Lady Delfont) at the Stoll Theatre in Kingsway, now rebuilt and renamed the Royalty.

The flying bombs directed at London were now getting a bit too close. I remember when we were in the middle of the duet "Deep in My Heart" in

The Student Prince one dropped very near and the whole place shook, and we and the audience were showered in debris from the ceiling, but we kept going and when the dust had settled the audience broke into spontaneous applause.

Later I was rehearsing a musical play, *By Jupiter* with the great Bobby Howes, when I was asked to "guest" with the Glenn Miller Orchestra. Miller said that if I was able to join him I could stay with him when he went into France once the second front had opened. Everyone will know the tragedy that later befell Miller flying out to do a concert in Paris. But to get back to *By Jupiter*. I could not be released to join Glenn Miller and the tour of *Jupiter* got under way, but in fact only lasted six weeks.

My calling-up papers arrived in 1944. Now you may wonder why I hadn't been called up before then. The answer is I don't really know. I had never applied for deferment, so I can only presume that I was probably regarded as "technically" a refugee from Jersey. Just before my call-up I had been offered my first film part. The film company hoped that I would be able at least to finish the first film, as people in entertainment at that time were still considered to be in a morale-boosting occupation. However, I was told to report to Brancepeth, the headquarters of the Durham Light Infantry.

Once in uniform as a Durham Light Infantryman I started on the familiar basic training and was then transferred to the Royal Engineers, first based at Chatham and then back up north to Ripon in Yorkshire. It was while I was at Ripon that I got called to the adjutant's office and told there had been an application from the War Office for me to join the Central Pool of Artistes' Stars in Battledress unit. This order had been initiated by Colonel Bill Alexander and his assistant Phyllis Rounce. So it was down to London for a "home" posting. It was nice because I was able to "live in" with the family, my wife Mary and two children, for part of the time.

The first thing I did with SIB was to resume some broadcasting for the BBC who I had worked for before call-up. The army incidentally got the fee I was paid and I had to put in a chit just for expenses. I travelled the country with various units and all the performers got on well together, and the shows were received with great enthusiasm by the service audiences.

I was eventually demobbed in 1946 and was lucky to continue my career in the theatre almost immediately, first with a tour of *The Student Prince*. I followed the *Prince* with a tour of *Goodnight, Vienna* in which the leading lady was Sara Gregory, the wife of Richard Stone, later to become a most prominent London theatrical agent.

I then went into *Brigadoon* at HM Theatre. I had taken over from the American lead, and it was during this show that I worked with Canadian tenor Bill O'Connor. It was a happy occasion for me as I struck up a long friendship with Bill. At this time I was invited to take part in the 1950 Royal Variety Performance.

Other West End productions Bruce was involved in included *Wish You Were Here* and *Camelot*. These days he is still singing in concerts, and he puts his piano playing to good use with the Grand Order of Water Rats, of which he is a very respected member.

Michael Denison

I didn't join the SIB unit until May 1945, and until then my only skirmish with army entertainment was taking part in a few battalion shows when I was doing service in the Middle East. I had been attached to the Intelligence Corps for the best part of the war and one of my duties was as an interrogator.

Because of this I was given an extraordinary job: it was to go to Odessa to collect ex-British prisoners of war who had been freed by the Russians when they had overrun the retreating German forces in the east. This would have been in 1945. On the ship out I had many ex-Russian prisoners who had been freed by the allies in Europe.

When we arrived in Odessa, the Russian prisoners were immediately labelled as traitors for having allowed themselves to be captured by the Germans. As you can imagine, the Russians were very dispirited about this, even though they were home, because they did not know what their eventual fate might be. Perhaps it's just as well we didn't know. The mood among the British ex-prisoners I was bringing home to the UK was of course quite different, very happy and quite convinced they were heroes.

I had to do a certain amount of interrogating on the ship, mainly to find out how they had been treated and what escape routes had been planned, if any. They didn't want to talk about the latter in case another conflict should break out. I must say because of this I wasn't the most popular man on the ship.

The base for the intelligence unit for debriefing ex-prisoners of war was at Beaconsfield and Latimer in Buckinghamshire, and when I arrived I met my new CO, a Colonel A. R. Rawlinson. He was a playwright and adaptor of Kipling stories for radio so we got on very well together. As I hadn't done any acting, well, not any serious acting, for six years I thought it would be a good idea to apply for a transfer to Stars in Battledress. After all, the war in Europe was now over. When I told Colonel Rawlinson this he said, "As a matter of fact I've just recommended you for a job with the Allied Control Commission in Germany with the rank of major."

I could speak German, which he knew, so I said, "Thank you very much, sir, but I would rather like to join the SIB unit. Would you release me?"

He said, "If I can find a replacement, yes."

He did this, and I was soon on my way to Upper Grosvenor Street and involvement in something that I knew about and would enjoy: entertainment. There were a lot of youngsters in various battalion concert parties who wanted to make performing their post-war career, so I was to be in charge of a sort of stage school with SIB. I had would-be actors, comedians, singers, dancers, acrobats and even conjurors. I had to maintain service discipline of course because they were all still in the services. I was a producer of various shows that went out under the SIB banner, and I remember I also had to take the ballet rehearsals! I think we once nearly fell into the planning department below – we were rather a heavy ballet class. [Is there no limit to Michael's talents?]

During the period I was with the unit I was given a chance to break into films, which came about purely by chance. I was able to live at home with my wife Dulcie (Gray) who was by now on the up and up in the film industry, although she was paid practically nothing in those early days.

Dulcie herself had been part of wartime entertainment through rather unusual circumstances. In 1944 she went to France, Belgium and Holland in a commercially sponsored tour by the Linitt and Dunfee Management in association with ENSA. This was prior to the production opening at the Playhouse Theatre in London, an unusual "prior to London" tour, to say the least. The company were in Eindhoven on New Year's Day 1945 when suddenly the air appeared to be full of parachutes. Dulcie and her party thought they were going to be besieged by German troops landing round them. It was a little worrying until they were told that they were Germans who had been baling out of their aircraft after being shot up by allied planes, and would be captured on landing.

My entry into films was prompted by an incident that happened in the early forties when I was on the intelligence staff in Northern Ireland. I came back to London for a short leave just as Dulcie was about to be tested for a film out at Welwyn in Hertfordshire. I said I would go along with her. There were five more girls being tested with Dulcie for a Ben Travers film, *Banana Ridge*. There were no actors available to go through the lines with the girls so Dulcie suggested to the casting director that as I was an actor she felt sure I would help them. This I did.

Much later, when I was finishing my duties in Stars in Battledress, Dulcie was contracted to do a film called *My Brother Jonathan* and the casting director, the same one who had worked on *Banana Ridge*, was looking for someone to play Jonathan. He said to Dulcie, "We want an unknown actor for the part in this instance. By the way, do you remember who the actor was who helped us with lines in *Banana Ridge*? I think he would be most suitable. I think he was in the army, but we can't remember his name." Dulcie said, "I do, he's my husband." I did the film and that was the real start of my film career.

Michael Denison's career in theatre, cinema and television has spanned more than fifty years, and he and his wife Dulcie have a unique place in this country's entertainment scene. They are two super people, and by coincidence their lovely home in Buckinghamshire is within a stone's throw of my birthplace.

I have had first-hand experience of Michael's jolly company in the London theatre when we appeared in the play and film version of *See How They Run* in which his Bishop of Lax was a joy of a performance.

Television viewers will remember Dulcie recently in the series *Howards' Way*, which also featured Michael in its latter stages.

Reg Varney

Reg Varney joined the Royal Electrical and Mechanical Engineers (REME) in 1942. It was almost inevitable that Reg would eventually become a member of SIB. He had been a part-time entertainer since the age of fourteen, playing the accordion in the many social clubs in and around the area of his home, Canning Town, in London's East End. His musical career was almost brought to an end when war broke out due to a job he had taken as a sheet metal worker. His hands were cut to pieces handling the rough metal, but being determined to carry on he managed to overcome the injuries and his hands hardened and healed up, allowing him to continue his accordion playing.

Like all East End families the Varneys were part of a close-knit community, and this certainly saw them through the horrendous bombing of London's dockland in 1940 and 1941. He and his family had their fair share of close shaves as family houses were knocked about, some of them reduced to rubble.

Once in the services Reg became involved in regimental entertainment and it was because of this that he started playing the piano on stage, which was to become an integral part of his post-war theatrical career. He also developed a liking for comedy during this time, performing in the NAAFI (the "regimental tea rooms") where the lads could relax, write letters or just chat.

A certain commanding officer suggested that he might be able to get a whole show together involving other service men in the area. Reg set about this task with an enthusiasm that was eventually to lead to SIB. He wrote comedy material for the regimental shows and became the principal comedian, not because he particularly wanted to at that stage, but because the other performers persuaded him that he was best qualified. He was writing the gags and sketches, after all, and his bubbling personality made him the obvious choice. He naturally finished the shows playing the piano or accordion which never failed to "raise the roof".

The production was taken round to various other camps and depots, on occasion some distance away from the REME base at Ashford in Kent where Reg was stationed. Believe it or not, the agent who fixed the dates for the show was the regimental padre. The bulk of any money earned from these service shows went to the Regimental Benevolent Fund, but a small amount also went to the performers. As a result of the padre's expertise and the show's success, quite a lot of money was given to regimental welfare funds.

A service recommendation that Varney be transferred to SIB came about in 1944 and he was almost immediately put in charge of a show called *Jamboree*. The leading lady was Stella Moray and the group did a tour of bases in the UK, led by Reg who had now been made a sergeant. After this they were despatched to British garrisons overseas, first to Malta, Libya (Sidi-Barrani and Tobruk), and Cairo, and then on to India and Singapore.

When they arrived in India nobody was expecting them because their papers concerning details of the group had been sent by mistake to Italy. Nobody knew what to do with the *Jamboree* company for some time, and they were left kicking their heels until officialdom sorted it out. However, all was eventually successful, and the show was received with the usual tremendous enthusiasm.

By the time Reg came home and was demobbed he had become a very experienced solo comedy and musical performer and was able to play the variety theatres in the UK. He did several more tours abroad as a civilian entertainer under the banner of Combined Services Entertainment (CSE) at service bases which were still manned well after the war had finished. He became the principal comedian in summer shows, several of them at Margate in Kent where his comedy feed was Benny Hill.

In the 1960s Reg was featured in television's *The Rag Trade* with Miriam Karlin, followed by yet another TV success *Beggar My Neighbour* with actress Pat Coombs playing his wife. But perhaps his biggest small-screen success was yet to come. Late in the 1960s London Weekend Television began a series, *On the Buses*, which very soon became a must for the viewing public. Besides Reg it also featured Anna Karen, Michael Robbins, Doris Hare, Stephen Lewis and Bob Grant.

Reg Varney had now become a big name in entertainment. He made several trips to Australia where *On the Buses* was also very successful, doing his now brilliant solo act of comedy and music, including a very funny send-up of a ventriloquist's dummy (Reg being the dummy).

Reg is still entertaining audiences with reminiscences about his life and also treating his loyal fans to his musical prowess. He recently played a theatre musical director with Joan Collins in her successful TV series *Tonight at 8.30*.

He lives now with his family overlooking the sea in a glorious part of South Devon.

The first part of his autobiography, *The Little Clown*, was published by Hodder and Stoughton in 1990.

Stan Hall

When Stars in Battledress finished it had among other things produced some fine performers of the future, many of them you will now know about, and well – if that woman hadn't stepped out in front of my car . . . I might never have been involved in one of the most interesting periods of my life.

One brilliant comedian who was in SIB was a chap called Ted Gatty, a marvellous comic, who began his post-war civilian career at about the same time as Danny La Rue, and I helped them both with their wigs and make-up. At that time Danny was a window dresser in Oxford Street, and doing shows in a sort of cellar just off Leicester Square. From there he went on to Churchills and other London nightspots and eventually his own club in the capital. Even in those days Danny was always meticulous about costumes and make-up, and would spend money buying the best, whereas Ted Gatty couldn't be bothered, and although he did some good work, and for many years was a very popular chairman of an Old Tyme Music Hall show at Margate, he never realised his full potential.

One of the most talented people we had on the music side was George Melachrino. He could play any instrument and was a fine singer and orchestral arranger. He and Eric Robinson got together and did a lot of broadcasts. Later they were to be household names for the BBC, both on radio and later television.

After my release from the army I went back to Denham where I noticed that it was very difficult to obtain certain things that before the war we took for granted, particularly wigs. So I decided to set up my own business with a partner from my service days, Norman MacGregor, and together we started Wig Creations.

Wig Creations became a huge and successful business and brought Stanley Hall into contact with practically every British and American actor and actress, and over the years many became close personal friends. Several used to spend weekends at Stan's country house just to relax and get away from the pressures of the film studios and theatres, among them Vivien Leigh and Coral Browne.

I talked to Stan at his charming and unusual cottage situated in woodland in the heart of Sussex, a cottage that has been the tranquil harbour for a lot of theatrical history.

Norman Macleod (and Little Johnny) in India

After a night's stay at Poole in Dorset the British Overseas Airways Corporation Dakota took off from nearby Hurn Airport with the SIB unit in slightly apprehensive mood, as none of them had ever flown before.

Our first stop was Marseilles for refuelling, and then on we went to Malta and eventually to Cairo. This was a two-day stop where we lived like lords in a posh hotel. Before we left we had been given a letter signed by Sir Alan Brooke, Chief of the Imperial General Staff, stating that as entertainers we were to be given first-class treatment where possible.

After our rest we flew on to Basra and then Sharjah in the Persian Gulf. The following day it was off to our final destination, Karachi. We arrived in India to find nobody knew anything about us. Little Johnny phoned HQ in New Delhi to find out what was to be done. He was told we were to go to Calcutta, right across the other side of India.

Next day we were driven to the docks, where moored nearby was a BOAC flying boat, which was to be our transport. We were shown to our seats in a luxurious cabin where there were already four other people, three men and a lady, all Indian. The doors of the flying boat closed and we were off, an extraordinary sensation taxiing across the water in a flying boat. Refreshments were brought round as soon as we were airborne and conversation started with our fellow passengers. They were not going all the way to Calcutta, but to Allahabad. We told them that we had only just arrived in their country and our main job would be entertaining the troops.

As we approached Allahabad and the River Ganges we saw thousands of people gathered on either bank of the river, cheering and waving to our plane. They couldn't be cheering for us, we'd only been in India a couple of days. We asked one of our fellow passengers why the cheering crowds, and he pointed to the lady sitting opposite us. We all had the same thought: she was a famous Indian film star. When the plane had stopped we were asked to board a motor launch while the plane was refuelled. We then realised who the crowds had been cheering, for sitting in the launch was Pandit Nehru who had come to welcome his daughter Indira Gandhi home. The lady whom we thought to be a film star was India's future Prime Minister.

We were soon on our way again to Calcutta, and eventually "splashed" down on the Hooghly River. We were met at our destination by an officer who was representing SIB, ENSA and CSE which were handling entertainment jointly in the area at that time.

Our first week in Calcutta was spent organising our itinerary which was initially to consist of playing garrison towns and cities in the Central and United provinces, an area covering several hundred square miles. The journeys were to be done by rail, and to our amazement we were given our own Pullman coach, complete with staff to do our cooking and washing. Each time we reached our venues like Nagpur, Bhopal, Jabalpur and Jhansi our coach would be shunted into a siding and would be used to eat and sleep in until we had done our shows, and then we'd move on to the next place.

We completed our first tour and returned to Calcutta just as the troubles started concerning the future partition of the country. The whole place was rioting, Moslem against Hindu and both against the British, especially those in uniform. Soon we had to forget entertaining for a while. We were once again serving soldiers. Our area of patrol was the Howrah Bridge. It wasn't too bad there. The civilians mainly swore at us and tried to catapult us with large pieces of stone, rather like doughnuts, which they put on a pole and spun in our direction.

When things had quietened down a bit we got ready for our next tour in which we would be visiting smaller units well off the beaten track. We had a coach for this, a truck which could be converted into a stage and take our props and mini piano, etc. So off we went into the Bengali hinterland.

By now the show was well organised, Little Johnny and I doing two-handed gags and other comedy routines with Joe Melia and all of us, including our ATS girl, joining in the singing. We did all the tested and tried gags, like someone coming on with a large outsize medal on his tunic and someone would say, "Where did you get that?" and he'd say, "On the Frontier," then he'd turn round with a similar one on his back and say, "I've got another one on the back here." All clever stuff!

After the shows we would chat to the blokes on the unit, mainly about things back home. We now had a pretty young girl in the show which was a real attraction for the lads, some of whom had been out in India for years. If the lads tried to get too friendly with her we would discreetly close ranks and usher her away to another group of men.

Although it was hard work, travelling on bumpy roads over long distances and sleeping in bamboo huts in the jungle areas, I think this part of our Indian tour was the one that gave us most satisfaction. When it came to an end we were told we would be going to Bombay to await a troopship home.

While we were waiting in Bombay for our ship, the SS *Franconia*, to arrive, Little Johnny was roped in to do a broadcast by a visiting Shakespearean company who were doing *Twelfth Night*. Johnny played Sir Toby Belch. Typecasting again!

The *Franconia* was packed to the gunnels by the time we left port. Civilians and service men in their thousands. Rather than go below we opted to sleep on deck, where it was much cooler and less claustrophobic. This was okay until we had gone through the Suez Canal, when very cold winds forced us to go below. We arrived in Liverpool twenty days after leaving India and without wasting too much time we were on the train to London.

After being debriefed at SIB headquarters in Upper Grosvenor Street we were told to go to the Battersea Park depot and wait for demobilisation. After demob, Joe Melia, Johnny and I teamed up with an ex-RCAF singer called Al Harvey, making a barber shop-type quartet.

It was while we were doing some shows before our demob came through that we met an old mate Pete Warren, who had been a stage manager for SIB. He told us that George Black (the same George Black who was one of the originators of SIB) was looking for acts to go out on tour with the two big stars at the time, Nat Mills and Bobby. We went to the Prince of Wales Theatre in Coventry Street, and after singing one song unaccompanied we got the job, and this touring show opened up all sorts of opportunities for us in radio and stage work.

Eventually Henry Hall, the famous band leader whom we also worked for, gave us a new name, the Maple Leaf Four (it had something to do with our Canadian connections and Al Harvey). We later had our own radio series for several years called *Smoky Mountain Jamboree*. After the Henry Hall show we worked as a group, as I've said, in radio and revues all over the UK and the Continent until the mid 1960s. In the 1960s I went into the straight theatre which included a long run in *Mame* with Ginger Rogers at the Theatre Royal, Drury Lane, where my parents had first met, and the *Dad's Army* stage show at the Shaftesbury Theatre in London, while Little Johnny went into the pop music business and had at least three number one hits, "Let the Heartaches Begin" and "Baby, Now That I've Found You" among them.

It had all been a wonderful time for us, and we wouldn't have missed a minute of it.

"If I Only Had Wings"

Part of the story of the RAF Gang Shows belongs to twins Fred and Frank Cox, and they probably know as much about most of the Gang Show's activities and, dare we say, its unique "Governor" Ralph Reader, as anybody. Their involvement with the RAF Gang Shows has spanned fifty years, much of this time spent as welfare and entertainments officers. It is not always easy to be part of a team, but the two boys learned the importance of working successfully with other people while they were still cutting their teeth.

The 1930s was an era of experiment and ground-breaking ideas. When the twins were fourteen they began a career that would lay the foundations for their activities as entertainers during the Second World War and for many years after. They became involved in the 1930s in the ambitious scheme of a conductor and pianist by the name of Steffani. (His country of origin is a little obscure.) Steffani was keen to form a choir of youngsters who he thought could become bill-toppers in the big variety theatres in this country, and hopefully pursue successful careers as broadcasting and recording stars. (The 1930s was the era which saw a boom in the popularity of gramophone records.)

Eventually Steffani's stage production was running parallel with Ralph Reader's Boy Scout Gang Shows, the forerunners of the RAF Gang Shows. Both men were adept in spotting raw talent that they could mould into the type of performer that suited their particular production.

Steffani greatly admired an established and successful group of youngsters known as the Vienna Boys' Choir. This choir was always a smash hit wherever it played, including the London

Palladium, so why not a home-grown one? The obvious place to look for good voices was Wales with its great natural singing talent and its well-known Eisteddfod competitions. It was not long before Steffani had found the sort of voices he needed. With their parents' permission all the young lads were only too pleased for a chance to experience the bright lights of show business, even though it might be only for a short time, as of course their voices would eventually break. Broken voices would not have greatly bothered Ralph Reader as he not only had Boy Scouts in his early shows but also the more senior Rover Scouts and Scout Masters. In any case Reader's shows were slightly broader than Steffani's and rather more varied in their content with musicians, comedians, dancers and speciality acts such as ventriloquists and impressionists. As we will find out, some of them rejoined Ralph Reader and the RAF Gang Show in the 1940s.

Steffani had been told about a singer who lived in the Rhondda Valley reputedly with a magnificent voice and who should be heard. The trouble was the singer had only one leg, but so enthusiastic were the reports about him that the maestro decided to go to his home and see for himself. When he arrived the singer was obviously handicapped by his leg problem but was quite happy to give an audition there and then. Someone said, "Who's going to play the piano?" The singer shouted, "Kenny", and a small boy appeared who straightaway proceeded, without music, to give a performance of extraordinary talent. The singer was not taken on, but little Kenny at the piano was offered a job with the choir as soon as he was old enough. He was then about eleven.

So now, along with some wonderful vocal talent, were the young Cox twins, Fred and Frank. Although they were not singers, they were brilliant clog dancers whom Steffani thought could be an unusual addition to the stage presentation. Steffani took a London theatre for one performance to show off the whole production which by now he had entitled *Steffani's Silver Songsters*. The result of the one-off audition show was more than he could have hoped for: two whole years' work all round the country.

Some young members of the choir later went into other areas of entertainment. Norman Vaughan was one. Another was Ken Morris (little Kenny, the pianist from the Rhondda Valley) who, after serving with the Stars in Battledress companies during the Second World War, made a name for himself in radio and stage productions. Another member of the Silver Songsters was the jewel that Steffani had always been looking for, a solo top of bill. He was Ronnie Ronalde who had a light tenor voice and was a brilliant yodeller. By the 1950s, long after the disbanding of the Silver Songsters, Ronalde had become a huge radio, recording and stage personality, managed exclusively by Steffani, and his recording of "In a Monastery Garden" sold well over a million copies.

Eventually the twins left the choir and started working in other shows, one of them starring songwriter Billy Reid and his wife Dorothy Squires, later married to the actor Roger Moore, and who has been a singing personality for fifty years. It was from this show that the Cox twins started their service in the Royal Air Force. Billy Reid and Dorothy Squires gave them a very generous farewell pay packet so off they went to RAF Padgate for their initial training.

The boys were not only dancers but also exceptionally good electric guitarists. (Very unusual fifty or so years ago.) They had bought the guitars from the top bandleader Felix Mendelssohn, he of the Hawaiian Serenaders. When it was known that the lads could play musical instruments they were immediately asked to do a "turn" in the Sergeants' Mess. This they did and were a big success. An officer heard about it and invited them to play in the Officers' Mess for a "musical evening". Again the boys were a terrific success, the audience dancing and jiving like crazy. Entertainment had now singled them out as something different, and when the first postings came up they were asked where they would like to go, not told as was customary, by a senior officer. They chose Blackpool, because they knew from their theatre days that Blackpool had the best fish and chips. Fish and chips, bread and butter, ice-cream and a cup of tea cost 3s (15p).

In Blackpool they quickly made friends with a lot of the other recruits, because the boys were able to treat them to fish and chip suppers and packets of fags bought with the wads of money they had been given by Billy Reid and Dorothy Squires. They had money, their general duties finished at five o'clock, and they didn't have to worry if they would be working the following week, as they often did in the theatre. Their jobs in the RAF were secure as long as they behaved themselves, so for the moment everything was rosy.

They were asked to entertain a service audience at one of

Blackpool's theatres, and were again received very well. This brought another bit of advice from an officer called Captain Bell. He said, "You boys are wasting your time here, you ought to join Al Fredo and the RAF Gang Shows." They thought Al Fredo was a conductor of a gypsy band or something. A sergeant whom they had become friendly with said he would write an official letter on their behalf. Well, Al Fredo as it turned out was Ralph Reader (Captain Bell had got it slightly wrong).

They were then ordered to Bridlington on the Yorkshire coast. They weren't quite sure why, but thought it would eventually lead to the RAF Gang Show HQ. At Bridlington they got their first taste of the hard RAF regimental sergeants. One of them kept walking up and down at the various lectures telling them how best they could kill every German soldier they met: strangulation, stamping on their faces, kicking them, etc. This man was like some maniac, shouting and bawling all over the place. The boys had soon got the corporals in their pockets with and more fish and chips and fags (the money from Reid and Squires still hadn't run out). They hadn't got short hair (by service standards) and the sergeants wanted to know why they hadn't had their hair cut. More ranting and raving: "The boys will ruin the Air Force."

They did the odd entertaining spot in the NAAFI canteen and presumably as a result of this were told by a sergeant that they had been posted to Adastral House in London, and they'd only been in the air force ten weeks altogether! Everything seemed to be happening so fast.

It is worth mentioning here that whenever you entered or left a camp you had to sign a lot of forms. In the case of the RAF history was being made all the time because they had no long traditions to adhere to. The service was barely twenty years old in the early 1940s and, unlike the other services, Prime Minister Winston Churchill had stated that RAF personnel who were twins could stay together. The Cox twins therefore always had to make sure they signed their various papers together. The other lads knew of this rule and always made sure that no matter where the twins were in the queue they would be able to sign together. The reason that the other services did not abide by this rule was that in the case of the army, for instance, if twins were in the same trench and one got killed, the other twin was liable to start screaming his head off and simply go to pieces and give away their position to the enemy.

Before leaving Bridlington the twins were shown into the CO's office where various other officers, sergeants and other ranks were waiting to give them a rousing send-off. The CO himself told them how proud he was that they were going to join the Gang Show, and perhaps they would come back some day and do a show for them. The twins readily agreed and got into a big staff car "with a flag on the front, mind" that had arrived to take them to London. They had no idea what the Gang Show was but whoever ran it must be very important. Can you imagine what the boys were thinking, fresh from general duties of a none too pleasant kind and into a posh and very comfortable staff car headed for London? When they arrived at Adastral House the driver was told that Ralph Reader had gone on to Debden Air-field in Essex. Off they drove and found a house on the base where they would be staying. The door was opened by a very smart ordinary aircraftman who said his name was Rudi Mancini and that the boys' rooms were ready (complete with fires and carpets on the floor). They could have a hot bath if they wished, and then they should come down for a meal. The twins thought this was all a dream. "The meal was taken and Rudi Mancini said we should say thank you on behalf of the Gang Show." This Rudi Mancini obviously held the Gang Show in same awe.

The morning after their arrival at Debden the lads were told that Ralph Reader would be arriving to talk to them and that they should wait outside to give the great man a salute. They waited two hours with cold hands and aching heads until a figure came up the drive looking like someone out of a Hollywood B picture. Camel coat done up with a belt, cap on the side of his head and walking like the film star Jack Oakie. The lads thought somehow this must be Reader. As he got close they brought up the smartest salute they'd ever given. Reader's reaction was, "Hi, kids, let's go and have a drink." From that moment on they understood why "Ralph Reader and the Gang Show" were magic words in the air force, and the Cox twins became faithful fol-lowers.

Reader's close friends included Winston Churchill, General Eisenhower, Air Marshal Tedder and "Bomber" Harris. He would arrange to do shows for them, and afterwards all these great figures of the time would come up and congratulate members of the Gang. Reader also knew General Montgomery, but they didn't quite see eye to eye. In fact Montgomery wanted the Gang Shows disbanded as he thought the airmen should be fighting alongside their colleagues instead of trying to amuse them. Reader decided to go right to the top to see if he could sort out the problem before it went any further. He flew to Cairo where Tedder was then based and was met at the airport by Lady Tedder who was driving. He got into the back of the car and, once they were on their way, she said, "It's nice to see you again, Cocky." Reader was startled. He'd never met Tedder's wife before. She then told him she had been in the chorus of a C. B. Cochran revue before the war for which Reader did the choreography. Nothing more was heard from General Montgomery on this matter. Reader was too powerful. "Member of the RAF Gang Show" was eventually printed on their identity cards and even military police showed great respect to members of the "Gang" if they happened to stop one of them in the street or elsewhere.

Ralph Reader had many friends in the entertainment business including Noël Coward, Binnie Barnes, Ivor Novello and Anna Neagle, and they were often invited to the Gang Shows.

Reader's theatrical career matured in America after he left England as a youngster. From being a Broadway chorus boy he progressed to choreographing some big musicals, including the Al Jolson shows. When he returned to England he was asked to present a show for the Boy Scouts' Association. This he did, and it was so successful that it became an annual event and was called the *Boy Scouts' Gang Show*. The chaps in those shows idolised Ralph, as later would the RAF Gang Show personnel. He had this way of firing the boys with enthusiasm.

It had been noticed that Reader's reputation had got as far as Germany. In fact Hitler's Foreign Minister over here, von Ribbentrop, was a fan of the Scout shows and had actually remarked to Reader when they met that he "ought to come to Germany and produce similar shows with the Hitler Youth Movement".

Having joined the RAF before the war Reader was now in a position to start planning RAF-type shows for the predicted war. These could be used, and go on being used if war came, as a cover for his investigations on behalf of the Special Branch over here and abroad. He would never admit to any activities outside this country except for one operation in France he was involved in which resulted in a female spy being shot for treason; apparently she was a hat-check girl in a restaurant who was a recipient for a spy ring, and that was all Reader would say about it.

The first Gang Show the Cox twins saw after joining Reader had no dancers; comedians and singers yes, but no dancers. The twins pointed this out to Reader and he said, "Blokes don't seem to be interested in dancing." The boys said, "We are trained dancers." They were immediately put into a show, and this was the start of their wartime entertaining.

The Gang Show performed all over the country, entertaining service personnel, mainly on RAF stations, sometimes in some danger. On a visit to Tangmere Aerodrome in Sussex they had barely left their lorry when they were machine-gunned by a lone Messerschmitt 109 fighter. All the lads jumped over a wall into the vegetable garden belonging to one of the officers on the station. The lady of the house came out and remonstrated most severely with them, "Trampling all over my cabbages that have taken me months to grow." (People's reactions are never quite normal in wartime.)

On another entertaining assignment at a Lincolnshire bomber station, practically the whole squadron were leaving that night (actually two in the morning) for a raid on Germany. Most of the air crews had been to see the Gang Show earlier in the evening and "Bomber" Harris, head of Bomber Command, was also present on the station. The Gang were asked whether they would like to go on to the airfield as the aircraft took off. Normally this was forbidden as it could be deadly dangerous if an aircraft were to crash on take-off and its bomb load blow up. However, the lads wanted to see them off, so it was arranged. As the aircraft taxied down the runway all the tail-gunners swung their guns from side to side and up and down to salute the Gang who had entertained them that evening. As the Cox twins said, "It was a very moving moment, and showed just how much affection the services had for them." They in turn had a tremendously high regard for the air crews, as did everyone during the war.

Some members of the Gang Show were a crazy lot. Dick Emery had his moments, and on one occasion gave a classic performance in trying to "win the lady". The lady in question was the daughter of General Lord Ironside. She lived in a very large house near one of the venues the Gang Show were working and invited them all over to lunch. When they arrived she had just been for her morning canter, and the sight of her in her riding gear was too much for Dick Emery. He said to the boys, "You see if I'm not making love to the lady before the day is out." During lunch Dick gave the lady all the chat, and also comic business at the table with serviettes and cutlery, all the time winking at the other lads. He proceeded to go through various comedy characters which the boys all identified years later when they saw Dick on TV: among them his old man, his short-sighted lecher and his blonde lady ("Oh, you are awful – but I like you"). It seemed this was beginning to have an effect on the lady when one of the company, who was not quite as masculine as some others in the room, got up and went over to the piano and proceeded to play a musical comedy medley which completely captivated the lady who never looked at Dick again. Incidentally the lady and the pianist lived together for many, many years until quite recently.

Dick at one point decided he was fed up with the air force, and the Gang Show presumably, so he decided to make himself scarce. He got a job in the chorus of *The Desert Song* in London. One evening his corporal had taken his girlfriend to see the show and recognised young Emery in the back row of the chorus, heavily made up with a long droopy moustache and desert headgear; very observant of the corporal, considering the disguise. He went out in the interval, phoned the RAF station, and Dick Emery was taken back to the air force by the military police, still in make-up. Dick was confined to something or other for six months. When Dick eventually left the air force legitimately he climbed the show business ladder pretty quickly.

The Gang Show had a mild mid-war crisis when various station COs made it plain to the authorities that they thought there was some homosexuality occurring within the show units. This criticism began when one member, who often played the girls' parts in the shows, went into a canteen still dressed in costume. On another occasion when the lads went for a drink outside one of the camps they were playing, the "lady" went with them in costume just to see if, surrounded by the other lads, "she" could get out, which "she" did. After a few drinks it was too late to get back to the camp the normal way so it was over and through the barbed wire. This resulted in a lot of noise and laughter and the game was up, causing reactions like "Now we know there's at least one bloody 'poof' in the company!" In those days there was little sense of humour about an event like that, and to some observers if you dressed up in women's clothes you must be a "bloody poof". Actually it was pretty obvious the Gang were rather butch in their outlook and views, and in any case although there was some gossip, the higher authorities would not have the RAF Gang Show undergo a smear campaign. Strangely enough Ralph Reader would not let any actual female impersonations occur in the Gang Shows. He said that all audiences must know and be secure in the fact that "It's a bloke dressed up as a woman. That's the way you get your laughs. That's the difference."

There were two superb female impressionists (a very different attitude of performance from impersonators) in the Gang Show units. One was Rex Jameson, known then as Rex Coster and later during his successful post-war career as "Mrs Shufflewick". "Shuff", as he was known in the business, did a stand-up chat act as a charlady commenting on local gossip and the friends "she" used to have the daily drop of gin with at the pub. Unfortunately Rex liked the gin too much in his private life, which perhaps curtailed his chances of becoming a very big star.

In the RAF, Shuff was in a Gang Show unit stationed in Cairo, where his flight sergeant was Tony Hancock. Shuff's post-war theatrical manager for many years was journalist Patrick Newley. He once asked Shuff when he began having a tipple or two. Shuff said, "It started in Cairo. Tony [Hancock] and I had our afternoons off and we used to visit every bar we could find – ah, happy days." Patrick told me, "Once Shuff eventually began his radio career he was rarely off the air." Patrick said one of his first theatre jobs after the war was with the famous Alfred Denville Repertory Company. "He was sacked from the company for falling off the stage." Was it an accident, or the gin?

He was a big favourite with Windmill Theatre audiences in the West End and in fact did eight seasons at that little palace of entertainment. I remember playing the Windmill with him during one of those seasons and his delivery and timing were superb. Ralph Reader said many years later, "Rex could have been one of the really big stars alongside Hancock and Sellers and the like if he had disciplined himself and kept away from the gin bottle." I believe that some of the man's brilliance and unique talent might have disappeared into mediocrity if he had been disciplined.

So many people had a warm affection for Shuff, not just for the character of Mrs Shufflewick he portrayed on stage but also for Rex Jameson, the gentle alcoholic he became. The pleasure he brought to his audiences certainly outweighed any problems he might have brought to theatre managements. When Rex died a few years ago, two bottles of Guinness were placed in his coffin. At the funeral the organist played the congregation out with the Shufflewick signature tune, 'My Old Man Said Follow the Van'.

Ralph Reader has to take a lot of the credit for discovering talents who began their careers in the RAF Gang Shows. We know Dick Emery was one. Others included Billy Dainty, Joe Black, Tony Hancock, Michael Moore, David Lodge, Peter Sellers, Cardew (the Cad) Robinson, Clifford Henry, Arthur Tolcher and Peter Reagan, to name but a few.

I know by talking to various ex-members of the Gang Shows that they all had a high regard for Reader. He was even known affectionately as "God" by some of them. Even now, after his death in 1982, the lads speak of him with affection. He had fostered their raw talents and was certainly responsible for a lot of their post-war success. He wrote comedy material that suited them, particularly in the team sketches, a lot of which eventually found its way into the famous Crazy Gang shows.

Comedian Jack Seaton, who nowadays presents many variety bills all over the country, was an established performer at a very young age, and was fired to greater enthusiasm when he met Ralph Reader after the war. He decided he would like to be part of his "team". He eventually became one of Reader's assistants and later on, when Ralph was asked to recall some of his Gang Show memories and anecdotes on stage, he asked Seaton to produce the show. It toured the country with great success, filling theatres wherever it went. Seaton said, "At some venues whole contingents of ex-Gang Show members would take a block booking and give the 'Governor' a tremendous reception."

Reader was a talented songwriter and Seaton remembers the birth of a huge song hit Reader wrote for Bud Flanagan and the Crazy Gang called "Strolling". This was tried out in a small room by a pianist on a not too brilliant piano. In that instance Jack Seaton was the encourager. When Reader wasn't sure about it, Jack told him he was certain he'd got a walloping hit on his hands. Max Bygraves was very keen to have the song, but he had to wait until the Gang had finished using it in one of their shows.

His other major songwriting achievement, "On the Crest of a Wave", became the anthem, not only of the RAF Gang Shows but also, before that, for the Scout Gang Shows. Gang Show members, whether ex-Scouts or RAF, still greet one another with the first line of the song, "We're riding along on the crest of a wave . . .". The royalties from "Strolling" and "Crest of a Wave" alone must have been considerable, but even so Ralph Reader was never a rich man.

He played a silly prank on some of the Gang, including the Cox twins, when they took off from Northolt Aerodrome just after D-Day to entertain the troops during the Normandy landings in 1944. Ralph came to see the boys off with handshakes and "Hoping to see you soon, boys; I hope everything goes well for you, boys; I'll miss you, boys," and then just as the plane was ready to go he hopped aboard the aircraft himself. The aircraft came in over the Channel and had to put down on a makeshift landing strip. As they came in to land, looking out of the aircraft they spotted Charlie Chester on the ground giving them the V sign. So Charlie and a Stars in Battledress company had beaten them to it by a few hours. However, the Gang had got to their destination as planned, the Cox twins, Frank and Fred, clutching their valuable guitars.

The boys had read a book some months earlier called *They Died With Their Boots Clean* which made a great impression on them. They were determined to look as smart as possible when they landed in France. Before leaving Hucknell, just outside Nottingham, they went to a Chinese laundry to have their shirts washed and ironed. As a sort of throwaway comment when relating their story to me they said, "I remember Clark Gable came into the laundry to have some washing and ironing done while we were there. He was a nice, unassuming fellow."

The Gang arrived in Normandy at noon and the cleanliness didn't last long. The plane landed on a makeshift muddy airstrip, so their good intentions of being smartly turned out were rather thwarted. They were immediately greeted by a barking army NCO with the advice, "Get yourself some weapons as soon as possible and dig yourself a big hole if you want to live after six o'clock." They duly found some service men who were willing to part with some bayonets and guns for a little remuneration. They had also been warned that German parachutists were operating in the area. Their imaginations started to run riot as they thought about huge supermen dropping from the skies. In fact most of the German paras were quite small, but it didn't stop the lads feeling apprehensive about the possibility of them dropping in on the entertainers. The unit duly dug a hole to a depth of six feet, climbed in and covered their bunker with some corrugated iron they had found.

Ralph Reader returned from making various local contacts after they had landed, and asked the boys whether he could join them in the hole. At that point German Stuka bombers (Junkers 87s) came out of the sky and started strafing them from low level. The bullets were making a terrible noise hitting their corrugated-iron covering. They looked out through a small gap and saw all these coloured tracer bullets coming towards them. Reader said, "If we come through this, boys, you'll never want for work. When we get back home I'll look after you." When the raid eventually finished the silence was eerie and nobody talked for a moment. Suddenly there was a knock, knock, knock on the roof. This is it, the lads thought, German parachutists.

Then a voice with a broad Scots accent said, "Is Squadron-Leader Ralph Reader there?"

Reader said, "Yes."

The voice said, "This is Sergeant Macrrrr . . ." rasping the indecipherable name. "Would you like to see a film, sir?"

Reader said, "What sort of film is it?" (As if anyone cared after the terrific air-raid that had gone on.)

"It's Errol Flynn in the *Seahawk*, sir."

"Where is it being shown?" asked Reader.

"In a tent in the next field," said the sergeant.

"So Reader took our tin roof off," said twin Frank, "and we all marched into the next field to see the film. It was full of Errol Flynn shouting 'Charge' all over the place. We started joining in the dialogue and shouting 'Charge' whenever Flynn did. We seemed to have forgotten we could be killed at any moment."

Within hours the Gang were giving their first show at Arromanches.

Before the Gang Show unit tour through France began a generator had to be found for the Cox twins' electric guitars. This was eventually supplied by one of the army units in the area and was added to the Gang's equipment. The amusing moments that always seemed to be occurring started at Arromanches. It concerned Jessie Matthews, one of Britain's top dancing and singing stars of screen and stage in musical comedy. She was visiting the zone to make guest appearances with various units, one of them with our intrepid boys in blue. The RAF Gang Shows were very popular wherever they appeared and Ralph Reader could do no wrong. Jessie appeared a little unhappy with the itinerary of the tour and wanted to make several alterations which seemed unnecessary as everything was going well. Just before her first guest appearance she contracted gippy tummy (a bout of the runs). As Frank said, "She walked on stage, did one high kick, vanished into the toilet and we never saw her again. It was the talk of Normandy."

A little later on when the unit was at Eindhoven news went round that German soldiers were infiltrating the area dressed as American officers. The lads were billeted in a school at the time, and peering out of the window they saw some Americans and, not knowing whether they were Germans or the real thing, they all hid for the night under very large radiator pipes, which weren't working at the time. Fred said, "The cold was intense and being in such a cramped space for so many hours made us so stiff and cold that the next morning we could hardly move our limbs, but we had a show to do and somehow 'doctor footlights' got us going."

Cardew Robinson

Cardew, or as he was later known, "Cardew the Cad", would readily admit that Ralph Reader had a tremendous influence on his life, and performing in the RAF Gang Shows shaped his postwar career in stage, radio and films.

One has to go back to the 1930s to find the source of Cardew the performer. He had been involved in school concerts as a youngster and his leaning was to acting or writing when he left school. He tried the latter first, but the newspaper he worked for closed rather rapidly after Cardew joined them so he thought he would try the insecurity of the stage. He bought a copy of the *Stage* newspaper and saw an advert for lads to join a theatrical group called "Joe Boganni and his Crazy College Boys". He applied for the job and got it.

It was a sort of down-market Will Hay team. It consisted of Boganni himself and his dog, whose sole purpose was to walk across the stage with a dog's head (not a real one of course) tied to its backside so it looked like a freak, with a head at both ends. His act also consisted of three boys of which I was one, and two dwarfs.

Boganni said to me, "You will be taking over from a very small lad [Cardew is over six feet himself] and the small costume will look very funny on you, so you can be the comic." I said, "What do I have to do?" and he said, "At a certain cue you come on stage and I say, 'You're late, where do you come from?' and you say, 'From a little place called Cookeroff,' and I'll hit you on top of your head and say, 'Well, cookeroff back again,' and then you sit down." I said, "When do I do this?" and he said, "Tonight." It was the middle of the week and the act was playing the Lyric Hammersmith.

I rang home and said, "Mum, I'm on the stage." We did the first house at the Lyric and then Boganni put all the props, the dog, the dwarfs and us lads into a car and went over to the Balham Hippodrome to do two shows there, and then we went back to do the second house at the Lyric. This was all in the late 1930s.

After that we went down to Swansea to do a week and we all stayed in the same digs there, and on the very last night of the week, very tired and hardly a pro yet, I was awakened in the early hours by Boganni. He said, "Get up, we're going to scarpa the letti" (leaving without paying the digs' bill, I learnt later), "we've taken no money this week." So we all traipsed out to the kitchen and through the window: dog, dwarfs, the props and the rest of us, followed by Boganni. I thought, This is great, I've only been in the business a fortnight and I'm a crook already.

I got out of that set-up and was lucky to get into a repertory company, and followed that with a part in *Peter Pan*, and then the war broke out and I joined the air force. I was stationed at Uxbridge for about eighteen months and I met a chap there who became a lifelong friend, and post-war a fine film director, Lewis Gilbert. His films have included *Sink the Bismarck*, *Reach for the Sky*, *Alfie* and *Shirley Valentine*. His duties in the RAF were mainly in 11 Group Headquarters, Stanmore.

On one occasion, after an unexploded land-mine had been found at Uxbridge, we were all playing football, and I took a kick at goal just as the bomb disposal squad were dealing with the mine. It went off with a terrific bang, and everyone stopped still like statues, including the goalkeeper, and my shot went into the back of the net, so I reckon I scored the only land-mine-assisted goal during the war.

While I was at Uxbridge Ralph Reader and his Gang Show paid us a visit. He saw one of our camp shows (not camp, or precious, as we know it now), and I got the chance to join the Gang Show units. There were quite a few of these and I finished up in No 5 unit for a while. We were of course still serving airmen and I was eventually made up to flight sergeant and put in charge of No 5 unit. I spent the rest of the war with the unit, and Ralph taught us an awful lot. We played to RAF audiences all over Britain, and then when the second front opened in Normandy we went there, and up through Belgium and Holland.

I remember one instance when we were playing for a Spitfire squadron in Normandy. We used to have a stage on the back of our lorry because we had long distances to travel at times to do our shows. At night we used to sleep under the lorry because you never knew when there would be a few bullets or shrapnel flying about. During this particular show on the Spitfire base I was doing my "turn" and three Spitfires took off. The noise was horrendous and the lads in the audience couldn't hear a word I was saying. When the noise had died away I said, "I'm the only comic who carries his own Spitfire cover." It got a big laugh and I was able to carry on okay.

Joe Black was in my unit and of course after the war we worked in various shows together so we never lost touch. I do remember we had a terrific row on stage one day in the RAF. We each took a swing at one another and missed, and both of us fell off the stage and into a big prop basket. We finished up in hysterics, not even remembering what we'd been fighting about. We also had a wonderful accordion player called Rudi Mancini, who is now a hotel owner in Blackpool, plus a great Cockney jazz pianist by the name of George Weedon.

When the war in Europe was practically over we were sent out to the Far East, although we didn't know exactly where we would finish up. It was a marvellous journey, all through the Panama Canal and on into the Pacific. Eventually we heard we were going to lay off Okinawa and await further orders. The day after our arrival the Americans dropped the atom bomb on Japan, so they rerouted us to the Marianas. We were only there for a day and a show had been fixed up for us to do for a huge contingent of American service men, about ten thousand in all. We were the only airmen allowed off our ship. The other three thousand or so, mostly flight engineers, had to stay on board. I had never played to an American audience and I was first "turn" on and I got a few wolf whistles when I walked out, which was really unnerving. I said to the audience, "I'm an Englishman so you'll probably expect me to say 'Cheerio, pip-pip, chaps, etc'," and they fell about laughing, then I said, "I've played to some audiences of your comrades back in Britain so I'll just say 'Hi-ya, fellas,'" and they applauded, so I just about got away with playing to my first American audience. I then introduced Rudi Mancini with his accordion and he absolutely paralysed them.

We then got new orders to go to Hong Kong. Our lads ran everything there, including the post offices. Some commandos arrived at this time and we did a show for them using the pavement near our quarters as a stage, and the audience sat in the road and the pianist sat in the gutter. Hardly the Palladium! We were in Hong Kong for about five weeks serving primarily as reoccupation forces, and then we came back with the first repatriation troops from the Japanese prisoner-of-war camps. We came back via the

Suez Canal and we did shows on the ship for everyone, including some repatriated civilians, so we were kept pretty busy. It was amazing, we had done a world tour within three or four months.

When we arrived back in Britain after the tour we were demobbed and for a while became the civilian version of the Gang Show. It of course had been formed before the war as the *Boy Scouts' Gang Show*. We did some weekly touring, including a week in London at the Stoll Theatre in Kingsway. We also played a season in Blackpool and it was there I wrote the first "Cardew the Cad" routine, and that changed my life. I had in fact tried it out briefly when I was in the RAF Gang Show in 1942, but once I had written it properly during the Blackpool season it really went well.

I started doing a solo act in variety and on radio in shows like *Variety Fanfare*, where I did "News from St Fanny's" fictitious school every week. Then I felt "Cardew the Cad" had really arrived when the character went in the comic *Radio Fun* with its seven million circulation worldwide. Then a film was made based on the comic strip. That wonderful and large comic actor Fred Emney played the headmaster Dr Jankers. Claude Hulbert was the senior master, and Miriam Karlin was the matron. Boxer Freddie Mills was the sports master, the small but beautifully formed comedian Davy Kaye was the cook, and that wonderfully funny comic actor Peter Butterworth was also in the cast.

I have been lucky to be cast in something like fifty films myself, including *Shirley Valentine*. I was also in *Pirates* with Walter Matthau which was filmed in Tunisia, the Seychelles, Paris and Rome.

Cardew is certainly aware of all the experience he gained in the Gang Shows and of the help he received from his colleagues during those years.

Ralph Reader was a remarkable man, and I remember him saying to us before we were demobbed, "Some of you, Peter [Sellers], Tony [Hancock] and the rest hopefully, will have your name up in lights when you get back into Civvy Street. I won't take credit for it, but perhaps you'll forgive me if I just take the credit for screwing in one of the bulbs."

I can assure you he was being very modest. He was a great Guv'nor.

Joe Black

Young Joe Black, who was also a member of Cardew Robinson's No 5 unit of the Gang Show, remembers one of the productions they were involved in on the Orkney and Shetland Islands. Their costumes and props were carried in skips (theatrical baskets) and there was a mishap with one of them when they were being unloaded from the ship.

A most important one fell into the water as it was being unloaded, and the last thing the lads saw of their precious cargo of funny hats, funny noses and funny wigs etc was it gently bobbing away into the mists of time in the North Sea.

Once the second front was open in 1944, on D-Day plus eleven, Unit 5 was on the march in Europe.

After entertaining the 2nd British Airborne Division near Nijmegen we were ordered to do a similar show for an American contingent nearby. Off we went with all our paraphernalia loaded on the lorry. Before long we were stopped by a British soldier who asked us where we were going. We told him the name of our destination and the soldier said, "That's the place up on the hill where the windmill is, but I shouldn't go any further because it's still held by the Germans, the Americans haven't arrived yet."

A hasty retreat by the unit was the order of the day.

At another forward area they were entertaining a group of Americans in a huge farm building and halfway through the show it was shelled by the Germans.

The Yanks got under the seats, their helmets making a hell of a clatter on the floor. Singer Tony Davenport carried on with his rendering of "Santa Lucia" with the barrage in progress. The American staff sergeant shouted at everyone to "get the hell out of here", which we did. We hadn't gone very far when we realised one of the lads was missing: it was Jim Skilling. We went back to look for him; perhaps he was injured, we didn't know. When we got back to the building it was practically demolished but Jim was okay. He was selling fags and chocolate to the local villagers – the little bugger. He wasn't very popular with us for a while.

Once the war in Europe looked like coming to an end the unit was told they were going home for a spot of leave and to get ready to go to another destination. Very soon they had embarked on the *Empress of Australia*, along with two and a half thousand airmen and soldiers, for an unknown area. Also on board were a lot of navvies, which no one quite understood why at the time. Eventually the ship arrived in the Pacific where it met up with the British battleship *Indomitable*. The unit were asked to do a show on the battleship, so they were transported from their ship for this purpose in a naval cutter.

We hadn't gone far when the cutter's engine failed. We started to float away from both ships. Someone shouted, "Where are the oars?" The naval pilot said, "We haven't got any." The cutter kept drifting further away. It was quite frightening: here we were in the Pacific Ocean without an engine, nobody seemed to be doing anything. All of a sudden the engine was restarted and we made it to the battleship.

During the voyage on the *Empress* the unit's singer, Tony Davenport, gave singing lessons to anyone who was interested. One of his pupils was a young Welshman, already the possessor of a good voice. His name was David Hughes. After the war David became a top of the bill entertainer on radio, stage and records. He unfortunately died quite a young man, at the peak of his career.

Eventually we reached the Admiralty Islands and were told our destination was Okinawa, but as the war with Japan had just finished we wouldn't be going there, but on to Hong Kong. When we got there the navvies, who we now found out had come along to mend the runways (they knew not where), were given the job in Hong Kong of policing the city. [The establishment certainly works in a curious way.]

On board the *Empress* with us was a contingent of the Green Howards, and somehow or other they got on to the Chinese mainland, broke into an empty bank and stole several bars of gold. One of the soldiers was overheard talking about their booty and when the ship arrived at Suez on the way home they were arrested. We never did hear what happened to them.

Just outside Hong Kong was a Japanese prisoner-of-war camp called Chamshupau. British prisoners were still there, and by tremendous coincidence someone I knew. His name was Albert Stevenson, and he had been the stage manager at the Shepherd's Bush Empire when I used to play there in variety before the war. Like other prisoners Albert had suffered at the hands of the Japanese; suffering that plagued him for many, many years. I believe he eventually had something like thirty operations. In the post-war world of entertainment he rose to be a television director and producer, one of his big successes being the long-running discovery series, *New Faces*. He became a King of the Grand Order of Water Rats, and despite his ill health, which he coped with by recalling some very funny stories of incidents during his hospitalisations, he was great company until he died.

Another coincidence that happened in Chamshupau was that the brother of one of the army sergeants in the camp had been strung up by a Japanese sergeant, and he was still there, now a British prisoner. The army sergeant took revenge and blatantly ran the Japanese fellow down with a truck. The sergeant was taken to his superior British officer, and when the officer had heard what had happened he said, "Leave the office. I haven't heard a word you've said, you have never been in my office." It was a funny time to be around then.

As entertainers we just kept quiet and carried on trying to keep the various units and prisoners awaiting repatriation happy. After all, we were still trained airmen and we didn't want to get mixed up in anything requiring us to revert to that role.

I must say the RAF Gang Show gave me and a lot of other lads like me a chance to see the world, and get paid for it.

For nearly fifty years the diminutive Joe Black has been entertaining variety and pantomime audiences all over Britain. His panto dame is exquisite.

David Lodge

Hardly a month goes by without David Lodge cropping up on our television screens in the reshowing of some of the great films of the past thirty years. If you did not know it, it is difficult to imagine that the tall, well-dressed David could ever have "mixed it" with some of the great comedy actors such as Peter Sellers, Norman Wisdom and Spike Milligan, as well as being an actor of dramatic merit.

He had that special ability to act as the straight foil in comedic situations, something he has been interested in since he was a young boy singing comic songs in school concerts. It is a bent which he probably inherited from his parents, his father being a great orator, and his orphaned mother a winner of singing competitions as a child.

David's introduction to the RAF Gang Shows was preceded by his joining the Boy Scouts movement in the 1930s. Here he was able to do some entertaining as many Scout troops did. As he says, "I wasn't really interested in tying knots or making camp fires, I just wanted to join in their concerts."

In some cases those concerts were the jumping-off ground for inclusion in Ralph Reader's famous Boy Scout Gang Shows, the forerunner of the RAF version.

In my early days in the RAF I did my basic training at Blackpool and I was asked whether I would like to go on a physical training instructor course. After thinking about it I turned it down because I wanted to stay with the rest of the lads who were going on to a bomber command base at Dishforth in Yorkshire. At that time Dishforth was a Whitley bomber base. [Now there's a coincidence: my brother was killed flying from there as a pilot in 1941.]

My maths let me down on my pilot's course. I was then transferred to the RAF police but that didn't last long because I lost a prisoner; well, I didn't try and stop him when he escaped is more to the point, because he was a huge, rough guy and I knew he was trouble. I was then put in the cookhouse – where else could I go! – and while peeling hundreds of pounds of potatoes each day I used to sing to myself, and one day a corporal bandsman was listening and he asked me whether I'd like to come down to the bandroom and sing a couple of numbers with the band.

There were two bands on the camp, and this corporal, Edward Bruback, was with the RAF Adastral Orchestra (the other band was Macari and his Dutch Serenaders). Anyway I did my two numbers with the band and they said you're in. Now this meant that life could be easier if I became part of the station entertainment. I was only nineteen then and I wasn't a bad-looking fellow, so they thought I would be an asset to the band. The two songs I sang were "All The Things You Are" and "The Ferryboat Seren-ade" – funny how you remember these things.

We travelled all over the place giving concerts, not just to RAF establish-ments but in theatres in some of the big towns like York. We made quite a lot of money for various organisations, and some for ourselves too in expenses.

I then got an act together, a few gags, some impressions of the well-known people, Charlie Chan, Bing Crosby and suchlike, which meant I could do solo spots in concerts. Then all of a sudden I was posted to RAF Melksham in Wiltshire as an instrument repairer. Why, I don't know, because I'm the least mechanically-minded fellow you could find. In fact, how many people could do a simple thing like putting a bulb in a holder and blow himself across the room? I did! Anyway, at Melksham they had concerts every week in the mess and I started performing regularly. I listened to the radio for new gags to do, and I had my impressions to which by now I added Max Miller and one or two others. After sixteen weeks doing the instrument course my flight-sergeant said to me, "You are the worst instrument repairer I've ever seen; however, I like you, but don't ever touch an aeroplane because it will be disaster."

I was soon on the move again, this time to Henlow in Bedfordshire. This was a good move for me because there was a lot of entertainment going on at the station, including auditions being held there for a radio series called *Aircraftsman Smith Entertains*. What a title! Anyway I did an audition and got a four-minute spot on the show doing my Max Miller impressions. This was where I first met Dick Emery, Ron Moody and Alfred Marks. The station seemed a boiling pot for a lot of service entertainers.

All of a sudden there was a directive from somewhere "on high" that certain RAF and navy personnel were to be transferred to the army for training to go out to Burma, and I was among a lot of lads who received the order. We were put on a train to a base training camp not too far from Blackpool. When we got there half the trainload were marched off but quite a lot of us were shunted into a siding and left there. Some of us decided to leave the train and walk back along the track and disappear into Blackpool to see a show. When we got back to the railway station our train was still in the siding and nobody seemed to have missed us. We asked the sergeant in charge what the next move was, but he didn't seem to know so we said, "Why don't you send us back to Henlow until things are sorted out?" He said, "Fair enough." I think he wanted to get rid of the responsibility of looking after us. So now we're back in Henlow, and I went to the air-commodore and said I thought I could do more for the war effort if I continued entertaining, and would it be possible to get a transfer to the RAF Gang Show? He was jolly nice about it, and arranged for me to travel to London for an audition.

I had to report to Adastral House in Kingsway, and the airman who watched my audition was George Cameron who after the war made a name for himself in variety and summer shows. He was a very funny man. Incidentally the man who played the piano for my audition was Norrie Paramour, who also later had his own wonderful orchestra and became musical arranger for many well-known names in the business. It appeared I had passed the audition and had then to go and see the "Guv'nor", Squadron-Leader Ralph Reader. I was sent to his office at nearby Houghton House and told to wait for him. Reader eventually came in and I stood stiffly to attention and gave the smartest salute possible. He breezed in, took off his jacket, threw his hat in the corner and said, "Sit down, son." He looked through my papers to see what sort of entertaining I'd been doing previously and said, "Welcome to the Gang Show."

For the time being I was to be put into a pool of artistes that would eventually become the basis of No 10 unit. In the pool we had Stanley Mortenson, a well-known footballer who lectured on the game and showed us how a football should be headed and controlled.

I had a short trip to Northern Ireland where I stayed in exactly the same place that my father had been during the First World War. After this I was sent to join No 10 unit in Gloucestershire, and the unit at that time was mainly musicians who also did some sketches and comedy routines. They were certainly fine musicians, and the drummer was a young man called Peter Sellers who used to bring the house down with his drum solo with the sticks flying in the air. My job was to play straight man in the comedy bits with the lads, compère the shows and do my own spot. It was all very enjoyable.

From Gloucester we moved into Europe, ending up in Denmark. Peter and I became great friends during the run of the show and I was sorry to leave the lads when my demob came through. Two of us, Georgie White and myself, were slightly older than the others, so we were first to be called home and we left Germany at Cuxhaven.

Some years went by and the act that I had joined in Civvy Street had just broken up and I was out of work. Suddenly I got a call from Peter Sellers, who was starting to make a name for himself, to say that he and Michael Bentine were going on tour with a revue-type show and although it was being presented by a well-known agent they were going to have to arrange the booking of the other artistes. They wondered whether I could manage it for them, pay the wages, do the advance publicity, and also work in a couple of sketches. Peter and Michael were great to work with, and always used to tell me, "David, you'll get a good break one of these days, betcher."

I had been at Windsor for pantomime and the third year I was there a note was put in my dressing-room asking me to contact John Redway at agents MCA. I went to see him and he told me a film was being cast called *Women Without Men*. It was about a women's prison, and I was to play a prison warder, which meant I would be in a lot of scenes, and it would do me good from the point of view of getting my face on the screen. I was to be paid £20 a week for this, and in addition I would be offered a seven-year contract.

The agent also told me that I was to meet a casting director called Paul Sherrington and actor José Ferrer who were going to be involved in making a big war picture about the Gironde River raid. Colonel Hasler of the Royal Marines, who was going to be adviser on the film and who had taken part in the actual raid, and the director, had asked to see me for a possible part in the film. I went to see them and the outcome was I got the part, a smashing one, and the film was *Cockleshell Heroes*. The film was a big turning point in my career, and was a giant step from my humble beginnings in RAF entertainment. Service entertainment had certainly given a lot of us the opportunity to become professionals later on.

After *Cockleshell Heroes* I did a lot of films with Norman Wisdom such as *The Bulldog Breed, On the Beat, Press for Time, Good for the Goose,* and then I worked with Peter Sellers again in films like *Two Way Stretch* and *Dock Brief*. I did thirteen movies with Peter altogether. I think *Cockleshell Heroes* and *The Long Ships* were milestones in my career. The latter was filmed in Yugoslavia and my wife Lyn and I got married there, so that one has to be a bit special.

Talking to David and Lyn in their comfortable London home is a very peaceful and pleasant experience. If you want to know more of David's life and career he has written a very readable autobiography, *Up the Ladder to Obscurity* (Anchor Publications).

Len Lowe

I have known Len Lowe for some fifteen years and in various conversations with him he has amazed me with his tremendous knowledge of the entertainment business. He has a wonderful memory for detail going back to the early 1920s, and you don't feel he is bragging in any way when he tells you of some of the biggest names in the theatre he has worked with. With all his experience it was a foregone conclusion that he should eventually join an entertainment unit as part of his service career in the Second World War. Brother Don Smoothey (he of Stars in Battledress) said, "Len was a West End actor when he was a very young boy," and Len told me:

At six years old I could sing all the comic songs of the day, and by the time I was nine I was performing at British Legion Clubs and suchlike in our neighbourhood. At thirteen I was able to go to the legendary Italia Conti Stage School to train in drama. It was a wonderful opportunity. I could always dance a little, but there we were trained to do ballet and tap.

My first appearance in a proper theatre was in 1929 at the Holborn Empire. After six weeks there I went out on tour in *Peter Pan* which starred Jean Forbes Robertson, a really big star, and a wonderful cast. I just seemed to go from show to show as a juvenile. I was in *St Joan* with Sybil Thorndyke, *All God's People* with the great singer Paul Robeson, and Flora Robson. I also appeared in the first two seasons of the Open Air Theatre, Regent's Park, in London. Greer Garson, who later became a famous stage and screen actress, had one line in a tiny part in one of the park plays. She was very young then and very pretty.

I had a change of direction in 1934 when I joined the very popular Jack Hylton Orchestra as a vocalist, guitarist and dancer. We opened at the Palladium in May and stayed there for six months. After this the band made a film, *She Shall Have Music*, and then immediately went on a continental tour where we played in thirty-six towns in thirty-four days, including theatres like the Paris Opera House and the Berlin Winter Gardens.

Then Hylton had a contract to go to America, so at the end of 1934 we boarded the SS *Normandie* for the States. Halfway across the Atlantic we were informed that the American Musicians' Union were going to bar us from working there. However, we got the opportunity to do a broadcast on the boat which was going to be relayed coast to coast in the States. Jack Hylton asked me to do the commercial introduction to the broadcast, and I said to Jack, "Do you want it in English or my best Hollywood accent?" He said, "Just do it, son." So in my best American voice, or what I thought was my best American voice, I started the broadcast. "Greetings, America, it's seven forty-five Eastern Standard time, Chicago. The Standard Oil Company presents Britain's Ambassador of Music, Maestro Jack Hylton." When we got to New York people started to ask Hylton who had done the chat on the broadcast they had heard, and he told them it was me.

After a fortnight the band had to return to England as there was no way they were going to be allowed to play in America. I however stayed on, and went to Chicago and got a job as a resident announcer with a radio station. I came back from the States and wanted my job back with Hylton but he didn't want to know. However, Buddy Rogers, the husband of the movie queen Mary Pickford, had just come over to England and one of the things he was going to do was conduct the Jack Hylton Orchestra for a concert or two. He remembered hearing me broadcast in America and took me on for his concerts with the orchestra. Hylton took over again after that and I stayed with him.

I worked in the Hylton set-up as Ken Tucker, and one week when we were playing the Metropolitan Theatre, Edgware Road (now the top-security police station in the capital), a dancer in a double act called "The Two Rogues" said to me, "Aren't you Len Smoothey?"

I said, "Yes."

He said, "I'm Bill Redman, we were at school together. Have you ever thought of doing a double act?"

I said, "I'll try anything once, but I'm contracted to Jack Hylton."

Anyway we talked about the possibility, and we used to write to one another and did a sort of postal rehearsal of what we'd do when I was free from the orchestra. Eventually we did it, in about 1938.

A chap I was friendly with was putting out a revue and I said, "Any chance of booking a double comedy and dancing act?" He said okay, but you'll have to feed the principal comedian who was Joe Pointer, and front the girl dancers in the routines. So now we're ready for a twelve-week tour to break the new act in, but first of all we have to find a name for it. It's got to look a catchy title on the bills. In conversation I happened to mention to Bill Redman, my new partner, that I had worked in Lowe's Theatre in New York and suddenly we both said, "That's it, Len and Bill Lowe." So now I am no longer a Smoothey (our family name) or a Tucker, I'm Len Lowe.

Bill and I worked in this revue for a while and then from there went into the Coconut Grove night-club in London (home of Edmundo Ros and his band for many years after the war) for nine months. After that we played a lot of variety theatres, including the Holborn Empire where I had made my first appearance in a proper theatre in 1929.

Bill and I had had our call-up papers just before this, and I remember we finished at the Holborn Empire at ten o'clock on the Saturday night and at eight o'clock on the following Monday morning we reported to Royal Air Force Uxbridge. After our initial training in Blackpool we were posted

121

to Swindon. We met up with a few entertainers in the Swindon area and we got permission to put a show on at the Savoy Theatre, Swindon, on a Sunday. We had been allowed to organise this show because the orderly officer knew we had been pre-war professional entertainers.

Bill and I then got posted to a fighter squadron near Bournemouth. It was a big aerodrome and they had a band there and, would you believe it, it was the one we had worked with at the Coconut Grove night-club. We did a lot of shows at this base, and then we heard that the RAF Gang Show were coming down, so we thought we might get a chance to join them. However, the group-captain commander of the station sent us away on leave so we wouldn't meet them because he wanted us to stay on at the station to continue entertaining there.

By 1943 we were at Fighter Command HQ at Stanmore where Air- Vice-Marshal Sholto Douglas was in charge, and we had just done a show with Bebe Daniels, Ben Lyon and Vic Oliver at the station. Afterwards Ben Lyon asked Sholto Douglas, whom he knew, whether we could be released for a time to do some shows for the American United Services Organisation. We worked for American service men and women for about four months, and then when we got back to Fighter Command HQ we were told we had been transferred to the RAF Gang Show. We reported to Houghton House in Kingsway, the HQ of the Gang Shows, and were immediately taken to see one of their productions.

There was a very funny comedian in the show, but he was doing a lot of material that we knew belonged to a pro called Laurie Howe we had come to know on the variety circuit before the war. When we were taken back-stage by Squadron-Leader Ralph Reader after the show he introduced us to a lot of the lads who were already members of the Gang Show: Reg (Confidentially) Dixon, Tony Hancock, singer Harry Dawson, Cardew Robinson, comedian George Cameron and this funny little comedian who was doing Laurie Howe's material. We tackled him about it, saying, "We think you're very funny, but the material you're doing belongs to Laurie Howe." He said, "Oh, I'm glad you like it, I'm Laurie's son, Dick Emery." We really felt foolish.

Bill and I eventually got our own RAF Gang Show unit with a cast of about ten, and we played aerodromes and other RAF establishments all over the country. We, Bill and I, were demobbed just after the war finished, and we went straight into a Tom Arnold show in London doing our double act. We were in this for a year, and then went into a variety bill at the London Palladium with film stars Laurel and Hardy. This was in 1947.

We kept our double act going until 1950 when we finished at the Prince of Wales Theatre in the stage version of the well-known radio show *Take it from Here* with Jimmy Edwards, Joy Nichols and Dick Bentley. Bill wanted to call it a day because in the meantime he had married the musical star of *Love from Judy*, Jeannie Carson. Bill became her manager and they went to live in America.

My agent said, "Why don't you get together with your brother Don [Smoothey] and form another double act?" So we did, and we called ourselves Lowe and Ladd (Don used the name Ladd for the sake of the act). We got some good work and stayed together until 1956 when I had a chance to join Charlie Chester's TV show, *Pot Luck*. Don went back to doing a single act, using his own name Smoothey, in variety and pantomime.

The boys, Len and Don, have led amazing lives, and their stories represent, in many ways, a catalogue of the history of twentieth-century show business. They are both still actively working, and they are involved in the organising of charitable events for the Grand Order of Water Rats, and the Entertainment Artistes Benevolent Fund.

Other Gang Show members included virtuoso harmonica player Arthur Tolcher had an exceptional musical ability, as I witnessed when working with him in a summer show in 1957. Arthur was born in a trunk, as it were; his parents were a vaudeville double act. His mother was known as "The Beef", for what reason I never found out. Arthur was always slightly anti-authority and particularly disliked military police. When the Gang were playing in Cairo during the war their lorry was challenged by the military police and Arthur jumped down from the lorry saying, "I'll sort this out, I hate the bastards." The "bastard" on this occasion turned out to be his brother whom he hadn't seen for many years.

In the 1970s Arthur was engaged for the Morecambe and Wise television shows. He would suddenly appear in any situation, play a few bars, and Eric and Ernie would say, "Not now, Arthur." He always played the same number, "The Flight of the Bumblebee". After a time the producer of the programme asked him to change the number just so there was a variation. Not Arthur, he dug his heels in and carried on with "The Flight of the Bumblebee" and got in quite a paddy over the situation.

Another was impressionist Michael Moore. Michael eventually made a big radio name for himself in a programme called *Ignorance is Bliss* along with comedians Harold Berens and Gladys Hay, Will Hay's daughter. The quiz-master of this show was Canadian Stewart MacPherson, a very popular radio personality in this country. Apparently Michael Moore rather ridiculed Ralph

Reader's Gang Shows, saying they were corny. I met Michael many years after his big successes on radio and stage when for nine years he was in the back row of the chorus (as they called themselves) in the *Dad's Army* television series. While watching the repeats of the show in recent years I see Michael's face appearing in shot pretty regularly.

Another member of the RAF Gang Show during the 1940s was Fred Stone. Later Fred appeared in *White Horse Inn*, many pantomimes, and was a regular member of the famous Players Theatre Company and their unique home under the arches at Charing Cross.

Cardew Robinson recalls a great Gang Show member, Terry Bartlett, who for many post-war years was part of an act called Bartlett and Ross, a superb female impersonation combination. Cardew remembers when he met Terry again after he left the RAF Gang Shows and was transferred to barrage balloons.

I asked him how he was getting on and he said, "Oh, you'll know my balloon when you see it, it's the one with sequins."

The position that Ralph Reader had achieved during his reign as leader of the RAF Gang Shows was quite extraordinary. He was a close colleague and friend of all the military top brass, and his influential position was in evidence when he wanted an entertainer by the name of Len Fearnehough to report to his headquarters at Houghton House in London in preparation to join a Gang Show unit. Fearnehough was at the time on active service in France and Fred Cox recalls:

Letters followed him around for three weeks until they reached him. He repeated the contents of the letter, and who it was from, to his commander who immediately laid on an aircraft to airlift him back to England. Fearnehough was still covered in mud when he left. He arrived in the same state at Houghton House to report to Reader. This sort of thing confirmed Reader's position of authority. He was certainly a father to the lads, always kept personally in touch with the various units, and also made sure the Gang got some leave occasionally. He would suddenly disappear every now and again to pursue his intelligence work, and a week or so later would appear again just as suddenly.

RAF Gang Shows played in many countries apart from the UK: Europe, the Middle East, North Africa and India. Clifford Henry was in a unit which gave a performance for King Faisal in

Baghdad when that city was rather more friendly than it has been lately. The Cox twins also performed in the Gulf area for long periods in such places as Basra. They performed in the presence of King Farouk of Egypt, and Iceland was another area of their activities.

Squadron-Leader "Ralph" was very popular with the Polish air force in Britain and in fact these airmen copied one of Reader's strange little idiosyncrasies. He used to illustrate his verbal intentions with a banging of his fists and the words, "Okay, lads, chickety snitch." This became the password for the Polish airmen he came in contact with. If something was okay it was "chickety snitch". Another of Reader's quirks was to lapse into a type of American dialect. Well, what was more natural. He'd met and been on intimate terms with such as James Cagney, George Raft, Joan Crawford, Jackie Oakie and Al Jolson so why not put on the style for his admiring young Gang Show members? They loved him for it, and in fact some of them believed he was American.

Ralph Reader actually came from Somerset and his folks still baked their own bread and cakes and lived a country existence in that lovely county.

The Cox twins, like other members of the RAF Gang Shows, continued their friendship with the "Boss" long after the war was over. There were annual reunions which were always looked forward to and very well attended. Reader is remembered in the Royal Air Force Church, St Clement Danes, in London's Strand. The Cox twins have been responsible for a tremendous amount of work at that church, creating a book of remembrance dedicated to the RAF Gang Shows, a lasting record for those involved in a very particular "theatre" of war.

Postscript

In November 1991 I was invited to a reunion dinner of the RAF Gang Show Association, and what a marvellous night it was.

I had the pleasure of meeting Ralph Reader's adopted son Bob Reader, OBE, who is the chairman of the association and his wife Diane. Sitting next to me was Moya Sutton, with her son and daughter-in-law. Moya's husband Bill Sutton had known Ralph Reader since the 1930s, and Bill, who died in 1990, worked alongside Reader during the Second World War and after, and was the president of the RAF Gang Show Association for many years.

Moya met Bill when she was in the resident ballet company at Drury Lane and he was a call-boy there. It must have been an amazing theatrical partnership, enhanced perhaps by the fact that Moya is the daughter of theatre historian W. Maqueen Pope (I have several of his wonderful books and anyone interested in the theatre should read them). Meeting this charming and intelligent lady at the dinner was a delight. There were, however, more goodies to come in the cabaret when some of the old RAF Gang Show members were introduced and showed us they had lost none of their sparkle, all, at seventy plus, giving us a taste of showmanship. The Cox twins doing a fantastically fast tap dance routine, great singing from Harry Herring, superb rope spinning from Rex Roper, clever impressions from Victor Seaforth and gags galore from Cardew Robinson.

I came away realising that the energy and enthusiasm of some of those Second World War veterans of service entertainment could show the youngsters of today a thing or two even now, fifty years on from their heyday.

"All the Nice Girls Love a Sailor"

As I have said, apart from their shore establishments, the navy was obviously the most difficult of the three services to cater for in the way of entertainment.

In the latter days of 1939 and early 1940, attention was drawn to the plight of some ships' companies in the base at Scapa Flow, by solo entertainers such as the lovely actress Evelyn Laye. "Boo" Laye, as she is known in the theatre world, organised at her own expense for some well-known friends of hers to make the trip to Scapa, and the reception they got was, as you can imagine, wonderful. The Navy Welfare Organisation did as much as they could in co-operation with ENSA, but this was naturally on a limited scale. Later on more organised concerts and full-scale productions were possible.

Some well-known artistes involved in naval entertainment had quite a nerve-racking time in London. Early in 1940 a very popular radio programme called *Navy Mixture* began weekly broadcasts which were to last throughout the war. The programme was hosted by a wonderful lady called Doris Hare, assisted by Petty Officer Jack Watson, the son of a music-hall great, Nosmo King. Later Jack became a fine film actor.

Dear Doris, as we call her, is still full of life and vitality, and has had a successful career in every department of the entertainment business, including her television appearances in the hilarious and much-loved situation comedy *On the Buses*. During the run of *Navy Mixture* she welcomed many guest artistes on to the programme, and she also had a few resident performers, like Claude Hulbert and his wife Enid Trevor.

Claude particularly was a very funny revue and musical comedy artiste. He and his brother Jack Hulbert were brilliant light comedians. Jack partnered his equally well-known wife Cicely Courtneidge, daughter of actor/manager Robert Courtneidge, in many stage and film productions. Collectively the whole family dynasty was a *tour de force* before and after the Second World War.

Doris Hare told me of many occasions during the blitz when the sound of bombs dropping on the capital almost drowned the noise of the broadcasts in the Navy Club in Rupert Street. In fact on one occasion Claude and Enid performed a sketch with plaster from the ceiling dropping all round them. It really seems amazing just how resolute wartime broadcasters were in making sure the show went on under the most terrifying conditions.

Jon Pertwee

Jon Pertwee is one actor who broke into comedy with his brilliant and original voices as a result of his wartime service in the navy. Jon and his late brother Michael were the sons of writer and actor/manager Roland Pertwee. My connection with them is that we had the same great-grandfather. My side of the family, by the way, were all farmers, engineers or commerce orientated. Michael followed his father as a writer and was responsible for some brilliant stage comedies. Roland and Michael also co-created the very first television "soap", *The Grove Family*.

Jon Pertwee, having now established himself firmly in radio and television, particularly as one of the best Dr Who's (in my opinion), and with his wonderful portrayal of the scarecrow "Worzel Gummidge", began his radio career in *Waterlogged Spa*, the navy version of *Mediterranean Merry-Go-Round*. The RAF version was *Much Binding in the Marsh* and the army *Stand Easy*.

Having been born just after the First World War finished, and hearing all the gruesome tales of trench warfare, I grew up thinking that if there was another war and I was involved I would join the navy. I volunteered for "bell bottoms" and by the end of 1939 I was in. I hadn't thought about seasickness, but did I suffer from it! After training I was posted to submarines as wireless operator, but being six foot two I was always bashing my head on girders and things. What with that and being sick all the time I was pretty useless, so I was posted to the battlecruiser HMS *Hood*.

I left the *Hood* for a shore posting at Portsmouth just before she was sunk by the *Bismarck*. At Portsmouth I was fire-watching one night during a heavy raid and the building was almost destroyed. I was blown off a staircase and against a wall and landed up in the crater the bomb had made. I woke up in the mortuary, or larder as they called it, and started shouting. The rating in charge said, "Blimey, mate, we thought you were dead."

After this slight mishap I was posted to the shore establishment at Hove in Sussex, HMS *King Alfred*, to take an officers' course. I passed out and my first posting as an officer was to HMS *Valkyrie* in the Isle of Man. While I was there I formed a play company which is still in existence today called the Service Players. It is now a highly respected amateur dramatic group. I had been a professional actor in a few repertory productions before the war so I had some experience in getting the group together on the Manx Isle.

My next posting was to the Admiralty in London and naval intelligence, so the entertaining went by the board, as it were. A group of us had to go round to various shore bases and ships lecturing on the dangers of careless talk, telling the lads, and particularly the Wrens, to stop yapping because "careless talk costs lives", as the slogan said.

In our group were John Paddy Carstairs, later a film director responsible for the Norman Wisdom comedy films, Lieutenant Harold Warrender the actor, Able Seaman Jim Callaghan, later Prime Minister Callaghan, and Bob Little, a dress designer by trade. We also instructed some of the lads in simple codes when writing to their loved ones. Civilians who had relations in prisoner-of-war camps would send certain numbers to the POWs who would then send corresponding ones which only we could decode. This told the military authorities over here certain details they wanted to know about, for example British air-raids on Germany.

I was also detailed at the Admiralty to assist Lieutenant-Commander Kim Peacock, the original Paul Temple in the successful radio series, in the naval broadcasting service to ships at sea and overseas bases. We had to have discussions with other service broadcasters like Peter York and George Melachrino. The whole thing was chaired by Harry Alan Towers who was later involved with commercial radio in this country. We recorded plays as well as musical shows, and I was able to take part in these. We used to be able to introduce young service men into the organisation, and one of them was David Jacobs who eventually went out to Ceylon to run Radio SEAC (South-East Asia Command).

Lieutenant-Commander Peacock said that he'd had complaints from high-up Admiralty brass that a certain radio programme in the *Merry-Go-Round* series with Eric Barker was being irreverent about them and certain politicians. Peacock told me to go to a recording of the show and find out about it. I sat in the audience watching the show which was very funny, and suddenly Eric Barker said, "Now I want somebody to shout out a line here." I said, "I'll do it," and he said, "Good, who are you?"

I said, "I'm Lieutenant Pertwee, and I've really come down to spy on you and your naughty jibes at the Admiralty."

He said, "If you tell them I'm behaving myself you can do this line," which was in answer to Pearl Hackney's (Eric's wife) tirade at Barker: "Why don't you leave him alone, you're always picking on him, the poor perisher," in a Cockney accent. Eric would then say, "Oh, the Ministry of Education is in tonight."

Eric Barker seemed quite pleased with what I did and asked me whether I would like to join the show when I came out of the navy. That was my introduction to radio comedy and I stayed with *Waterlog Spa*, the naval contribution to *Merry-Go-Round*, for five years.

One of Jon's voices in that show was the Devon Postman with the catchphrase in answer to the question, "What do you do with the letters you don't have time to deliver?" "Tear 'em up. Well what does it matter what you do as long as you tear 'em up?" This voice of Jon's was the one he also used as Worzel Gummidge, the scarecrow.

Also in the show with Eric and Pearl were Wren singer Barbara Sumner, Humphrey Lestoqu (Flying Officer Kite) and George Crow and the Blue Mariners Orchestra.

I met Jon for the first time in 1948 during the run of *Water-logged Spa* when the recordings were done from the BBC Paris Studios, Lower Regent Street in London. I was then working as a salesman in Burberry's store in the nearby Haymarket, long before I had any thought of becoming an actor myself.

Much later, at the beginning of the 1980s, I appeared in the stage musical of *Worzel Gummidge* with Jon for two seasons in London playing Sergeant Beetroot, painted in red from head to foot. This was a really happy show, and it was nice to do a whole production with JP. Of all the things that Jon has done, including a marvellous characterisation in *A Funny Thing Happened on the Way to the Forum* and TV's *Dr Who*, I think his Worzel Gummidge is the best. By the way, Jon and his wife Ingaborg's son Sean is going great guns in his acting career, and their daughter Dariel is just starting out on hers.

Donald Hewlett

A schoolmaster in Herne Bay who, at the time of writing, is ninety-five, appears to have been responsible for Donald Hewlett taking to the "boards". The fact that this gentleman bought a ticket to the moon in 1930 may give some indication of his, shall we say, slightly eccentric outlook on the world! The master put Donald in a play at school when he was twelve, and from that time on there was absolutely no other profession to follow as far as young Hewlett was concerned.

I met Donald many years ago, but only in the past two or three years have I spent much time with him, during the making of the BBC TV series *You Rang, M'Lord*? After the usual schooling, Donald went up to Cambridge and was quite soon involved with the famous *Footlights* revue, a springboard for so many actors. Then came the war: he joined the navy and was later posted to Scapa Flow for duties in a light cruiser moored to a buoy. The acting had had to be put aside during the early war years, but now with boredom rearing its ugly head from looking at a buoy day after day, he decided the ship could do with some light entertainment. He started a show called *On Board Tonight*, which was to be a parody of a well-known BBC radio programme called *In Town Tonight*.

It was a weekly programme, unless the ship was ordered off to sink something, which would be inconvenient, to say the least. We had the use of the sick bay where there were plenty of blankets for sound-proofing which made it an ideal studio. The show went out over the ship's loudspeakers. I was then a rating, a very ordinary seaman and I was now doing the sort of thing I liked best, even if it was in a small way.

I was later posted to a battleship off West Africa, having meanwhile received a commission. We organised concerts on board this ship and the captain's secretary, who used to type out the daily orders, would also mention our shows. We had a brainy chap on board we used to call the schoolmaster; he was a bit of a comedian and I included him in all the concerts. On one particular occasion there was a slight misunderstanding in the ship's orders. The schoolmaster liked to bring items of interest to the notice of the crew, and he dictated one such to the captain's secretary to be included in ship's orders. This particular one was, "We are off the coast of West Africa and as late as 1830 icebergs were seen in this area." The secretary typed it out wrong as, "At 1830 hours icebergs will be seen in this area." Eighteen hundred crew members came up from below decks and leaned over the side trying to see the icebergs, and the battleship nearly keeled over, with the admiral on the bridge yelling, "What the bloody hell is going on?" The typist was put in jankers for a couple of weeks.

After the West Africa trip I was posted back to the Orkneys at a naval air station helping with the weather reports. The first time I went into Kirkwall, the capital of the Orkneys, I found there were thousands of army, air force and naval personnel in the area, and only one tiny cinema offering any form of entertainment, so I had the idea of starting an Arts Club. I was able to get hold of a room beneath an old theatre which I thought would be suitable. I advertised in the local paper, offering membership to the services at one penny a day. I got permission for personnel to be allowed to wear civilian clothes when they came to the club.

I received an enormous response and we were in business. I enrolled the assistance of set designers within the service personnel and we were soon making use of the stage area upstairs. We presented plays which we also took to the island of Flotta, not the most salubrious place to be, but they had a fine theatre there built especially for King George VI when he came up. There were theatres of sorts on most of the little islands so we were able to tour some of our shows. I had to fit in my theatre work with my service work, which at that time involved weather forecasting. Sometimes after seeing to the theatre business I'd be a bit late and I would walk back to my office through huge gales. I would get to the microphone and say, "Gales are imminent!" which was quite obvious as they'd been raging for some time before I broadcast the fact.

I think the navy quite liked the club I had started. At least it was some-where for people to go and relax and make friends. I asked John Gielgud to be our president, and as we were an air station some people used to fly in to entertain certain garrisons and I used to go and meet them and per-suade them to pay the Arts Club a visit. We had Sybil Thorndike, Eric Linklater, Gertrude Lawrence, Puishnoff, Yehudi Menuhin, John Mills, Will Hay and Bernard Miles among our visitors.

Later I was drafted to Singapore and I started the same sort of thing there. One person who had been in the Orkneys saw my advert in the Malayan newspaper and said, "Bloody hell, I've come ten thousand miles and Hewlett's at it out here as well."

They had the Raffles Theatre in Singapore next to the famous Raffles Hotel. We put on a production of Ian Hay's *Middle Watch* for a special visit of Lord Louis Mountbatten and his staff. Lord Louis came backstage afterwards and insisted on meeting everybody personally: actors, stage staff, lighting men, etc. He was that sort of man.

The commanding officer in Singapore asked me whether I could put on a Christmas show, so I thought a circus might be a good idea for the festive season. I'd seen a small one that travelled around Malaya. There was a huge aircraft hangar we were able to use so I got some large wooden crates and made a ring. We also did it for the New Year with the addition of a baby elephant. One night we painted the baby elephant pink with "slosh" and took it into the mess at midnight. Everything went fine until the elephant started drinking all the drinks on the tables. Suddenly it let out a terrific bellow, charged through the huge doors and out into the open air. All night you could hear it bellowing. It kept coming back into the building where the men were sleeping, and they would wake up from a heavy sleep after a night's drinking in the mess and be confronted by a pink elephant. After that incident I was hastily drafted back home.

When I got back to Britain I was demobbed and immediately applied to RADA. I actually did my audition in naval uniform, as I hadn't had time to get my civilian clothes. Anyway, by 1947 I was into that great college for actors.

I think if I hadn't been in that school play I would have gone into my father's factory in Manchester. It was a factory for processing rubber tyres, which strangely enough is the sort of factory I am supposed to be running in the television series *You Rang, M'Lord?* If I had gone into the factory I expect I would have made a lot of money, but I wouldn't have had such a joyous time as I have had in the theatre, meeting people like Ronnie Barker and the writers Jimmy Perry and David Croft, creators of *It Ain't Half Hot, Mum* and *You Rang, M'Lord?*, two of the television productions I have been involved in.

Donald is full of fun, and you would never imagine that he was actually a real-life lord, so the role he plays in *You Rang, M'Lord?*, Lord Meldrum, is quite apt. He lives with his actress wife Therese (Therese was one of the nurses in TV's *Emergency Ward 10*) on the Kent coast – at the time of writing, that is. You never know with Donald: he could by now be up the Amazon somewhere.

Arthur Lane

If ever one person deserved to be the subject of a documentary it is the late Arthur Lane. I have been very fortunate in obtaining extracts from his diaries from his widow Audrey (Lupton). Audrey is incidentally now on the management committee of Brinsworth House in Twickenham, a retirement home for theatrical performers, a post Arthur would certainly have approved of as most of his life was spent among theatre people.

The first major experience of his life came on a sheep farm in Australia, and then later, after various extraordinary adventures down under, he made a home for himself for a while on a park

133

bench in Sydney, having walked the thousand miles there from Cootes Crossing. Arthur's "neighbour" on the park bench had heard of an amateur theatre company who were preparing a production of *The Constant Nymph* in honour of a visit from Sybil (later Dame Sybil) Thorndike and her husband (Sir) Lewis Casson. Arthur obtained a part in the production, and afterwards Sybil and Lewis suggested to him that if and when he returned to England he might try his hand at acting for a living.

Before he went to Australia as a very young man in 1928, Arthur had been given a night out in London on the eve of his sailing by his father, and as his diaries relate:

[We had] A wonderful meal with plenty of wine at Pinoli's in Wardour Street, followed by a performance of Noël Coward's *This Year of Grace*, the cast of which included Sonnie Hale, Jessie Matthews, Douglas Byng, Tilly Losch and Marjorie Robertson, who later changed her name to Anna Neagle. I enjoyed this show immensely and always believe it planted the seeds for my future fondness of the theatre . . .

After my meeting with Sybil Thorndike and Lewis Casson I was able to save the fare to get back to England, and very soon after this I began my acting career in the UK . . .

The 1930s were spent learning some of the arts of acting, and also the intricacies of management, and by the time the war broke out in September 1939 I had become an actor/manager. [In those days actors didn't wait for someone to employ them, they employed themselves, and other actors, if they were out of work.] I performed in melodrama, farces, old-time musical hall, etc . . .

In 1939 I was running two companies, one at Gravesend the other at Woolwich. On September 2nd I went to see my production of *The Prisoner of Zenda* at Woolwich. I was standing outside the stage door in the interval, getting a breath of fresh air, when a Rolls-Royce drew up. A famous agent at the time, Mike Lyon, jumped out, ran straight through the stage door and into the wings just as the curtain was going up. He grabbed his daughter Pat who was in the company, dashed out again to his car with her and shouted at me, "We're going to be invaded, I'm taking her up to Scotland for safety." I said, "What about the costume?" (you can always find actors and actresses but costumes are more difficult) and he shouted back as he drove off, "Don't worry, I'll send it on to you." The next morning I was listening to Neville Chamberlain's "state of war" speech with my theatre manager. When Chamberlain finished, my manager, trembling like a leaf, downed a whole bottle of my sherry, rushed out of the house, and I have never set eyes on him since . . .

All theatres closed at the outbreak of war, but some outside the major cities were allowed to open after a few weeks. I got my companies together again and we carried on in a fashion until Hitler overran the Low Countries and France . . .

I remember getting a call from the police one night at the digs where I was staying in Gravesend asking if I could make up a crew with another pal of mine who had a small boat, to go to Dunkirk. We went over to the French coast, joining the rest of the armada in the rescue operation of the allied armies. We were away for about three days, and when I got back I realised we would not be able to carry on in the theatre as German planes were beginning to make a nuisance of themselves with daylight raids even before the Battle of Britain had started in earnest. I phoned an old friend of mine, Charlie Denville, and told him I was going to disband my companies. He said, "Oh, for heaven's sake come up to Halifax [Yorkshire] as all my actors are being called up." This I did, acting, producing and helping Charlie run his repertory company up there. There were thousands of service personnel in the area, and we did a tremendous amount of shows, plays, Sunday concerts and even a pantomime in aid of service charities. I stayed in Halifax for over a year, and the amazing thing was we missed all the big raids, even though there were these concentrations of troops all round us. Coventry, Birmingham, Liverpool, Hull and Manchester were being bombed nearly every night, but Halifax was spared . . .

Late in 1941 I got my call-up papers to report to HMS *Collingwood*, a naval training establishment at Fareham in Hampshire. No sooner had I arrived there than an officer sent for me and said, "I believe you are a professional actor." I said, "Yes," and he said, "Right, put on some entertainment for the lads here." I started auditioning folk and with the help of a Wren who was also a professional dancer we got some shows together. We had a professional musician at *Collingwood* by the name of Bobby Pagan. He had been an organist pre-war when he used to broadcast regularly with the BBC from the famous Trocadero at the Elephant and Castle. He rehearsed the resident Royal Marines band with all the music we wanted and we had some terrific shows . . .

135

When I had finished the training course at Fareham I had a week's leave, so I went back to Halifax and spent it with Charlie Denville. Charlie, knowing I was coming, had done some advance publicity and outside the theatre when I arrived was a big notice

SPECIAL ENGAGEMENT – FOR ONE WEEK ONLY
ORDINARY SEAMAN ARTHUR LANE

And in brackets underneath (ON LEAVE!).

I went straight into *Jane Eyre* having to read most of my part, even though I knew the play pretty well. It was difficult for the rest of the cast, particularly the leading lady Betty Baskomb, a very professional and well-known actress. However, we managed somehow and it was a marvellous week for me.

My new posting was at Portsmouth naval barracks with my mate Bobby Pagan. It was at Portsmouth that I learnt all the service tricks, how to get out of this duty and that parade, etc. At one point I acquired a hand-cart with a centre shaft to be pulled by four ratings, the sort of thing you see at the Royal Tournament, and on certain days of the week we would gallop up to the front gate of the barracks and I would shout, "Shore patrol." A rating would open the gates and we would disappear down the road, put the cart in a hiding place we had found, and go off for the day, have some lunch, write a few letters and then in the afternoon gather for the return journey to the barracks shouting, "Shore patrol returning . . ."

We had one particularly bad air-raid on Portsmouth when, among other things, a bomb fell on our detention barracks and all the inmates escaped "over the wall" and disappeared, never to be seen again. The office containing their files was also destroyed, so all their criminal records were blown to smithereens . . .

The next posting for Bobby Pagan and myself was to the battleship *King George V* moored at that time in Scapa Flow in Scotland.

We got a show together that we were going to be able to produce at the Playhouse on the island of Flotta. This was a marvellous theatre with a good stage, dressing-rooms and everything. Bobby and I would go ashore every morning to the theatre to work out lighting plots, etc. Then suddenly we were told the *George V* was to move up into Iceland waters because it was rumoured that the German battleship *Tirpitz* was in the area . . .

We were at sea for several months, and when we eventually got back to Scapa we got our show under way and it was a big success. Admiral of the Home Fleet, Sir John Tovey, had apparently been in the audience one night and I was sent for the next day. What have I done? I thought. On meeting the admiral he said, "Mr Lane" (MR Lane – I was an ordinary seaman!), "Mr Lane, I saw your show, and it was wonderful. Now we are going to be up here for some time because of German naval activity so I'd like you to present some shows on board ship. You can have all the help you want, canvas, paint etc from the Rosyth dockyard. If you say something is essential you will have it." After the interview I thought to myself, this is a right turn-up!

I had previously got pally with a petty officer, "Barney" Barnes. He was a helpful chap and liked the theatre. I said to Barney, "I think we'll do a melodrama next, *Sweeney Todd, the Demon Barber of Fleet Street.*" I sent to Charlie Denville in Halifax for the scripts but unfortunately he didn't have a copy so I dictated it word for word from memory to a typist. I sent to London for the costumes from my old friends D. & J. Benjamin of Rupert Street. The ship's carpenters and painters got cracking on the scenery, and we finally produced it in the ship's huge aircraft hangar. It was very well received by the ratings and officers, and it must have looked realistic because one Royal Marine on board fainted when I "cut Mrs Lovatt's throat". After *Sweeney Todd* we did a revue called *Hello Flotta* which was also much appreciated by the lads . . .

After I had done my six months afloat I was posted to the *King Alfred* shore establishment at Hove in Sussex to do an officers' course . . .

I didn't finish the officers' course at the *King Alfred* and instead I was promoted to leading seaman on a newly commissioned rescue motor launch. We travelled from the Thames estuary to Weymouth, dodging some German gunfire from the French coast on the way, to await orders. We soon got them. We were to take part in the now famous Dieppe raid.

For several weeks before the raid the walls of the gentlemen's toilets in Weymouth carried graffiti signs saying "Dieppe, here we come". Churchill and Mountbatten took most of the blame for the failure of that operation, but what about the security staff? If Weymouth knew about it so must have the Germans! . . .

Before long I was commissioned and told to report to Combined Operations. (Was all this because of the shows I had produced? I asked myself!) . . .

After a short spell in hospital with some eye trouble I was posted back to Hove in Sussex, this time to HMS *Lizard*. When I got there I asked what I would be doing and was told I could pick my own job. The only one left open to me was "Officer of Drains". I was given a bike and I used to ride up and down the front at Brighton inspecting the drains. I had a rating with me who lifted the drain covers while I peered in and said "Okay, next one," and so on . . .

Early in 1945, while I was on leave, I went to a concert in Croydon and the band was the Royal Marines, some of whom I knew. The naval officer in charge of them was one Jon Pertwee, later to become famous on radio and television. Pertwee said to me, "Did you say your name was Lane?" I said, "Yes." He said, "The Admiralty have been looking for you for over a year!" (They must have known where I was. After all, they sent the orders each time I was moved on.) Pertwee said, "They want you for an entertainment ship they are building." . . .

I went to an office at Queen Anne Mansions by St James's Park and met Lieutenant-Commander Kim Peacock. Peacock later became the first Paul Temple in the hugely successful radio serial of that name. He told me that the Admiralty were converting a merchant ship, the *Agamemnon*, into an amenities vessel. They thought the war in Japan would go on for another couple of years and they wanted to provide a floating base for naval personnel who were being rested for short periods in fleet battle squadrons. The *Agamemnon* would have a theatre, laundry, shops, sports facilities and even its own brewery.

The whole idea of an amenities ship was first thought of during the 1914–18 war but had been shelved then; now it was to become reality. Kim Peacock's assistant was a two-ringed lieutenant called Harold Warrender, a professional actor. When the war was over Warrender went back to the theatre and also became a well-known name on radio. One radio series he was featured in was *Waterlogged Spa*.

I was to be the entertainments officer on board *Agamemnon* and my number one was Lieutenant Michael Mills who before joining the navy had been the sound-effects boy on the famous radio series *ITMA* which starred Tommy

Handley. Michael became my right hand, and we gradually got the company together.

Our revue was to be called *Tokyo Express*. We had six chorus "girls", six good-looking young seamen. The navy did not allow us to have any real girls in the show. Wrens were taboo because of course we were all operational seamen and our eventual destination lay in the seas around Japan. Among the people we auditioned for the show was a rating called Tommy Rose. He was a brilliant female impersonator and we immediately made him our "leading lady". Post-war, Tommy was a huge success in stage revues and pantomime . . .

Early on I had heard a pianist with an unusual touch and asked him to join our company. His name was Trevor Stanford – remember that name. My last professional encounter with Trevor was a delightful tour I did with him in *Golden Years of Music-Hall* which I produced at the Nico Malan Opera House, Cape Town, in 1975. No matter where he appeared he was a crowd-puller . . .

After visiting various naval establishments in the UK, *Tokyo Express* went on a pre-Pacific tour to Germany. We opened in Minden and then travelled throughout Europe playing to service audiences, and finished up in Brussels where we spent our last night before returning to England. By this time we had collected a great deal of Belgian and French bank notes, bartering our sweet and cigarette allowances for them as we travelled round. We were not allowed to bring the currency home, so we spent the night in the Brussels hotel eating the finest food and drinking the most expensive champagne. What we had left we threw overboard the next morning as we left.

One amusing little episode in Germany was when we had stopped at an inn in the Black Forest for a drink. It was a place straight out of *White Horse Inn*. We drank the local brew out of beer *steins* and of course the navy lads decided to keep them as souvenirs when we got back on to our coach. The innkeeper went mad and said he would report us to the British naval authorities. We recovered them all except one. Where it had gone I do not know. The only way to placate the innkeeper was to tell him that I thought the thief was one of our able seamen – in fact it was Bill Clayton – and that because of his misdemeanour he would be taken into the woods and shot for having let down the British navy. We then enacted a melodramatic scene in front of the innkeeper with Bill begging for mercy as he was taken into the woods where, before long, a couple of shots rang out. This seemed completely to satisfy the innkeeper, and once he had thanked us

139

and gone back inside his inn, Bill Clayton came out of the woods, got back on to the coach and off we went. The navy had obviously gained enormous respect from one Black Forest citizen.

Back in England we were told that the *Agamemnon* was not quite ready and that we were to join her in Vancouver (British Columbia). After doing a few more bases in the UK we eventually embarked on the *Ile de France*. Although it was a luxury ship it was pretty overloaded. Apart from us on board there were also seven thousand Canadian service men returning home. I was lucky, I had a cabin to myself, but the conditions on the rest of the ship were pretty grim.

We landed at Halifax, Nova Scotia, and then had to start working our way across Canada to Vancouver by Canadian National Railways. When we pulled into a town that had a navy, army or RAF establishment in the vicinity we would do a show for them.

When we finally reached Vancouver we got the news that the atomic bomb had been dropped on Japan and they had surrendered. As there was obviously now no need for the *Agamemnon* and our show, I decided to get in touch with the Canadian navy about a charitable organisation which they were involved in, and we had the idea that we could help the charity with our show. London quickly agreed it would be a good idea, and our show was performed for three weeks, to start with at the Lyric Theatre in Vancouver. We played at theatres all the way back to Halifax to packed audiences, eventually raising fifty thousand dollars for the charity. On reaching the east coast we were all suddenly put into quarantine for fourteen days because one of the ratings had diphtheria.

We eventually left Halifax on the SS *Mauretania* and this time I didn't just have my own cabin, I had a suite. After landing in Liverpool I travelled down to the Admiralty and the next day I was demobbed. Before I said goodbye to the navy I asked the authorities what was going to happen to the production of *Tokyo Express*. They said if you want it make us an offer for Royal Navy funds. I suggested three hundred pounds, they said done, so I got the entire production, costumes, scenery, a set of band costumes that the Royal Marines band had used and a Hammond organ, which alone must have been worth a thousand pounds, and now it was all mine. I was now ready to continue my civilian career as an actor/manager . . .

I went into partnership to present a commercial tour of *Tokyo Express*, and to help with the finance of the tour I sold some of the items. The organ went for four hundred pounds, and the band costumes went to Harry Roy, and with other bits and pieces I found I had made a profit of about fifteen hundred pounds on my original investment.

I used as many ex-navy personnel as I could in the show so that I could justifiably call it *The Royal Navy Show Tokyo Express*. Michael Mills stayed with me on the production side until he was enticed away, almost against his will, to the BBC to help with the reopening of television services. I was delighted to see him get this job although sad that we were parting company.

Michael Mills later became Head of Comedy for BBC Television, and it was he who thought of the title *Dad's Army* for the long-running series.

After *Tokyo Express* I presented a production of *The Dubarry* at the Princes Theatre, now the Shaftesbury, but because of the disastrous winter of 1947 I lost money on it, and also on one or two other shows I had on the road. I must say the 1940s had been an extraordinary time in my life.

I first met Arthur Lane when I was working at the Wimbledon Theatre in the late 1960s. Arthur then had a lease on it and put on all sorts of exciting productions including some spectacular pantomimes. He was also presenting seasons of his *Golden Years of Music-Hall* not only in this country but also in other parts of the world. These shows were tremendously popular and included the real stars of the music-hall and variety heyday such as Bob and Alf Pearson ("My brother and I"), Sandy Powell ("Can you hear me, Mother?"), Cavan O'Connor (the "Cavalier of song"), Peter Cavanagh (the "Voice of them all"), Margery Manners, a large, good-looking lady with a great voice, and our old friend Don Smoothey.

Arthur was a larger than life character, the sort of person the theatre lacks nowadays. I remember going to see one of his shows at the Royal Hippodrome, Eastbourne, and as I walked into the bar the famous voice rang out: "Dear boy, how are you?" I said, "What are you going to drink, Arthur?" and he replied, "A large brandy, what else?" Nobody left his company without some story or other about the business, and to buy him a drink was a small price to pay for the pleasure of his company.

When Arthur died a few years ago, a theatrical legend died with him.

Barrie Gosney

I first met Arthur Lane when I was playing in a repertory company at the Grand Theatre, Halifax. The company was run by a fine old actor, Charles Denville, and he was assisted at times by Royal Navy Lieutenant Arthur who came up to Halifax on his leaves to direct, produce and play at the theatre.

I went into the navy while I was there. I did my initial training at a North Wales Butlin's Holiday Camp, renamed HMS *Glendower* for the duration of the war. While I was there I received an order to report to My Lords the Commissioners for the Admiralty at Queen Anne's Mansions (what had I done?). I duly reported to two officers, Kim Peacock and Harold Warrender, who told me that a Lieutenant Lane (yes, Arthur from Halifax) wanted me to join his *Tokyo Express* company who were at that time in Germany. So after the various administrative papers were signed, and I had said goodbye to my mates at *Glendower*, I was sent to Hamburg to join the *Tokyo Express* show. Arthur Lane had obviously remembered me from the Halifax days and that's how my participation in it came about.

Hamburg Opera House was a wonderful theatre with five different revolves on the stage in full working order. The theatre did not appear to have been touched by the allied bombing raids. We also played in Nissen huts doing one-night stands all over France, Belgium and Holland. There was no actual time allotted for the shows to take place. It depended on when we arrived. We would set up the scenery, lighting, sound, etc, and after the show take it all down again and move on to the next venue. If we had time we were offered hospitality in the Officers' Messes, generally finishing up giving them an impromptu cabaret.

When we played the one-night stands we were given service rations of chocolates and cigarettes in the same quantity as service personnel who were there for a week. This way we had large stocks to barter with, so we always had plenty of occupation money in our pockets.

In Wilhelmshaven in Germany there was a black market operating in the local graveyard. We used to go to the cemetery at certain times, open our suitcases full of cigarettes and sweets, and do business. We got into a little racket, knowing we would never be able to take the money home, whereby we went to the Army of Occupation post offices and bought postal orders to send home. You couldn't do it too often, but it added up to quite a tidy sum when we eventually got back to the UK.

The shows we did in Europe were in preparation for the Far East tour with the amenity ship we were due to join at Vancouver, which was going to be a recreational vessel for the lads of the Far East fleet. As you know from Arthur Lane's diaries, this never came about.

Going across Canada to Vancouver we played in temperatures forty degrees below freezing in Manitoba. We went up the Alaskan Highway to

A programme cover for the
Navy touring revue.

Lieutenant Arthur Lane, R.N.V.R.

The *Tokio Express* company, including top row, second from
left, Gerald Edmonds (later radio and stage accordionist,
Delmonde); third from left, 'mystery man' Trevor Stanford;
fifth from left, Tommy Rose (female impersonator par
excellence); third row, fourth from left, Arthur Lane; fifth
from left, Michael Mills, and front row, second from left,
Barrie Gosney.

The Importance of Being Earnest

A Comedy by OSCAR WILDE

Directed by Donald Hewlett

AT

The R.N. Base Cinema

(by kind permission of Cdr. E. W. WOODRUFF, R.N.)

ON

Monday 9th, Saturday 14th and Sunday, 15th April

AT 8.30 P.M.

Sub-Lieutenant Hewlett's
early involvement in service
entertainment at Kirkwell
in Scotland, 1942.

Donald Hewlett as
Robinson Crusoe – centre,
second row from top.
Hatston Royal Naval Air
Station, Orkney.

Obviously a concert for a naval audience, probably a shore base.
Left to right: Phylis Calvert, Eric Portman, Carol Ray, Eric Barker and
Godfrey Harrison. The face peeping over Phylis Calvert's shoulder is
George Crow, conductor of The Blue Mariners Orchestra which
continued together after the war.

Extracts from a programme for the
Stage Door Canteen which opened
in London's Piccadilly in 1944.

Jimmy Perry outside the Royal
Artillery Theatre. Simla, 1945.

I wonder if he knew what he was advertising
– 'Tis a puzzlement! India, 1945.

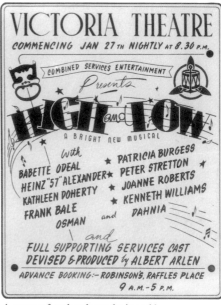

A poster for the show designed by
Kenneth Williams.

The nose is unmistakable! Kenneth
Williams (left) in drag in the revue
High and Low. Combined Services
Entertainment. Singapore, 1945.

Major James H. Howe, M.B.E., at the time of his retirement from the Army in 1974.

Jimmy Howe (centre) and his famous band at Stalag VIIIB, Lamsdorf. Note the carved music stands with initials "J.H." made out of Red Cross parcel boxes.

Jimmy Howe's Band in a German publicity picture.

Stalag VIIIB,
Lamsdorf.
The Housemaster.

A postcard to be sent home from Stalag VIIIB. A quite wonderful piece
of artwork, and what a lovely title: *Snow White and the Seven Twirps.*

Surrey artist Alex Cassie
sketched various scenes in
Stalag Luft III where he was
imprisoned after ditching his
Whitley bomber into the Bay of
Biscay in September 1942. The
sketch shows the building of
the theatre in the camp. Note
the orchestra pit in the
foreground. Alex was involved
in producing fake documents
and papers for the infamous
'great escape' from the camp.

Entrance ticket Stalag 344,
formerly VIIIB, Lamsdorf.

S.L.C. PANTOMIME COMPANY
PRESENTS ITS THIRD ANNUAL PRODUCTION

ROBINSON CRUSOE

BY
A. CARMICHAEL

CHRISTMAS 1944

Above and below: Scenes from the *Robinson Crusoe* pantomime. Stalag IXC, Nordhousen. What about the wonderful costumes, and where did the black make-up come from?

Programme cover for *Robinson Crusoe*. Stalag IXC, Nordhousen.

Tons of Money on tour, Glenshagen near Berlin, 1944, during the heavy allied bombing raids.

French Without Tears. Glenshagen near Berlin, 1944.

British prisoners, hands chained, one receiving his Red Cross parcel, the other peeling spuds. Photos taken with a 'button' camera smuggled into the camps. See the Denholm Elliott piece.

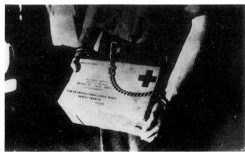

Stalag XVIIIA, Austria. *The Student Prince* production. The 'females' are doing fine 'boys' and what about the Bavarian students' costumes; pill box hats in evidence.

Stalag XVIIIA, Austria. A Pierrot show complete with full costume and banjos. Amazing.

Full orchestra! Breath-taking scenes! Ballet and chorus! All this in a brutal and hostile atmosphere. Unbelievable.

entertain British troops based near Yellowknife. Another entertainment company called "Pacific Showboat" had already gone ahead of us and we were both doing shows for army personnel. One of the sailors in that company was John Hewer. After the war John played many seasons at the Players Theatre, under the arches at Charing Cross. More recently he has become famous for his Captain Bird's Eye character in the TV advert.

When we eventually got back to England I had another two years to do in the navy and was sent out to Malta as a despatch rider! Having quite a lot of free time on the island I put on a few shows for the garrison, and was eventually asked if I would like to become the naval representative for the CSE (Combined Services Entertainment), which was then starting up operations to combine all the service shows into one. It would have meant me becoming an officer and signing on for a further tour of duty which, although it sounded very nice, was not what I really wanted to do. I wanted to get back into the acting business I had known since a young boy.

Life in the services had been good to me. I made a lot of friends and saw some of the world that would normally have been out of my reach.

I first started my theatrical career when I was seven years old. I was sent, unwillingly at first, to a dancing school run by two sisters, Joan and Barbara Andrews. Barbara was the mother of the now great actress and singer Julie. I used to perform at festivals and won medals and cups. From there I was sent to the Cone-Rickman theatrical school in London. Julie Andrews had also just started there; she was then four years old. I used to catch the train from Walton-on-Thames, where I was living, change at Surbiton and wait for Julie who was living there and escort this lovely little girl every day to London. Julie eventually moved to Walton with her parents Ted and Barbara.

Strangely enough, many years later I married a girl called Jennifer Walton who had a brother called Tony who later married Julie, so I became her brother-in-law.

My first professional show after the war was called *Calypso* at the Playhouse Theatre in London and, believe it or not, I played a matelot, along with Billy Dainty and Australian actor Bill Kerr. Billy Dainty became one of the finest pantomime dames, and Bill Kerr made a name for himself in radio with his catchphrase, "I'm only here for four minutes" and then later in the Tony Hancock shows.

Barrie has been one of those actors who have rarely been out of work, and quite rightly so. I have worked with him in pantomime where his dame character is lovely and warm and full of fun. Recently he has been in several Ray Cooney productions, including the record-breaking *Run for Your Wife* and *Out of Order*. He has also had a successful spell as a BBC radio presenter.

The Mystery of Trevor Stanford, DSM

I joined the navy in 1942, having altered my birth certificate. I was sent to Plymouth for my initial training in HMS *Impregnable* for a signals and telegraphy course. One of the first things I did at Plymouth was find a piano. Not only did I enjoy playing, but it was also a way of getting some free beer and cups of tea. There was another rating who always seemed to be around the piano. He had a great voice and I used to play for him. I lost sight of him after we finished our course, but we met up again quite by chance in 1955 when he was climbing the ladder of fame.

Before I joined the navy I used to play the piano in the YMCAs around my home town of Bristol. I met a lady at one of these places and she became a second mother to me, my own mum having died in 1941. Her name was Mrs Lewis and she encouraged me to entertain the troops who were using the canteens. I was about fifteen and a half and Mrs Lewis used to travel around the RAF and army bases giving film shows, always good family films. I used to help her hump around the projectors, etc, and if the film broke down, which it often did, I would fill in on the piano until she had sorted things out. Later on Mrs Lewis also taught me to drive.

She gave me a wonderful send-off party when I joined the navy. Almost as soon as I was in, there was drama. I lost the top of the third finger on my right hand. I did it with a bread slicer. To me this was a tragedy; I didn't think I'd ever play the piano again. I did, however, although I had to develop a different style of playing. Little did I know at the time that it would actually help me. Life's a funny thing.

One of the officers aboard HMS *Impregnable* was a Commander Whitehead. There was a beautiful upright Steinway or Brinsmead piano in the wardroom and he used to say, "Play the piano for us." It was a lovely instrument, and sometimes I would spend an hour or so doing just that. Whitehead was a charming man and I remember one day, just as I was going ashore he said, "There's a car waiting to take you to HMS *Raleigh* at the other side of the base. Noël Coward is over there giving a performance and his pianist hasn't turned up yet." So off I went to *Raleigh*, and when I got there I was asked to do a fifteen-minute solo spot and an introduction to Coward who then did the soliloquy that he had created in *In Which We Serve*. He was very pleased with what I did, but his pleasure was not so noticeable when the lighting went all wrong during his performance. They got the colour gelatines mixed up and Coward went from white to blue to green to red to yellow. He certainly let fly about that with some extreme naval language when it was all over.

A lovely lady called Judy Campbell was with him and I accompanied her in "A Nightingale Sang in Berkeley Square". She had apparently sung this song with great success on the London stage. It really was a big thrill for me, playing for such famous people.

144

After Plymouth I was posted to Lowestoft in Suffolk, and they had their own concert party run by a petty officer. We used to play at various service bases in the area and really had a good time. I had a great piano to play on, a big sturdy upright.

In 1943 I was sent to Scapa Flow. I was due to go on leave for Christmas from the base ship I was on, but I missed the ferry to the mainland and had to wait until the next day. Talk about fate. The ferry I should have caught turned over in the rough seas and several hundred service men were drowned, just a couple of days before Christmas.

I was actually serving on HMS *Iron Duke* then, and the ship looked like the *Bounty* and the captain like Captain Bligh. I remember at one of the concerts I was playing a sort of jazzed-up version of Tchaikovsky's Concerto and this Captain "Bligh" came over to me and said, "Don't ever let me hear you playing that tune in that way again"!

After my period on the *Iron Duke* I was posted to one of the little drifters called *Sunnyside Girl*. The skipper came from Yarmouth and the bosun from Buckie near Aberdeen, plus there was an assortment of other fishermen, all of them speaking in different dialects. I couldn't understand any of it. Because of wartime regulations drifters had to have a trained signalman on board and that's why I was there. This wasn't the best period of my naval life. It was certainly very different from Scapa Flow. I really enjoyed my time up there. You see, there was a purpose-built theatre at Lyness and quite a few theatre and radio stars came up to entertain, Tommy Handley, Arthur Sandford (a fantastic musician) and Vera Lynn among them. I used to play the organ while the audience came in. Although I'd never learnt how to play this instrument, I had in fact played it once before in the Colston Hall, Bristol, when I was ten.

It was great seeing all the concerts at Lyness like West End shows. The only difference was you caught a boat to the theatre instead of a bus. In March 1944 I was sent back to Lowestoft for a couple of months before being posted to the Mediterranean.

In Alexandria in Egypt they had a place called the Fleet Club, and there they used to have talent competitions. I won a couple of these, not playing the piano, but singing. You see, my voice still hadn't broken properly and I had listened to my mother who was a contralto and I copied what I'd heard and sang contralto. Actually I was threatened by some matelots who said I should give the other lads a chance or else they would do me physical damage. I didn't sing any more.

I was drafted on to minesweepers in the Med and almost immediately Britain invaded Crete and Greece, so off we go to the Aegean Sea and I was seconded to the commander of the entire minesweeping fleet in the Eastern Med as his signalman. Where he went, I went. Some of the secret signals I was involved in would shake you if I was to repeat them. Maybe they'll come to light some day, but not from me.

We dropped anchor in Piraeus, the port of Athens at one point. One day we walked into Athens because we had seen the enemy troops fleeing into the mountains and everywhere seemed chaos. The Greeks didn't have any money but they had plenty of vino, Retsina and Ouzo. I passed a warehouse and went inside. There were thirty or forty concert grand pianos lying around. I started playing one of them and some Greeks came in. They began to drink and I joined them. I can't remember which piano I woke up in!

Eventually I was posted back to the UK, to Lowestoft again. The navy's show *Tokyo Express* was in the area and I gathered it was on its way to the Pacific area of operations via Canada. They were looking for a replacement pianist for the show and I auditioned for Lieutenant Arthur Lane who was the producer.

I was accepted and we were soon on our way to Canada and then right across the country from Halifax to Vancouver by train and doing shows for the Royal Navy Benevolent Fund. We carried three mini pianos and the Royal Marines Band, of which Norman White was the musical director. Later Norman became Head of Music for Television Wales.

I got into trouble with our commanding officer and producer Arthur Lane at one show we did in Vancouver. I'd had a couple of drinks before the performance and three of us were playing in unison. The music was "All The Things You Are" and I decided to play it in a slightly different key. I kept to the right harmonies, but it certainly caused a rumpus. When I came off stage Lieutenant Lane turned to somebody and said, "Put this man under close arrest." After a while it got forgotten, I think because the commanding officer needed the appropriate dress uniform to officiate at a Naval Court. He needed a white plumed hat, white gloves and a sword, and they couldn't find them in Canada, so I was let off and continued to play piano.

One of the most wonderful sights in Canada was going through the Rockies. We had a great time there, but having said that we had to observe discipline because we were serving sailors wherever we were. The plan to serve aboard *Agamemnon* never came about as the Japanese had surrendered, so off we went back across Canada.

When I got back to Civvy Street I read in a theatrical paper about film extras needed. I joined a lot of other folk in the queues outside the agents in Charing Cross Road. I got one job in a film with Anna Neagle and George Baker and then who should I meet up with again but Arthur Lane. He told me to be careful about trying to make a career in show business. "Very precarious," he said. That was in 1946. In fact I didn't start professionally until 1955. I got a job at Chappells, the music publishers in Maddox Street in London. I used to play the songs that Chappells published to singers and band leaders in the hope they would use them on the radio or in the theatre and produce royalties for writer and publisher. I met Dickie

Valentine, Dennis Lotis and Lita Rosa there, who had all been with Ted Heath's famous band. I eventually went on tour playing for Lita Rosa. It was at Chappells that I met up again with the matelot from Plymouth with the great voice. He was then Michael Holliday, the amazing Bing Crosby sound-alike. He went on to greater things, but unfortunately died too young.

I started touring all over the place accompanying people like Joan Regan, Adelaide Hall, Shani Wallis and Dorothy Squires. At the same time I was dashing back to the EMI studios in Abbey Road (where the Beatles and many others began their recording careers) in St John's Wood. My job there was to accompany the auditions for record producer Norman Newell. Adam Faith, Frankie Vaughan, Toni Dali, the King Brothers and Peter Egan, who is now an actor, all came to Abbey Road to see and sing for Norman.

One day Norman suggested I make a record in my honky-tonk style, a style I had adopted to accommodate the missing tip of my finger. The number I recorded was "Roll Up the Carpet". Norman liked it, and next day when I went to the studio he said, "You are no longer Trevor Stanford. I've changed your name to Russ Conway."

The mystery of Trevor Stanford is solved!

Russ has never been anything but a great entertainer. I suppose it was "Side Saddle" that put his recording career on the map. His many television appearances since then with the *Billy Cotton Band Show* together with literally hundreds of broadcasts and theatre appearances have made him a much loved entertainer.

He survived a serious illness a few years ago and on returning to the theatre his popularity if anything increased. His concert performances are sell-outs all over the country, and he has helped to raise thousands of pounds for charity. Apart from that he's also a really nice bloke.

His Distinguished Service Medal was awarded "for services while minesweeping in the Aegean during the invasion and reoccupation of Greece".

Combined Services Entertainment

CSE came into being in 1946 to maintain the morale of the various service garrisons stationed abroad, of which there were many, during the immediate post-war period, and was a natural successor to all that had gone before in terms of army, air force and naval entertainment.

For the first few months or so of 1946 the various existing entertainment organisations, particularly in the Far East, worked together with CSE before the latter took over sole responsibility.

As hostilities in Europe were drawing to a close in 1945, some service chiefs had advised that entertainment should be included when discussing the future of Army Welfare. They foresaw the problems that would naturally be encountered within the liberating armies in the period between the end of war and the return of stable governments. The service welfare departments were made aware of the importance of continuing organised entertainment.

Richard Stone

Major Richard Stone had been an actor pre-war, albeit not a well-known one. In fact after leaving the Royal Academy of Dramatic Art he had had little time to establish himself before joining the army. He had, along with his wife Sara whom he met at RADA, joined the Little Theatre at Saltburn in Yorkshire. He went on to do repertory seasons at Huddersfield and Colchester. From there he began his service life in January 1940. In those early days of the phoney war he even had time to direct his first adjutant John Leather, whom he had known as a friend in peacetime, in a play called *Close Quarters*. The venue was

Leather's Little Theatre in Bromley, Kent, which he ran with his wife Betty, who held the fort, as it were, while her husband was in the army.

Richard Stone was then a gunner in the Royal Artillery. (It was a strange case of a gunner directing his adjutant, but then in early wartime Britain many strange things happened.) After that Richard did an OCTU (Officer Cadet Training Unit) course at Aldershot, and then joined the Royal Horse Artillery. He was eventually to fight right through the African campaign with the 7th Armoured Division, the Desert Rats, and then go on to Italy.

At the end of the Western Desert campaign in 1943 and before moving into Italy, Stone, who was by then a captain, was ordered to organise some entertainment in the huge amphitheatre at Homs, about a hundred miles east of Tripoli. Along with Captain Cecil Clark, much later to become Head of Drama at Thames Television, they had to put on a show every night. Any entertainers who appeared on the scene were quickly recruited, such as touring ENSA concert parties. These sometimes included star names, such as Beatrice Lillie and Leslie Henson. The amphitheatre with its stone benches is still there to this day.

After the Italian campaign I was sent back to England, and when I got back home I heard there would be a job going at the War Office for an entertainments officer in the 2nd Army in Germany once the second front was opened. Colonel Basil Brown, who was then in charge of Army Welfare, wanted to get Stars in Battledress units on to the mainland of Europe just as soon as possible after the invasion, and he needed to have army personnel on hand who knew something about entertainment and could organise arrangements on the spot. The RAF with Ralph Reader's Gang Shows were doing the same. I got the army job and this was the start of a long association with Basil Brown that was to continue well after the war when he became Billy Butlin's right-hand man, and I produced many shows for the Butlin organisation.

I was eventually sent to Normandy on D-Day plus five with one of the SIB parties, and I was standing on the Normandy bridgehead, having been put ashore from a tank landing craft. There we were trying to keep pianos and drum kits and other entertainment necessities from getting too wet. In the group, if my memory serves me correctly, were Eddie Child, comedian; Boy Foy, juggler and unicyclist; Arthur Haynes, comedian and leader of the group; Syd Millward and his Nit Wits, a crazy musical band; and a couple of ATS girls, Janet Brown, impressionist, and Frances Tanner, singer.

Cyril Nagey, the very funny black drummer and dancer with Syd Millward's band, was leaning on a piano looking after his drum kit with shells bursting not far away when a high-ranking officer came up to him and said, "What on earth are you doing here?" and Cyril said, "Sir, that's what I've been asking myself all day."

As the allied advance began to gain momentum we established entertainment areas at the various bases and also in a few theatres. ENSA too were sending out parties by now and some individual artistes also arrived on the scene. Flanagan and Allen and impressionist Florence Desmond actually reopened the ABC (Garrison) Theatre in Brussels for me.

The 21st Army Groups had by now acquired about six colonels in charge of entertainment. I was just one captain on my own doing it for the whole 2nd Army. It certainly was a very exciting time, and I remember sitting in Lüneburg, Germany, with my colonel just after the surrender of the German forces, and he said he had heard somewhere that a certain division had captured two elephants. He said, "Stone, let's have a circus." Now two elephants don't make a circus, but I managed to get hold of one (a circus) called Berrie's. One of the difficulties was that you couldn't use German artistes just after the war had finished, you could only use displaced persons: Latvians, Estonians and the like whom the circus employed as clowns or other performers. I requisitioned the big top belonging to Berrie and we were in business, complete with the elephants. We established the circus in Hamburg and on the night we opened we had Laurence Olivier, Ralph Richardson and Margaret Leighton in the audience. They had come out to play at the Opera House in the city with an Old Vic company sponsored by ENSA.

It was at this time that various branches of entertainment started crossing one another's paths. SIB units, ENSA, RAF Gang Shows and battalion concert parties all played their part. The 2nd Army was now being disbanded and divided up into areas: 12 Corps, 8 Corps and 30 Corps, and each one had a major in charge of entertainment. I was sent to 30 Corps with the rank of major and strangely enough this was the corps I had fought with in the desert.

Actor Ian Carmichael joined me from the 30th Armoured Brigade and became my staff captain. Ian and I had met at RADA pre-war. So we started auditions for a pool of artistes that we could call upon. We had a 30 Corps dance band conducted by a soldier, Bombardier Ray Martin, and I remember a colonel who was playing on third trumpet. Funny situation, a bombardier giving orders to a colonel, only musically of course. Frankie Howerd auditioned for us: he was a transport driver at the time, and we made him the comic in one of our shows.

Ian Carmichael and I had about thirty shows running, which was incredible. We used to go to Berlin to audition acts, and bring them back, and it wasn't easy, as you had to get through the Russian zone. We would have a load of chorus girls from Berlin in the back of a three-ton truck. When we got to the Russian zone we used to have to cover them up with sacking and the like to get through, otherwise they would have wanted to know what we were doing taking entertainers away from Berlin. So we had shows with an English sergeant in charge of a *Continental Follies*, or whatever the show was called, which was made up of all these acts that we had found all over the place.

We had an agent in Hanover, and an agent in Berlin booking artistes for us, and how we paid for it was quite simple. We let them perform for the Germans in the afternoon, from which they earned their living, and for that we provided them with rations and the means to get around. They then played to our troops free in the evening, which as far as we were concerned was wonderful.

Now we come back to John Leather, whom I have mentioned in connection with the Little Theatre at Bromley. John was now at the War Office in the Army Welfare department with the rank of a full colonel. Early in 1946 I was waiting to be demobbed and I had already decided to go into the agency business with Felix de Wolfe who was my counterpart in 21st Group RAF. We had met on various occasions in the service to discuss entertainment issues within our group.

John Leather sent for me in London and asked me whether I would like to stay in the army and start a worldwide entertainment organisation for the forces who would for some time to come be staffing British garrisons abroad. I told Leather I would do this job for a short time only as I was waiting to join Felix de Wolfe who had already been demobbed. I said I wanted the rank of honorary colonel, and that I would put on my uniform and fly to any part of the world as an officer to set things up for him, but I must have some time to myself to help get the agency going with de Wolfe.

I did this for about a year, and I called this new organisation Combined Services Entertainment (CSE). You see, ENSA was finished by now and there were just a few SIB units still in existence, travelling to Italy and the Middle and Far East. I remember seeing Reg Varney and Stella Moray in one SIB company in Singapore. Benny Hill was the second comic in a show I saw in Germany, but I'm not sure that it was an SIB unit.

Ian Carmichael, who had now been demobbed, was helping get the CSE tours together. We sent out plays like *Worm's Eye View* and *See How They Run*. We had Ivy Benson's all-girl band, along with Hugh Lloyd and the Beverley Twins (before they became the Beverley Sisters). Jack Douglas's father, John D. Roberton, who was in theatre management, provided the scenery and costumes, costing a total of a hundred and forty pounds.

When I was in London I used to go to the War Office in the mornings and to my office of de Wolfe and Stone in the afternoons. A lot of the artistes who had been in the services were now demobbed and used to go back abroad under the banner of CSE as civilian entertainers. I did this until 1947 when George Brightwell took over the running of it. Several of the wartime performers I had known asked my advice about getting an agent and I suggested to some of them that I would handle their business if they so wished. I signed up Reg Varney, Benny Hill and Norman Vaughan, and the agency already had people like Bernard Miles, who at that time used to play the halls as a country yokel long before he inaugurated the Mermaid Theatre Trust.

I was then asked by Billy Butlin to present some revues for him at the camp theatres. This brought me back into contact with Basil Brown, who was by now Billy's right-hand man. I did the first show for them at Clacton in 1948 with Vic Gordon and Peter Colville, who now live in Australia. Terry Scott was in our next show, and after that Terry teamed up with Bill Maynard at Skegness.

Ian Carmichael was now being handled by us (de Wolfe and Stone) and he produced some of the Butlin shows. His assistant was ex-Major David Croft, who has since become the hugely successful producer, director and co-writer of so many television shows like *Hugh and I, Up Pompeii, Dad's Army, It Ain't Half Hot, Mum, Hi-de-Hi, You Rang, M'Lord?* and *'Allo 'Allo*.

Round about 1949 I booked several of our artistes into the London production of *Wild Violets*, including Ian Carmichael and David Croft. So things were going well for me.

Richard Stone has had a remarkable career as an agent, and has at one time or another handled the careers of many famous artistes, guiding them to the top of the theatrical profession.

Ian Carmichael

Ian Carmichael was very much involved in Army Welfare entertainment in the latter part of the war.

I began acting just before hostilities broke out in 1939, after attending the Royal Academy of Dramatic Art. The last theatre job I had before joining up was a ten-week tour in a Herbert Farjeon revue which was due to finish up at London's Criterion Theatre, but the week before this happened I received my "papers". That was the end of my career as an actor, at least for some while, apart from a very brief excursion into performing and co-producing with Captain Nigel Patrick in a play called *Springtime for Henry* while I was stationed at Helmsley in Yorkshire. We became good friends there, but shortly afterwards Nigel left to organise service entertainment in Italy.

Post-war Nigel Patrick became a very successful screen and stage actor. Ian did at a later date produce a revue at Warminster in Wiltshire with an all-army cast and some spectacular stage effects, before moving on with his regiment, the 79th Armoured Division, to East Anglia and a period of rigorous training in preparation for the second front. He eventually landed in France on D-Day plus ten.

Once the fighting in Europe was over my thoughts turned to my acting career, which hopefully I could continue when I was back home. While I was stationed in Germany a letter came round to all units saying that auditions were being held at the Garrison Theatre in Neinburg for service personnel who were interested in theatrical entertainment, so I applied to be included. I quickly learned a song and presented myself at the theatre. I was just getting up on stage when a voice from the stalls said, "Don't I know you?" and I looked down and sitting there was Major Richard Stone.

I said, "You probably do. I think we were at RADA [Royal Academy of Dramatic Art] together."

Richard said, "You don't need to audition. Come and sit down here with me," and that was the beginning of a long relationship with him. I became his production assistant at 30 Corps where he was now in charge of entertainment. Early on I made one big goof concerning someone who later became a very big name in our business. I have told this story many times before and I'm sure people must have got bored with it; I'm sure the bombardier in question has.

We had broken for lunch after the morning auditions and the bombardier came up to us as we were leaving and said, "Can I do an audition for you?"

Richard Stone said, "Is your name on the list?"

He said, "No, I'm the NCO in charge of the lads who've come from my unit."

He eventually auditioned for us with a song called "A Tisket a Tasket" which he interspersed with jokes.

When he had finished Richard said to me, "What do you think?"

I said, "Oh no, no, he's too raw, with no timing, and I don't think he's particularly funny."

Richard said, "I think you've got it wrong. I'm going to book him for one of our shows" – and that was Frankie Howerd!

Other would-be entertainers came to see us, and we were also able to put together a big band and a string quartet. We had plays to deal with and we imported some ENSA girls to help with this. We booked some existing German variety shows and reproduced them because they were rather slow and laborious. We then sent them out to places such as Wilhelmshaven, Cuxhaven, Hanover, Hamlin and Brunswick. The use of German acts was illegal, strictly speaking, because a non-fraternisation policy was in force and you weren't supposed to talk to Germans. But General Horrocks, commanding the troops in Germany, turned a blind eye to what we were doing because he was so anxious that we got entertainment to the troops.

I of course wanted to act, but to do so I would have had to drop a pip from captain, and as by now I had a wife and daughter in the UK, I needed to keep my rank for financial reasons. So I became Richard Stone's staff captain, assisting him in the organisation, which was now growing very large with a big theatrical pool of artistes. A lot of the performers in the variety shows claimed that they were Latvians or Estonians and suchlike because they were entitled to slightly better rations than the Germans. Most of them denied they were of German origin but they had no papers to prove it, and we had our doubts. However, our job was only to get them routed to all the various battalions and existing theatres as quickly as possible. The arrangement was that they gave a free show in the evenings for the British troops but were allowed to play anywhere nearby in the afternoons and they would take the "box office" money. Everything ran smoothly for about a year and was marvellous.

We had an agent in Berlin who used to obtain performers for us, and he and the British Welfare officer would arrange for us to bring the artistes out.

Richard Stone was now recalled to London to start organising CSE and so I took over Richard's job with 30 Corps until I was demobbed. When I finally came out I went to see Richard who had told me he was going to start in the agency business after the war, and at that time he was my only connection in the theatre. He certainly kept me working in the early years after my demob. If I wasn't acting I used to produce shows for him at the Butlin Holiday Camps, and also some of the shows that were now going abroad for CSE, and so I slowly picked up the threads again of my theatrical career.

Ian's career has certainly been varied. Films, television, radio, stage plays and a remarkable number of hugely successful revues. He appears to be the Peter Pan of entertainment.

He lives in a most beautiful part of the country, high up on the North Yorkshire moors, where his garden overlooks a river, and on the day I visited him there the sun was shining on this most idyllic spot.

The first volume of his autobiography, *Will the Real Ian Carmichael . . .*, was published by Macmillan in 1979.

Frankie Howerd – No, don't laugh – poor soul

"An impact on radio audiences seldom experienced in such a short space of time" . . . "One of the funniest stand-up comedians of our age". . . "A performer in the true tradition of the clown."

All these things and many more have been said about Frankie Howerd. Another adjective that could be used about him is determined. The road to success in the entertainment business is not easy but to some laymen "a star overnight" means just that. Hopefully the majority knows it usually takes several years to achieve success, if it is to be achieved at all.

This is the second book of mine that Frank (I am not quite sure why I am still inclined to call him Frank) has played a part in. My main concern this time was his early life, his army career (though I'm sure he'd agree there was little chance of his being a great success as a soldier) and his subsequent rise to fame. On this occasion we had a forty-minute telephone conversation – a conversation I might have had with my next-door neighbour about life and its ups and downs ("Well, you've got to keep going, haven't you?"). A chat is what Frankie Howerd is about. Radio, television or stage are places for him to have a chat, and it's also his irreverence, particularly to the show business establishment, that is so funny, letting us in on the secret, as it were ("I got a phone-call from Lord Delfont; he was up to his old tricks, reversing the charges . . .").

It is always a pleasure to talk to Frank because you know there are no hidden thoughts, no silly illusions about the word "star" that has been placed on him. "It is a difficult business to be in just like any other which you have to work at, and hope you will still be needed again even after you've done a smash hit performance." Show business is a fickle profession (some folks don't even think it is a profession), and learning your trade is not easy, particularly if you are hoping one day to make people laugh for a living.

Frankie Howerd came from a poor but loving home in Eltham, south-east London. He was a gawky, nervous boy with a slight stutter (his description), not the best credentials for a career in the theatre. However, he didn't relish spending the rest of his life in an office, and what would he do there anyway? Perhaps he would be able to hide the nervousness and rather "ordinary" person behind theatrical characters. RADA (the Royal Academy of Dramatic Art) seemed the place to start. Frank applied for an audition there and got one, but failed it horribly. The nerves and lack of confidence let him down, and the auditioners at RADA weren't quite sure what to make of him. But his ambition to become a professional entertainer burned on.

He presented himself on two or three occasions at Carol Levis's discovery shows that were touring the variety theatres. Carol Levis, a Canadian, had become hugely popular on radio in this country presenting would-be comedians, impressionists, singers, instrumentalists and so on, who were hoping it would put them on the first rung of the ladder towards the "bright lights". Levis always used to sign off with the phrase, "Remember, ladies and gentlemen, the discoveries of today are surely the stars of tomorrow." His successful radio shows made him a big attraction on the theatre circuit where he presented some of the better performers heard on the air. He would also audition a few local people with hopes of appearing in the theatre in their area.

Frankie tried his luck with Levis at the Lewisham Hippodrome (not far from his home). He told some elaborate stories about events that had presumably happened to him, heavily embellishing them in a way that was to become his style in later years. At this time, however, it was an unheard-of technique (stand-up comedians were supposed to tell straightforward gags), and in any case his nerves let him down and he was shown the door. He tried again at the New Cross Empire, another theatre in south London. This time he tried impressions, with the same result. Although unnerved by these failures, he was determined to keep trying. A third time he decided to try a different tack at the audition, doing a straight (or as near to straight as Frank could be) monologue. That also proved a disaster.

The turning point, although Frankie may not have known it at the time, came with his call-up into the armed forces, soon to be Gunner Howerd of the Royal Artillery. While he was stationed at Shoeburyness Garrison in Essex, a garrison I knew well, playing a lot of my early cricket on the beautiful ground there, it became apparent that some sort of entertainment was needed to relieve the boredom of the service men and women. A few of them, including Frankie, got together with the idea of producing a show or two. Well, it was a start, and Frankie began knocking the idea into shape. He wrote a few sketches, persuaded the few good musicians on site (in fact pre-war professionals) to take part, and of course made sure he himself was shown to advantage. Frank was frightened. The old nerves had come through, but his determination to succeed gave him the enthusiasm to produce, write and star in the revue-type shows with titles such as *Fine Goings On*, *Talk About Laugh* and *Rise and Shine*.

The garrison concert party appeared to have taken off, and in his own way so had Frankie. Of course the garrison all knew one another and were rooting for their mates on stage, but could there be success elsewhere? Frankie was soon to find out. He was transferred to South Wales and he immediately applied to audition for Stars in Battledress. He now felt that with the little experience he had had at Shoeburyness he was ready for the more organised entertainment that Stars in Battledress represented. He was told to report to the cookhouse where he would be seen by an officer who might or might not have had any idea about entertainment. With rows of empty canteen tables between himself and the officer he very soon felt the return of that nervousness and lack of confidence. Well, who wouldn't? It was like being on trial. At the end of the audition the officer just said, "Very good, Howerd", and that was the last he heard of his attempt to become an entertainer with Stars in Battledress.

Frankie was soon on the move again, this time to Germany. He became part of 30 Corps and he began, unofficially, to do some entertaining when the chance came about. Essentially his posting was to work in the office of the corps and, to his surprise, act as an interpreter! He muddled along in the office, trying to cope with the filing system and operate the typewriter, activities which had never been his forte. Frank good-naturedly did not complain, but this could not be said of his superior officer who shared the office with him. The situation became a sort of Laurel and Hardy double act with the officer playing Hardy to Frank's Laurel. The officer eventually had a nervous breakdown and was removed to a "safer place".

Once the war in Europe had finished it was more important than ever that the service men and women in Germany should be saved from boredom, particularly as opportunities for leisure activity were scarce owing to the fraternisation laws with the local German population. Frank devoted his energies to the organisation of unofficial concert parties in the Hanover area. The authorities were not wholly against his activities, but having heard of Frank's organising prowess, or lack of it, grew anxious that his proposals might even upset the peace, and possibly reignite hostilities between the two countries!

However, Frankie was obviously making his mark in Germany and was soon auditioning again, this time for two officers who certainly knew something about entertainment, Captain Ian Carmichael and Major Richard Stone. Their reaction to Howerd was complimentary (well, Stone's was anyway) and he was sent off to compère one of the productions, then later run it.

Early in 1946 Frank returned to England. While waiting for his demob he did the rounds of the agents' offices in London, showing each one a letter of recommendation Major Stone had given him in Germany, but his efforts were unsuccessful. There was now a chance to go back to Germany solely entertaining the forces there, and with his confidence and experience of knowing what the service audiences liked he was again successful. He was even able to instil a certain amount of confidence into the other performers.

After a time it was back again to England and final demob. Armed with his free suit and army gratuity the quest began again for a chance to show civilian audiences over here what he could do, but this still eluded him and his determination began to wane, to say nothing of his confidence. In Piccadilly there opened in 1943 a Stage Door Canteen where service men and women could meet and see a show. Frank heard about this and, putting on his discarded uniform to give himself confidence in front of an audience who might then regard him as being "one of us", Frank presented himself for an audition.

The powers that be thought he was funny, but they hadn't got a space in any of their immediate shows and said, "We'll let you know" – a phrase the author and thousands of others have heard at some time or another. Frank decided he had better look for a "proper job". Money was running out, his widowed mother needed looking after and he couldn't just hang around waiting for something to happen. He did meet some nice agents on his travels who encouraged him to stay with it. They liked his style, he was a pleasant and friendly fellow, and one agent particularly urged him to keep on trying. His name was Robert Layton.

Robert Layton used to book a lot of acts into small concert parties all round our coasts, and he was a gentleman. This Frank and I both agreed upon. In fact he gave me my first break into concert party in 1955. Frank didn't forget Robert's kindness and encouragement and when, much later on, Robert needed a little help Frank was able to give him just that.

Then came the first break. Someone had to drop out of one of the shows at the Stage Door Canteen at the last minute and the gawky, slightly nervous, but funny fellow who had auditioned was remembered, and was asked to come in at a moment's notice. Frank agreed. He had nothing to lose, and anyway had almost resigned himself to finding some other occupation.

He was a big success at the Stage Door Canteen that night, and in the audience was a representative of Jack Payne's organisation. Agents and managers were often popping into the Canteen looking for talent and Jack Payne, one of the biggest names in pre-war radio with his band, was putting out a revue for the summer. Frank was engaged to appear in this show sharing bottom of the bill with another comedian, Max Bygraves, himself only just demobbed from the RAF. They were both fairly successful in the show in their different ways and after ten weeks someone had obviously heard about the "gawky" boy and his unusual style because he was invited to audition (by now he could almost have made a career out of auditions alone) for a radio series which was already running, called *Variety Bandbox*. He was to alternate on Sunday evenings with another comedian, Derek Roy, who had a very different style to Frank's.

Frankie got the job, and soon the whole country would make a point of staying in on Sunday evenings to listen to the programme, and woe betide any member of the household who dared breathe while it was on. Millions of people regularly listened to the radio – remember there was hardly any television then. Frank's chatty style caught on almost immediately, and people identified with the situations he described, larger than life, rather like a cartoonist's portrayal of an event or a person. People on buses on a Monday morning or in the shops were soon talking about his *Bandbox* appearances. He was being impersonated by all and sundry and within a year Frankie Howerd, from being a bottom of the bill artiste in a touring revue, had his own show on the road and his name over the title.

Frank didn't forget the Stage Door Canteen, and on several occasions put on whole shows for them as a thank you for that first break he had there. He has had his ups, and a few minor downs, since those days, but Frankie Howerd has surely made a place for himself in theatrical history.

I think I've had this flu, you know – I've not been well – plays the old joints up [to the pianist] what, dear? – yes chilly – I said it's chilly – no, don't laugh, she's a bit mutt 'n'jeff – poor soul – anyway I'll have a chat with you for a minute or two . . . well, you've got to keep going, haven't you?

Bryan Burdon

For a young man who had learned his trade as a stooge to his father and other comedians, the many tours that Bryan Burdon did for CSE between 1958 and 1968 was the jam on his bread and butter life in show business.

Bryan's father, Albert Burdon, was a very famous Tyneside comedian who was brought to London by the great C. B. Cochran, and in the capital he stayed. He made many films for the Gaumont British Company and toured in revues and variety, often using young Bryan as his assistant in his various comic routines, one being a send-up of an Oriental magician and the disappearing person in the cabinet, who inevitably appeared or reappeared at the wrong time, with hilarious results.

CSE gave me an opportunity to see the world, which I doubt would ever have been the case in my career at that time. I started the tour feeding actor Brian Reece, who had made a name for himself as radio's PC 49. CSE was then based in Dean Stanley Street, Westminster, just a stone's throw from the Houses of Parliament, and all the preparations and rehearsals took place there under the administration of George Brightwell, who had taken over from Colonel Richard Stone. The shows had super costumes, and all the artistes involved were professional entertainers. We played to various holding garrisons in Libya at Tripoli, Benghazi and Tobruk. We also performed at a sort of staging-post in the Maldive Islands where about five hundred men were stationed on an atoll rather like Treasure Island. This was where the troops could get acclimatised before flying out to trouble spots, if need be, like Singapore, Borneo or Belize.

I was eventually given principal comedian status in the shows, and I remember when we went to Singapore all the garrison troops were out on manoeuvres so we got sent up the Malay Peninsula to Penang and Ipoh and Kuala Lumpur. In Penang we stayed at the European and Oriental Hotel, a beautiful place overlooking the Malaccan Straits. The whole scene was like a willow pattern plate with junks going across the water.

When we got back to Singapore the manoeuvres were still in progress, so we were sent off to Guam Island in the Marianas. There were RAF and army personnel on Guam and during the day we had the chance to go scuba diving which they taught me in seven days. We also went out big game fishing in RAF torpedo boats, and we even did some hang-gliding.

On another CSE trip, to Kenya, we went to the George VI game reserve where, armed with 8mm cine-cameras, one of our African drivers took us in his open-sided jeep on a tour of the reserve. We had to stop at one point as there was an ostrich in the middle of the road laying an egg. The egg was huge, and I've never seen such pain on anybody's face as I did on that ostrich, and I've got it all on film. We got out of the jeep at one point to film more of the wonderful scenery, unaware that there were lions and cheetahs roaming about. When we got back to our base the folks there said, "You must be crazy, driving round in an open jeep. It's not Richmond Park, you know."

Another tour I did was to Aden. Ted Rogers (*3-2-1* and "Dusty Bin") was in the show, and when we flew to the Radfan Mountains we saw the rebels fighting round Beau Geste-like forts. Of course the oil exploration hadn't started in those areas when we were there in 1960. We had to do our shows in daylight and then fly off before nightfall as the rebels used to come close to the airstrips and lob a mortar bomb or two at any moving vehicle, including aircraft. I remember one show we were doing there and all through it there was rifle fire going on while Ted and I were working on table-tops, in the open air of course. We asked one of the service personnel what was going on and he said, "It's just the rebels trying to worry us." We said, "Well, they're definitely worrying us!" and we couldn't wait to go on to our next venue.

The airfield was in a kind of crater and our Andover transport had to take off almost vertically because there was always the chance the rebels would machine-gun the plane if it was in their sights for too long. Apparently there was a truce every Wednesday so that the tribesmen could come into town, which I think was called Dhula, to do their shopping. When they left, the fighting started again. It was a funny sort of war going on there! Since the oil explosion in the area it's all skyscrapers and motorways now. We also went to the lovely island of Bahrain.

Something that did impress me wherever we went, particularly in North Africa, was the British and Commonwealth cemeteries, looked after by the War Graves Commission. The German cemetery in the area was quite different, built like a fortress with every brick engraved with a name.

Sometimes we would have the same aircraft and crew with us for the whole tour, and they would help us with lighting at night and sort the props out for us. There were always at least two girls in the shows so that they would be company for each other and they were chaperoned everywhere. We worked hard on the tours, not only performing but also because there was a lot of travelling, and when time permitted we were also expected to socialise in the various service messes, but in general we were always well looked after. I certainly wouldn't have missed my ten years with CSE for anything.

Don Smoothey

Within a few years of Don settling into his post-war theatrical activities following army service and SIB duties, he was asked to go on tour for CSE. This was in 1956 in a unit headed by singer Dickie Valentine. Dickie was a big name then after his successful seasons in company with Dennis Lotis and Lita Rosa with the popular Ted Heath big band. This first trip was to entertain British garrisons in Germany.

Immediately after this Don was sent out to the Middle East during the Suez crisis and this included the first of three visits to Cyprus during the terrorist EOKA and Makarios troubles. He then went to East Africa with Alma Cogan's sister, Sandra Caron.

Following this he took his own show to Malaya in the company of Tommy Layton who had been his one-time comedy feed before Tommy became Dickie Valentine's manager. They played to small army garrisons situated in the jungle who were there to protect the communities from the rebel fighters operating in the vicinity.

When they had finished in Malaya they flew to Hong Kong and then on to Inchon in South Korea, just below the 38th Parallel, where they gave one show in a huge tent to thousands of UN personnel. Sixteen nations were represented.

Don teamed up again with Dickie Valentine for a trip to Nairobi and then on to Saudi Arabia and Aden where a small Valetta aircraft piloted by an ex-Spitfire pilot had to dodge the Yemenese tribesmen's bullets as they took off over the border. The pilot remarked to Don that there wasn't much to worry about, because most of the bullets didn't fit the rifles anyway, so it was a thousand to one chance they would be hit!

Don had terrible toothache when they started this, his last trip for CSE in 1960, so much so that it closed one eye and caused a huge swelling on his face. An African doctor was contacted in Nairobi who suggested he could inject Don with some kind of liquid or pass his hand over the infected area. Don opted for the latter! Within minutes of this doctor passing his hand across Don's face the pain disappeared and the swelling started to go down. I wonder why English dentists can't do that!

In most places that Don Smoothey toured, and at one time he was on the move for five continuous months without a break, the entertainment party slept within the service garrisons where, as

Don said, "We felt quite at home and considerably more comfortable than we had been with the SIB tours during the war."

Wyn Calvin, MBE

Wyn, known as "The Welsh Prince of Laughter", has had a long and varied career in the entertainment business, since 1945 in fact. He has been the principal performer in many summer shows throughout the UK, but naturally, perhaps, has found most success in his native Wales where he really is their "Prince".

For many years he has had his own radio show based in Cardiff but which has also taken him to every corner of the Principality interviewing his countrymen on serious as well as light-hearted topics. Wyn is a wonderful pantomime dame, and recently has been playing "Mother" Crusoe to boxer Frank Bruno in *Robinson Crusoe*. He is, and always has been, a tireless worker for charitable causes, and in recognition of this was awarded the MBE in 1990.

After the war, having joined ENSA and with CSE in full flow, Wyn Calvin did many trips to British bases abroad. He was probably one of, if not the most, travelled entertainer for that organisation in Europe and the Middle and Far East.

While entertaining garrisons on islands in the Persian Gulf in 1966 he remembers landing at Muscat, and the Emir of that state personally sending him a message of condolence on the death of "all the children in Wales". The Emir was a radio "ham" and had picked up a message over the airwaves about the Aberfan disaster, the avalanche of coalmining waste which roared down on to that little town killing over a hundred children. The Emir had thought that all the children in Wales had died, and was overcome with grief for Welshman Wyn. That was how Wyn first heard about the disaster that stunned our nation, thousands of miles away in the Persian Gulf.

Once Wyn had got the facts he was able to reassure the Emir that the disaster had been confined to Aberfan, ghastly enough though that was.

I know personally just how proud he and his wife Carol felt on a November night in 1990 when Wyn Calvin gained the highest honour the Grand Order of Water Rats could bestow on him when they elected him their King Rat.

Jimmy Perry

Actor and television writer Jimmy Perry had from an early age been bewitched by the theatre. When he was called up into the Royal Artillery in 1943 he was posted to Oswestry in Shropshire and immediately set about forming a regimental concert party. This was the start of his involvement in service entertainment.

He was posted to India in 1944 and soon after arriving in Bombay was moved to the Royal Artillery depot at Deolali. From Deolali he was sent to an anti-aircraft unit in Assam, in the heart of tea-growing country. Unfortunately the range-finders for the guns were quite old and by the time the distance of the enemy positions had been calculated the Japanese were out of range. Even in this small unit in the tea plantation, Jimmy Perry spent the unoccupied hours entertaining his comrades with jokes and impressions.

A short while later he contracted dysentery and jaundice and was sent to a hospital in Calcutta where it was also found he needed an operation to remove his appendix. A long convalescence followed in Kashmir and the rehabilitation was helped by a meeting with a major's wife who decided a little extra "comfort" on her houseboat would speed up his recovery. He was then sent back to Deolali where he joined the already established Royal Artillery concert party. However, the war with Japan had now finished and the concert party was disbanded, which appeared to please the regimental sergeant-major who said, "I'll have all you actor poofs sent back to the jungle."

For some reason Bombardier Perry was posted to Coimbatore (near Madras) on the southern tip of India. This was an RA unit, made up mostly of men from the Gordon Highlanders. Jimmy then heard that CSE would now be handling all the entertainment in India and Malaya with headquarters in Singapore and New Delhi. It would be run for the time being under air force, army and navy administration.

He applied to do an audition at CSE in New Delhi and was given permission to travel. It took him six days by train to get there, most of the journey in the company of Indian high-ranking army officers and princes who introduced the young Perry to a little "whacky baccy" smoking which he didn't enjoy, but for a few brief hours gave him the feeling of not caring whether he was in Delhi or up the Khyber Pass.

When he arrived at his destination nobody knew where the CSE headquarters were, but during his ride round the city in an Indian *"taxi"* he heard a ukelele playing and told his *"driver"* to follow the sound. The "uke"-playing came from an auditionee.

Perry met Squadron-Leader Charles Fletcher who had obviously never seen an aeroplane and made all the would-be entertainers sing "It's a Long Way to Tipperary". Jimmy became a member of a party called *The Ready for Action Road Show*. The opening chorus of the show went as follows:

We're ready for action, so on with the show –
Ready for action so here we go,
With music and laughter to help you on your way
To raising the rafters with a Hey Hey Hey.
So meet the gang, meet the gang, say how do you do,
Come on and meet the gang, meet the gang,
We hope to bring a laugh or two to you.
So getting around and going places,
Getting around to show our faces,
Getting around we're mental cases,
Yes, we're getting around.

From Bangalore to Singapore, from Rangoon to Bombay,
And if you really liked the show
We'll come again another day, hey –
Getting around and going places,
Getting around we show our faces,
Getting around we're mental cases –
Yes, we're getting around.

(Applause) . . . and into the comedy routines, etc.

This show was the start of the Combined Services Entertainment in the Far East. The show travelled all over India, Burma and Persia (Iran). They played to a regiment of Gurkhas on the North-West Frontier with a British officer with a cut-glass accent translating the jokes. This was quite difficult, to say the least, particularly when one of the comics with a thick north of England accent was telling his jokes. A routine such as, "Now, my wife's a funny woman, talk about a bad cook, she even ruins cornflakes", sounded ridiculous in its Urdu translation. It was even more ridiculous when the officer translated Jimmy Perry's impressions of Gordon Harker, Ned Sparks, Robb Wilton and Katie Hepburn to the mystified Gurkhas.

The members of the party were of course still serving soldiers and had some particularly hair-raising moments trying to keep the various factions of the population from killing each other in the lead-up to the partition of India and Pakistan. During a visit to entertain the British garrison at Lahore where there was terrific rioting going on, they drove through the streets in a caged lorry being pelted with stones and other missiles.

The female impersonator of the show, Julian Pepper, over all the noise and shindig said, "Take no notice of them, they're only jealous." During the actual show in the garrison theatre you could hardly hear yourself speak with the shouting, screaming and gunshots coming from outside.

Jimmy eventually left India in 1947, six days before the declaration of independence. His experiences there were stored away in his mind and reawakened in the 1970s when he co-wrote with David Croft the highly successful television series *It Ain't Half Hot, Mum.* This was incidentally their second collaboration as writers, the first being *Dad's Army.* Their holiday camp series, *Hi-de-Hi*, was immensely popular with television viewers, and their most recent BBC series, *You Rang, M'Lord?*, concerning family life in the 1920s, has already attracted large audiences.

Between them David Croft and Jimmy Perry have launched many theatrical careers.

Clive Stock

Clive's service career, which began in 1944, took in both the RAF and the army, a pretty rare occurrence, and began when he was posted to India in 1945. He was an established professional singer before he enlisted, having appeared in several West End musical productions, some of them working with and for the great Ivor Novello.

We had left Britain on the *Mauretania*, without convoy because the ship was too fast for the U-boats, and on the ship we did a few concerts. Charles Chilton, who was an authority on Western music, and was later to present a popular programme for BBC radio, was featured in the concerts.

166

On arriving in India Clive, like other performers, wanted to continue with his chosen profession, if only in a limited way, and he eventually formed a small cabaret unit to entertain at local garrisons. The RAF personnel were responsible to Combined Services Entertainment in India and the army likewise in Singapore. The South-East Asia area at that time was commanded by Major-General Stopford, and he had heard about Clive's entertaining activities and had him attached to the army so that he could become involved in entertainment in Malaya, hence his dual service.

Russell Braddon and Sydney Piddington had both been prisoners of the Japanese in Changi Jail and while they were there they invented a telepathy act which was the forerunner of the world-famous telepathy production staged by Sydney Piddington and his wife for several years. Coincidentally, several years later I was a guest on their show in Australia, my first meeting with Sydney since meeting him after he was freed from Changi. Russell Braddon eventually wrote a graphic account of his experiences under the Japanese occupation in Singapore and elsewhere in South-East Asia.

The Japanese had by now surrendered and I was immediately engaged in organising working parties of the prisoners of war under British jurisdiction. This was a tough job at first as the Japanese were not too happy about taking orders from their victors.

Very soon Clive teamed up with another ex-RAF service man, Albert Arlen, who was a composer of some repute. The two of them set about holding auditions, and had soon discovered a number of talents within the serving units. One of their first recruits was Stanley Baxter who had been doing some plays with his units north of Singapore. Stanley was to become a fine revue, pantomime and television performer in the post-war years, not only in his native Scotland but much further afield. Kenneth Williams also joined them and this was certainly the start of one of the most brilliant theatrical careers. I worked with Ken for eight years in radio's *Beyond Our Ken* and *Round the Horne* and he certainly was a comic genius.

Another service man who joined this newly formed "pool" of CSE artistes after entertaining in his unit shows in the Singapore area was John Schlesinger, then a very good ventriloquist. He is now a famous film and stage director. *Midnight Cowboy*, *Sunday, Bloody Sunday* and *Darling* have all won Schlesinger top awards, and the film industry certainly owes him a great deal of gratitude.

167

We also had Peter Nichols with us, who much later wrote the very funny and successful play *Privates on Parade* which was loosely based on his experiences in Far East entertainment.

The official CSE photographer was Morris Aza, the son of Lilian and Bert Aza, who as theatrical agents handled some of this country's biggest stars, including Gracie Fields. Morris now runs the agency since his parents died. Incidentally, Morris took my wedding photographs when I married my wife Gwen. The administrator for the CSE army activities in our area at that time was Captain Peter Ohmn, who later changed his name to Vaughan, and has become the well-known actor Peter Vaughan. Radio SEAC, which covered the whole South-East Asia area, was run by David Jacobs, now known to millions of radio and television audiences throughout the world, and Desmond Carrington, now a radio presenter in this country and, before that, one of the stars of television's *Emergency Ward 10*.

We had some wonderful scenic effects at our disposal for the shows, back projection even, and the costumes were made by a tailor in Singapore. We sent out several units from the base depot. Kenneth Williams was in a revue called *High and Low* which went up-country into Malaya, and I took another company to Ceylon, Malaya and Burma.

At times, when all the shows got back to the depot at the same time, we would put on a big show combining performers from all the units and this is where Kenneth Williams and Stanley Baxter really excelled. They would improvise and work out all sorts of routines, many of which I am sure became the basis for their later comic voices and impressions.

Reg Varney, later of *On the Buses* fame, came out with a Stars in Battledress company while we were there. He was best known for his impression of a ventriloquist's doll and his accordion playing, but at one show the pianist was off sick so Reg took over on the piano and played for the whole show. He was brilliant.

Tommy Trinder came out to Singapore with an ENSA show but was unaware that his brother Freddie, who was an army technician in the area, had been doing all Tommy's jokes round the garrisons. Consequently Tommy could only play a few places, so he cut short his visit and went on to Australia where he was a huge success, not just on that trip but on subsequent ones too.

Although, as I've said, there was initially a lot of hard work to do after the Japanese surrender, looking back it was a wonderful period of my life. I had not only been able to continue performing, which was my profession, but also, with the wonderfully consistent weather we seemed to have, I was able to play cricket again, which has always been a great love of mine.

Morris Aza

My father and mother were successful theatrical agents, and among their clients they managed Stanley Holloway, Gracie Fields and Bill Dainty. My father died in 1960 and my mother retired in 1972 so I took over the business, as I naturally had been closely associated with it during my younger days. I wasn't a performer when I joined the army in 1942, just an ordinary soldier. I was in fact a professional photographer and was almost immediately posted to the army film unit whose motto was "If in doubt, over-expose!" This was in 1943 and I did my training with them at Pinewood Studios in Buckinghamshire. I was then sent out to Singapore in 1945. There wasn't much for me to do at first, except take pictures of Japanese POWs. I then became Lord Mountbatten's personal photographer for a year. I used to follow him around, taking his photograph wherever he was and whatever he was doing. I went to Australia with him and so on; he was very conscious of personal publicity. I also took photographs of the entertainers who came out to India and the Far East to entertain the British garrisons. The local newspapers all carried my pictures.

As a photographer I was attached to CSE and the performers I remember well at that time, in and around Singapore, were Kenneth Williams and a fellow called Kirby, who was the son of the inventor of the now famous "Kirby's Flying Ballet". Reg Varney had also come out to Singapore from India with his SIB party, and Peter Nichols was in the area too.

We had a very strange sergeant-major attached to us in Singapore, and Peter Nichols based the sergeant in *Privates on Parade* on him. This chap had been in a lot of trouble one way and another in the army, and was due to do another term in service prison when he decided to commit suicide. He had been out in the East a long time, and could speak fluent Chinese and Malay. He was at one time dropped by the British army deep in the jungle and got caught up in all sorts of rackets. I was on leave when he died and the one who found him was Kenneth Williams. The sergeant had taken cyanide, so it was not a pleasant find for young soldier Williams.

CSE in the Far East was formed from various units. You could be posted from any regiment and would then be formed into an entertainment unit. They would arrive at CSE HQ and those in charge there had to find out what sort of performers these newcomers were. It was all a bit chaotic at first because some of the performers were not very good, they had just taken a chance they could get into the unit. Actor Jack Hawkins, who was an officer in the army, had arrived in Singapore from I think Ceylon at one point to try and pull it all together. I remember him saying, "I've never seen such extraordinary chaos in my life."

There were a large number of service units all over Malaya and the army, navy and air force authorities were very conscious that they should receive some sort of entertainment to help keep up morale, especially the lads in the middle of the jungle.

The shows would just turn up at these various units with a couple of lorries, put some scenery up and do a show. The audience loved it, even as small as some of the shows were. The entertainers also loved doing it. Shows were also presented at Neesoon transit camp. This was a huge camp full of thousands of fellows waiting to be posted home for demob; the last stop before going back to Blighty. Neesoon had its own big theatre and once again the shows would arrive unannounced and the performers used to have to show their pay books as they would be back under army orders for a few minutes. They were of course still fighting soldiers.

CSE also used to put on shows at the Raffles Theatre in Singapore, next to the famous Raffles Hotel. Kenneth Williams had previously been in the army map unit prior to his involvement in entertainment out East. He used to travel around with his colleagues mapping out the roads and jungle paths. Their transport was a large van carrying printing machines, and one day Ken said to me, "With all this equipment we've got we could print posters and programmes of our shows." Everybody thought this was a good idea, so we produced some fine, colour posters to send out as advance publicity for CSE.

I had a varied career in India and the Far East, first with the army film unit, then with CSE, and later, after some leave at home, I went back there as part of the War Graves Commission, which was quite a change.

Morris is a quiet, unassuming man and, I know, a very good manager of his clients. One who needs a bit of managing is Roy Hudd! I've known this crazy, volatile and extremely talented middle-aged "kid" and his clever comic inventiveness for over thirty years and both Morris and his mother Lilian Aza have steered him to the position of respect he now has in our profession.

Dennis Castle

I volunteered for the army in 1940, and, arriving at the recruiting office, I handed in my application form to the sergeant-major in charge. He said, "Castle, this is typed, TYPED!" I said, "Yes," and he said, "Just a minute." I naturally thought I had offended the army before I was even in uniform. The sergeant rushed into the back office and shouted, "Colonel, there's a bloke here what 'as typed 'is application. Typed it, sir. He's a bloody typist!" That little word "typed" guided my career through the army. I wanted to join the Royal Artillery because I thought you were safer with a big gun in front of you rather than a rifle, but I was a typist as far as the army was concerned and so the sergeant put me down for the Royal Army Service Corps.

I was posted to the regimental depot at Sowerby Bridge in Yorkshire where I learnt, as part of my basic training, to handle a rifle with some success, even hitting the bull on several occasions. The young lieutenant in charge of us recruits said to his sergeant, "We've a good shot here, we must remember this Castle chap." The sergeant said, "It's no good, sir, he types, and quite fast from what I've heard." The lieutenant said, "Ah, yes, damn useful, typists. I'll see him in the office. Damn useful, typists."

I was eventually posted to Portsmouth as a clerk and from there I was sent to India on the advice of the commanding officer who had served in India and knew that they were short of typists out there. I was part of a large contingent going east in a convoy of thirty-eight ships, accompanied for part of the journey from Glasgow by Sunderland flying boats.

On the way to our first port of call, Durban, I arranged a show on board our ship the SS *Ormand*. There was some talent among the other ranks on that boat. After we left Durban half the convoy split up, we on our way to India and the other half to the Middle East. After parting company we heard some heavy gunfire in the far distance so we put into shelter off Mombasa. We learned later that the German battleship *Von Scheer* had attacked the other convoy with severe losses, so we were the lucky ones.

After our arrival in Bombay I was posted to Poona. When the authorities knew that my peacetime occupation was in the entertainment business I was asked to put some shows on at the Officers' Club in Poona.

After a while I applied to go on an officers' training course, but my superiors wouldn't agree to this because I typed, and they needed me in the office to carry on clerking. After a time of frustration I got my opportunity, and finally got my one pip, second lieutenant. I was then sent to Army Public Relations. I remember the press boys used to come in late at night bringing us booze hoping that in an inebriated state we would pass on censored material that they could send back home to their newspapers in the UK.

Later I was sent on to Delhi and soon after arriving I was asked to organise a Hallowe'en dance for the troops, and knowing that the lower ranks hardly ever got a look-in at those sort of dances I put up a notice outside the club: "Out of bounds to officers". I didn't realise that only the Viceroy, Lord Wavell, or the GOC General Auchinleck could do that. I had made a terrible mistake assuming a second lieutenant could issue orders like that, but it was suggested that somebody got on to Lady Wavell to see if she could get me pardoned, as it were. Lady Wavell was Irish, with an apparently good sense of humour. She was quoted as saying at the time, "Someone been a naughty boy, have they? What fun. I'll straighten it out with my husband, but Castle can't stay in Delhi; send him to Simla." I was sent there and I really enjoyed myself. I joined a concert party made up of service personnel so I found myself playing in, and producing, shows with the Five Aces concert party at the Gaiety Theatre.

ENSA parties which arrived in India had been given very little knowledge of what they would encounter and just how different touring was in India. The finances of the ENSA artistes and their touring expenses all had to be dealt with, and I was promoted to staff captain to help with these problems. I acted as liaison between ENSA and military finance which was in the hands of that fine actor, Jack Hawkins, then a colonel. Jack really got to grips with all the problems of entertainment in the area and did a fine job.

There was this lovely little theatre, the Gaiety, in Simla in which we used to produce our shows. Kipling had played there, so had Lord Baden-Powell, so it had a long history, and it is still there as a tourist attraction. In 1945 the Wavell Open Air Theatre in Delhi was opened with a play, *The Late Christopher Bean*, with Edith Evans heading the cast that had come out with an ENSA party. The occasion was a great success with everyone.

As a result of my involvement with ENSA in India I was made production officer, co-ordinating all the entertainment in India and Burma under Jack Hawkins. I did this for six months while I was waiting for news of my going home and demob.

Stars in Battledress companies, RAF Gang Shows, and some CSE units did not arrive in India, Malaya or Burma until the war with Japan was all over bar the shouting. They were good, light-hearted shows, and that's what the troops wanted. There had been a fair amount of heavy drama put out for the service garrisons and, apart from John Gielgud, who the lads thought was marvellous, it didn't go down too well, so the arrival of the lighter shows was much appreciated. Some of the solo artistes sponsored by ENSA had already been out to the Far East when the fighting was still in progress, Leslie Henson, Gracie Fields, Duggie Byng, Vera Lynn, Roger Livesey and Joyce Grenfell, among them.

I was stationed in Calcutta before returning home and this was a very difficult time to be in India. Sergeant-Major Philip Hindin was in the ENSA HQ with me and was very brave on one occasion. The major in charge of our base had gone on a pleasure jaunt and forgot about the order not to leave unattended service vehicles in the area because of rioting among the Indian population. One afternoon I was sitting in my office and someone rushed in and said, "The lorries are alight." I looked out of the window and there was a mob of five or six hundred students all around the vehicles. Philip Hindin and I, together with one of the SIB units, went to see what we could do. Two staff cars were alight and tyres were blowing, a real mess. Philip got into one of the trucks and drove it away and then proceeded to put sand and gravel into the petrol tank. Phil Hindin had been a comic, and after the war went into theatrical management in a firm called Hindin, Richards and Hicks, and very successful they were too.

172

But back to our riot. We were being pelted with sticks and pieces of granite, anything in sight, and we'd left our steel helmets in the building. One of the ENSA girls suddenly appeared with my revolver, but I thought if I use it we're as good as dead because if the mob catch sight of it they'll go berserk and try to get hold of it for their own use. The ENSA girl took it back to my office and phoned GHQ. Very soon a troop carrier came trundling slowly down the road with a British sergeant on top behind a big Sten gun perched on the front. The mob suddenly went very quiet and retreated. I've never been so pleased to see anyone in my life. I'd like to meet that sergeant again just to tell him so.

Soon after this incident I was on my way home, I'm glad to say. As soon as I was demobbed I got back into radio. (I had broadcast a little before the war and quite a bit while I was in India.) I also started to get in on the early post-war television scene, writing scripts for Terry-Thomas, Arthur Askey and one or two others, and appearing in shows like *Dixon of Dock Green* and *Probation Officer*. However, writing seemed to be taking up more of my time.

Dennis's writing had always been "another string to his bow", and from 1960 he was rarely away from the typewriter. His book, *The Fourth Gambler*, a novel based on certain aspects of Indian life, was published in 1960 and was well received by the critics.

His grandfather, "Sensation" Smith, was responsible for many of the wonderful stage effects at the Theatre Royal, Drury Lane, and this was also documented by Dennis in his second book, *"Sensation" Smith*. In 1975 his book *Run Out the Raj* was based on his cricket experiences in India; being a fine amateur cricketer and keen follower of the game, he makes this one of the most amusing books on the subject.

Dennis is now living in retirement at Brinsworth House in Twickenham run by the Entertainment Artistes Benevolent Fund and Grand Order of Water Rats, a truly wonderful paradise for professional entertainers. He still meets up with old friends and colleagues from his very full life, including members of his old regiment, the 5th Mahratta Light Infantry in India.

John Horsley

Actor John Horsley, who is familiar to theatre audiences, Agatha Christie and *You Rang, M'Lord?* television fans, told me of an odd experience he had in 1945 when he was in a service entertainment unit performing in a Ted Willis/Bridget Boland play *What's Wrong with the Germans?*

I was playing a German officer, and had to make my entrance in the play through the audience from the front of the theatre. The play toured several military camps and the particular incident in question happened at the Caterham Guards Barracks.

I had walked from the backstage area on to the parade ground surrounding the theatre. The light was fading when suddenly I heard a voice: "What the bloody hell, there's a f...... Nazi here, call out the guard." I quickly had to explain the situation, just in time for my cue to walk into the theatre and proceed with my performance.

Luckily for me it was quite a good one, otherwise I would have had more than just a sergeant to deal with.

Alfred Marks

Spike Milligan told me briefly of an occurrence that happened to that very versatile entertainer, Alfred Marks. Alfred later recounted the incident to me.

I was a leading aircraftsman mechanic attached to an RAF squadron near Cairo. Just before the El Alamein push in the Western Desert a directive went round asking serving personnel whether they would like to audition for some small entertainment units that were being put together to go into the desert near to the various units who were waiting for the battle to come. There just weren't enough SIB or Gang Show parties available to cover the needs at that time and ENSA shows were not allowed near the front line for obvious reasons.

I went to Cairo and was auditioned in an infants' school by a general and a wing-commander sitting at little kiddies' desks. This was a comic situation in itself. I passed the audition and was told I would be the comedian fronting a small unit which was to include a small five-piece musical combination transferred from the much larger Royal Air Force band. I was put in charge of this unit as most comedians appeared to be, with the accompanying increase in rank, and given a slip of paper authorising me to go to the stores and pick up a set of flight-sergeant's stripes. This must have been the quickest promotion in the RAF. The corporal in charge of the stores had been in the service for about thirty years and grumbled about the fact that an LAC could come in and become a sergeant at the drop of a hat when he was still only a corporal.

Our first assignment was to go to a unit about half a mile behind the El Alamein fortifications and do several shows there, in daylight of course.

Before we left we were told that the show had to be well dressed and well rehearsed to as high a professional standard as possible. We were sent to an Egyptian tailor who would be making us evening tail suits, in tropical material because of the intense heat. When we found the venue, the stage area and audience accommodation were in a wadi, a depression completely surrounded by very high sand dunes, the whole effect being rather like an amphitheatre.

Before our first show I told the rest of the blokes in the group that I wanted to have a pee. I climbed out of the wadi and up on to the main road that ran back from Alamein. All round the area at hundred-yard intervals were large empty petrol cans sunk into the sand with holes punched in the bottom. The cans stopped the flies and other creatures swarming over an area which was the case if one peed straight on to the sand. Using the cans meant it went straight through the holes in the bottom of them and disappeared into the sand.

I was standing by the side of the road relieving myself in full evening dress and a five and nine make-up (long since redundant in the theatre) which made you look like a Red Indian, when I heard what I thought was some sort of a car. I was completely out of sight of the wadi and everywhere was silence, which made the noise of what I thought was a car even more eerie in the extreme quiet of the moment. Suddenly into view came a jeep, and as it got close I saw the driver was wearing a Scots beret and beside him sat an officer with his leg hanging over the side of the vehicle. It stopped, the driver looked at me standing all by myself in evening tail suit and red make-up and said "Christ", and turned the jeep round and went back towards civilisation.

Now my thoughts were focused on what went on when the Scotsman and the officer got back to their base.

"Well you see, sir, it was like this, I saw a man in full evening dress with a red painted face standing beside the road about half a mile from Alamein," and the chief medical officer replying, "These things do happen on active service. Let me give you another injection and you go and have a lie down for several months, there's a good boy. The war affects people in all sorts of different ways."

Postscript

As I have stated, Combined Services Entertainment continued to operate from its headquarters in Dean Stanley Street after the war in Europe and Asia was over, and since that time there has been close co-operation between CSE and the British Forces Broadcasting Service (BFBS).

British entertainers were prominent in the Cyprus and Aden trouble spots and many star artistes, male and female, made tours to Korea during that tragic war.

Jim Davidson, under the auspices of service welfare organisations, went out to the Falklands, and the troops in Northern Ireland have not been forgotten either, by Frankie Howerd for instance, who incidentally also volunteered to visit military bases in the Gulf during the recent crisis there.

I suspect that wherever trouble spots emerge in the world that involve British service men and women there will be generous support for them from members of the entertainment profession.

The Barbed Wire Follies

Battledress also applied to allied prisoners of war which they still wore proudly in captivity whenever possible and, despite these men being confined to a war behind barbed wire, it didn't stop them from producing some great theatrical moments.

About two years ago I was invited to see an amateur pantomime in a Surrey village hall. It happened to be a very good production, and I was told on good authority that this particular society is among the top in amateur theatre. Afterwards I chanced to talk to a member of the cast who had played a pedlar selling "new lamps for old". You can guess from this that the pantomime was *Aladdin and his Wonderful Lamp.* This gentleman in question, Arthur Moss, confessed to me rather proudly that he was seventy-five, and that he had begun his amateur frolics in a German prisoner-of-war camp after being captured near Calais in 1940. Arthur then told me of some of the ingenious ways that the prisoners used to present entertainment behind the barbed wire. It set me thinking that this little-known activity was worth investigating further with a view to including some of the deeds in this book. Arthur put me in touch with a few friends of his who had also been in captivity and once the can of beans was opened I'm glad to say they spilled out from all directions.

This is certainly not a record of the deprivation, hardships and, in some cases, unbelievable cruelty inflicted upon prisoners of war during the Second World War. In-depth stories of their captivity have been documented by writers far more qualified than I am, in most cases from their own personal experiences. Books by Airey Neave, Sam Kydd, Clive Dunn, Ken de Souza and many more are all fascinating accounts of those years. However, I feel that I should explain briefly some of the situations that service men endured at that time. I hope in some way that it highlights even more their remarkable resilience and determination to keep up their morale and bring relief from the boredom and frustration felt by many of their comrades in the prison camps of Europe and the Far East.

Like Arthur Moss, many army personnel were captured in France before and during the Dunkirk evacuation. Together with some members of the original British Expeditionary Force (BEF), a great number of those captured were just territorials (reservists) who only a week or so before arriving in Calais were clerks, shopkeepers, and the like. Landing in France in May 1940 they found themselves four or five days later prisoners of war.

At that time there was a certain amount of chaos at the War Office, and lack of communication between London and the senior officers in France. Guns were shipped to the Channel ports without ammunition, tanks without guns, and transport sometimes did not leave with their regiments. In certain instances only searchlight battalions were available to engage advancing German tanks. The Queen Victoria Rifles, the regiment of which Arthur Moss was a member, suffered their fair share of what Airey Neave described as "shameful organisation". Arthur explains:

The QVR landed in Calais on Wednesday, May 22nd, and nothing really happened, apart from being machine-gunned on the beach at various times, until Sunday the 26th. I had gone sick with a head wound to a nearby hospital so I wasn't around when the Germans arrived to take prisoners. Three days later I joined the remainder of the battalion who were waiting to be marched off by the Germans.

They put us in cattle trucks, seventy men to a truck. We were in and out of them for two days, no toilets of course, and then eventually transferred to another train that took us to Lamsdorf in Silesia. We were by now very weak as we'd had no proper food, so we kept falling down. The first thing they did to us in the prison camp was to cut all our hair off. Then five hundred of us were transferred to another camp at Nikolasdorf. Here we cut down trees and dug trenches for drains. We were there for eighteen months and by now Red Cross food parcels were arriving, which was a godsend, and we started talking about eggs and bacon, and girls, and all the normal things again. Up to then it had been a case of just existing from day to day.

We put on concerts here. We had a pianist who also got hold of an accordion. We had a simple guard there called Joseph and we used to say, "When the British troops arrive you want to be an interpreter, not one of the lowly workers like a shithouse wallah, an interpreter." "*Ya, ya*," he'd say, and there was another group of our fellows with their guard Fritz and we told them to tell Fritz he must be an interpreter too. "Now," we said, "the first thing is good morning, and the English for good morning is Bollocks." And the other group told Fritz that when Joseph said "Bollocks" he was to say "Suck-em". The next day we watched these two guards shouting at one another, because they were so pleased with what they'd learnt, just these two words all over the place. They then started to teach the other guards the same thing, but of course the commandant of the camp heard about it and there was trouble, but we explained we were just having a bit of fun and he said no more.

We moved to another camp in Silesia where we were put out to a factory making windows. It was here we put on a revue called *Bubbles and Stars*. The backcloth was decorated with large coloured balls and stars, and at the opening chorus of the show we put our heads through a hole in the sheet in the middle of a bubble or a star. So this was the beginning of my amateur acting career.

It all went quite well, so we thought we'd do a pantomime. It was *Aladdin* [Which was a coincidence. Remember, *Aladdin* was the pantomime I saw Arthur in at the Surrey village hall], and we had a fellow in the show playing the genie who was as thin as a rake. Anyway we covered him with some rancid margarine from a Red Cross parcel and then put cocoa powder all over him. We made the flash for him to appear by taking the wires out of two of the fuses and putting them together in front of a sheet of silver paper to make the flash, then we had to put the fuses back together very quickly to bring the lights on for the rest of the scene until the next time we wanted them for the genie. It gave a marvellous effect. We also worked out a system for dimming the lights on stage.

Unfortunately the pantomime only lasted one night because one of the cast got carried away and put a comb on his top lip, à la Hitler as you've seen people do. Well the German commandant was sitting in the front row and banned the show, so all our trouble lasted only one night. Most of the German officers used to watch our shows because they got as bored as we did and they knew that if we were busy putting on shows we weren't planning escapes.

In the big base camps (ours was a smaller one) some of the good-looking young lads who played the girls' parts in the plays had to have an escort back to their compounds at night because the lads in the audience got a bit excited when they saw them on stage.

Towards the end of the war we were told that we were to be moved on because the Russians were coming. The German guards were getting worried and asked us to give them our trousers because they didn't want to get caught by the Russians or British or Americans when they eventually freed us.

We had a bit of a wheeze going with the German dentist who had his surgery outside the camp. He disliked Hitler and all he stood for and when we went to see him he used to drill our teeth and put a soft filling in so that we could brush it out when we got back to the camp and then we could go again the next week and he'd do the same thing. You could keep this going for four or five visits, which meant you could get out of the camp for a while and also get the rest of the day off from whatever work you were doing for the Germans. Actually the German guards we had, who naturally had to go with us everywhere we went – to work, or the dentist – were not too bad to us; we seemed to be reasonably treated by them and of course we kept them a bit sweet by giving them an item or two from our Red Cross parcels which pleased them because they were very short of cigarettes and choc- olate, for instance.

We started moving off towards Germany in March 1945. We parted from our German guards and were picked up by some Serbian folk who had a lorry and after we left them we got to Prague. Just outside there we were met by some Americans and after that we flew home to freedom. I perhaps had a better time than a lot of them. I was single and I hadn't left any immediate family at home, so I didn't have to worry on that score. Some of the lads naturally worried about their wives and children. Some of them had letters to say that their wives had gone off with other blokes and wouldn't see them again, so there were some desperately depressing cases in the camps.

Arthur Moss became a successful businessman after the war, and although now retired is still active in community life. In fact he started another business after retiring: growing Christmas trees.

The Flames of Calais by Airey Neave is a wonderful and detailed record of the final few days of May 1940 in France.

Sam Kydd

Also a member of the Queen Victoria Rifles, Sam tasted freedom for a little longer than Arthur Moss after arriving in France to defend Calais in May 1940. One day more, actually, then it was the almost food-less journey to Poland and five years of captivity.

Sam Kydd was an actor and post-war was as much a part of the British film industry as anyone. His unmistakable face seemed to fit any character he played. He was a friendly guy with a lot of charm, inherited from his Irish upbringing no doubt (he was born in Belfast), and he was as popular with the big movie stars he constantly came into contact with as he was with someone making a first appearance in front of the camera. Not long before he died he had become a *Coronation Street* favourite. His sense of humour and his distinctive, fruity voice impressed me when I met him on a television production in the early 1970s.

His mild acts of disobedience in the POW camp were generally ignored by the older guards, but the younger Nazis were inclined to be harsh, particularly when a little bartering was in progress with the Polish civilian population the prisoners came into contact with on days when they worked outside the camp.

One such incident in 1942 put Sam into solitary confinement for a month. He was carrying three bars of chocolate with him to exchange for a few eggs and was unfortunately seized upon by a guard when he tried hurriedly to hide the chocolate in a small hole in the ground.

After his solitary and a period in the sick bay he returned to his "billet" and became energetically involved in the entertainment programme which was by then in progress. An ambitious Christmas show was planned entailing five writers plus all the production expertise available. It was to be a pot-pourri of pantomime: all the traditional pantomime characters blended into one production to be called *Pantomania* with about thirty songs and gags for all the characters. Sam recalls the story of getting the production together in his book published in 1973 by Bachman and Turner called *For You the War is Over*.

The first half finale ended up with all the characters on stage, and quietly in the background under the John O'Gaunt speech from Shakespeare's *Richard II*, "this scepter'd isle . . . set in the silver sea . . . this England", was heard the strains of (at first very quietly) "There'll always be an England, and England shall be free, if England means as much to you as England means to me!" The chorus was taken up and swelled into a tremendous climax in that little theatre. I'll never forget seeing so many grown-up men standing there with tears streaming down their cheeks! The well of suffering, humiliation and frustration and loss of pride that everyone had experienced since capture was thrust behind them, culminating in this tear-letting public emotion.

It is not just this little incident that Sam relates so well in his book. It is touching and funny throughout and that sense of humour is undoubtedly the reason that he and his immediate comrades came through those five long years in such a good physical and mental condition. None the less, the scars of his experience did affect him later in life.

When I spoke to his widow, Pinkie, recently she told me of his love of cricket and football, the occasional visit to the betting shop, but most of all his love of people with a sense of humour. Incidentally Pinkie Barnes (her maiden name) was one-time UK table tennis champion, and represented this country in international competition. Their actor son Jonathan has inherited his parents' love of sport, and is a fine club cricketer.

If you can manage to obtain Sam's book you will find it a little gem.

Jimmy Howe

One of the really big successes of POW entertainment concerned Major James Howe, MBE, LRAM, ARCM. Young Jimmy was a lance-corporal bandsman in the Royal Scots Regiment with the secondary job of stretcher-bearer which bandsmen were trained for.

Part of the BEF in France in 1940, the Royal Scots were overrun by a German SS division in Belgium with severe casualties, particularly among the bandsmen. Jimmy's career in the army up to that point had been a little lengthier than the territorials who were captured at Calais: he had been a regular army bandsman since 1933.

After our capture we were marched three hundred miles through Belgium and Holland to the German border. Then for three days and three nights we travelled in cattle trucks into Poland, to Lamsdorf Stalag VIIIB near Breslau. It was a huge camp, the surroundings having a history going back to the Franco-Prussian war. There were already twenty-five thousand prisoners there when we arrived, many of them Polish. We were divided into groups of about three hundred in the various buildings. There were so many in the camp that the Germans left us to our own devices in some ways, under supervision of course.

The first six months were pretty grim. Apart from being continually hungry, we'd had no mail from home, and no organised recreation. This naturally made it a period of depression in our new surroundings, but gradually things began to change and some of us started to think about putting on shows for the lads. I acquired an accordion from a Polish prisoner of war. I gave him a wrist-watch for it which I didn't need because time wasn't important. We didn't know what was going to happen to us anyway. The first concert party we put on consisted of three accordions and a guitar

182

player, and we called ourselves the Scapegoats. The Germans allowed us to build our own theatre which we did, and we had our own stage manager and electrician.

Just after Christmas 1940 we were sent some musical instruments by the Swiss and Swedish Red Cross. When the Americans came into the war in 1941 we obtained some more instruments from their Red Cross. We bartered with the German guards for more with the *Lager Geld* (camp money) some of the lads earned from going out on working parties. This money could only be used in the POW camps and by the German guards. I was excused work because I was getting the band together. The Germans were glad to have people involved in organising entertainment because it meant we weren't trying to dig tunnels and it helped with morale.

There was another chap trying to get a theatre band together so he and I went round the various units in the camp with a home-made crown and anchor set and played the fellows for the *Lager* money so we could get enough to buy the instruments. We could buy a trumpet for a hundred and ten marks and after twelve months the Germans gave us a piano, which was very helpful.

I eventually got the dance band going and it consisted of five saxes, six brass and a rhythm section. We also had a theatre and a military band. Music stands were made by the camp carpenter from old packing cases, and our band uniforms by the camp tailors from linen bags that had been sent from various Red Cross organisations containing food and other items.

Our first big Christmas show was called *Snow White and the Seven Twerps*. The commandant and the censor always came to our dress rehearsal to see if there was anything that offended them. Then they would come again once we had started, to see if we had changed anything. There was a camp newspaper printed by the Germans and in one show one of the fellows was supposed to be reading it and he said, "Let's see what's in the *Comic Cuts*," and the censor jumped up and said, "No, no, you will not make fun of our paper." So we had to cut it out.

We only saw two films all the time we were in the camp and one of them was a German film that had an orchestra doing a comic version of "Poet and Peasant", so I thought I would copy the idea for our band. The commandant didn't like this as he said it was making fun of a German composer. I told him about the film but he still stopped us doing our version.

Our shows were becoming very popular, and as the theatre only held about five hundred we used to run for two or three weeks so that lots of the chaps could come and see it from other compounds in the camp. We had allocations of tickets that we sent to the groups. There were about five thousand in the RAF section and they got their bundle of tickets to distribute. Some of the guys used to get cross because they couldn't always get in on the night they wanted to.

In 1941 the Germans took us out to some of the smaller working camps scattered around Lamsdorf, places like Posen and Blackhammer. We went out on a three-week tour to these places by train. We enjoyed it because it got us out of the main camp.

In 1943 the Germans took the band up to Berlin and we were there for about three months playing at some of the camps around the city. It was really a propaganda campaign to get our lads to join up in a British Legion, and a Dutch Legion and an Irish Legion. They were trying to recruit the lads from various countries to join a sort of SS Legion made up of the soldiers they could brainwash into joining them. They used to give the lads lectures in the camps telling them why it would be good for them to join the German army.

In August, while we were there, the Americans and British started heavy bombing raids on Berlin and things really got bad so they moved us back to Lamsdorf.

At the start of our stay in the camp we used to take down music note by note from playing old gramophone records we had acquired. We borrowed plain paper from the Germans for this, a very painstaking job, but then later we started getting sheet music sent from home.

As far as food was concerned, as I've said, it was pretty terrible, but one little game we got up to to get some money from the German guards was to barter some of the tea we got in the Red Cross parcels once they started coming through in 1941. We would use the tea leaves over and over again for ourselves, drying them off each time. Then eventually we would put the used tea leaves back in the original packet, seal it up and sell it to the guards. That was another way of getting money from them.

We had to sign a parole book to say we wouldn't escape. We weren't keen on this because it was our duty to try and escape, so we all signed it with names like Greta Garbo, Charlie Chaplin, Douglas Fairbanks, etc. When there was an attempted escape for instance they stopped the shows and the Red Cross parcels. When we had been out on a tour of other camps they would make us play our instruments at the gate in case we were smuggling food or anything else into the camp inside them so we always used to play the Colonel Bogey March, and of course the Germans didn't know what it was or what the significance of it was.

When Jimmy returned home after the war he went to the Royal Military School of Music at Kneller Hall to study music, and then he was appointed bandmaster of the Argyle and Sutherland Highlanders. He served with them for nine years, visiting Hong Kong, British Guyana, Berlin and other places, and then in 1959 he was appointed Musical Director of the Scots Guards, and was with them for sixteen years. He then served as Senior Musical Director of the Household Division playing at the Cenotaph and Trooping the Colour, and with Ralph Reader at the Festival of

Remembrance. He corresponded with, as he puts it, "dear Ralph Reader, a great guy", for many years.

James Howe, MBE, retired from military service in 1974 since when he has been responsible for several anniversary concerts. Perhaps one of his great pleasures has been to head the ex-prisoner-of-war reunion concerts. As well as featuring many of his POW colleagues, there have been guest appearances from stars who were popular in the Second World War, one of whom, Anne Shelton, Jimmy has a real soft spot for. These concerts are a memorial to the ingenuity, courage and hard work POWs like Jimmy put into making other people's lives more bearable in extremely difficult conditions.

The signature tune of Jimmy's band was "The World is Waiting for the Sunrise". Jimmy certainly made it rise over Lamsdorf. He has made over twenty long-playing records, appeared in *Friday Night is Music Night*, conducted symphony concerts and presided over the BBC Concert Orchestra.

This quiet and humorous gentleman now lives with his wife in a delightful spot on the south coast, and receives frequent visits from his grandchildren whom I have met, and who are obviously very proud of "Grandad".

The Danny La Rue of Stalag VIIIB

Walter Parrott was with the 1st Search Light Regiment which played such a heroic part in the defence of Calais in May 1940. The regiment was ill-equipped for this but they knew that if Dunkirk was to happen, every hour that the Germans were delayed in the area the more chance there was of the evacuation being successful. They were eventually taken prisoner in Calais and started off on the long journey to Stalag VIIIB Lamsdorf via Holland.

As we have heard, the first six months in captivity were very difficult, but by December 1940 conditions had improved somewhat and thoughts were turned to devising some entertainment, the first production being a concert party. By 1941 *The Home Maker* produced by drama enthusiast Jock Mathews featured Walter as the young daughter of the house. This was the first of many female roles he was to play in various productions at Lamsdorf, later, by the way, to be renamed Stalag 344.

There were seven or eight large-scale productions in 1941 and 1942, all made possible by the ingenious tailoring of costumes and wigs. In 1943 one of his roles was the daughter Dinah in *The Philadelphia Story*. The reason that Walter became regularly cast as a female was because of his size (five foot), and slim build.

In 1944 he played Ella Delahay in *Charley's Aunt*. This production also "went on tour" to a civilian internment camp at Krenzberg. The Overture and Entracte music was played by the Krenzberg Novelty Octet under the direction of Victor Hammett.

Also in 1944 the Lamsdorf Gaiety Players were asked by the Germans, as part of a propaganda exercise, to take two productions to another rest camp, Glenshagen outside Berlin. They were *Tons of Money* and *French Without Tears* in both of which Walter played a maid. When they arrived at Glenshagen they met a British soldier, Bill Brown, who was the sergeant in charge. The Germans had always preyed on some of the prisoners whom they thought they could indoctrinate with their ideology. Some fell for it, including obviously Bill Brown whom the Germans had placed in a position of responsibility. The visiting company minded their own business and got on with the job of performing their plays.

At this time the allies were bombing Berlin very heavily and the company used to watch the raids on the city and they were quite happy when they were eventually taken back to the "comfort" of Lamsdorf.

It wasn't until much later that they learnt that Bill Brown was in fact a British agent who had been sending back reports to London of the bombing and other German military activities. He had well and truly fooled his captors.

Walter Parrott was eventually repatriated under a Red Cross exchange plan and now lives in a suburb of Nottingham. He has been very articulate in his correspondence and phone-calls with me.

Tommy Frayne

Tommy Frayne, Press Officer of the Barking, Essex, POW Association, very kindly loaned me a wonderful diary of theatrical events entitled *Interlude*, put together by a committee of POWs who were at Stamlager VIIIA Gorlitz near Dresden.

The principal actors and producers involved in the early variety-type shows at the camp were Ralph Griffin, Major Bronilow-Downing, Rod McDiarmid and Frank Young, with Len Skane and his dance band providing the music.

Fred Colly was responsible for orchestrating all the music for an ambitious and successful Ted Pearson revue.

Later, in 1943 and 1944, straight plays were produced with great ingenuity by the casts and backstage staff. Don Bosman and Herb Whitman were just two of the outstanding leading players.

Morry Cameron headed the backstage staff, who overcame great difficulties in making and assembling scenery and props including a suit of armour, a string of pearls and a life-size dog. Dyes for costumes, which were all made from scraps of odd material by the POW tailors, came from boiling down coloured book covers, and the tailors even made a "mink" coat. Some quite sophisticated lighting effects were organised by Ollie Squirrell.

Among the plays produced were Noël Coward's *Blyth Spirit* and *Hay Fever*, Patrick Hamilton's *Gaslight*, and George S. Kaufman and Moss Hart's *The Man Who Came to Dinner*. The drama department also staged Shakespearean and poetry readings. Perhaps it was the provision of music that gave everyone the impetus to produce the varied fare of entertainment that was a feature of Stalag VIIIA.

I was delighted to receive a letter from New Zealand ex-prisoner Wilf Brunt who lives in Whitby in that country. Wilf was in Stalag VIIIA and told me that *Interlude* was prepared in the camp and then brought out at the end of the war when it was printed in London. He says the quality of entertainment, sports and other hobbies in the camp was very high. Wilf also had some photos taken illegally in the camp during his capture. He says he'd be delighted to see me if I happen to be in New Zealand at some future date. Well, you never know!

Cliff Jones

Cliff was in the 2nd Battalion Seaforth Highlanders, part of the 51st Highland Division, when he was captured just before the Dunkirk evacuation.

He spent part of his captivity in Stalag VIIIB and was involved in making many of the props for the theatre productions there. He also had a hand in the construction and painting of the scenery which, as he told me, "looked pretty good from the front".

Cliff now lives in retirement with his wife at Bridlington in Yorkshire.

Eric Howe

Eric, known as the George Formby of Lamsdorf, was captured outside Brussels in 1940 and became yet another inmate of Stalag VIIIB. They say you can't keep a good man down, and Eric certainly made his mark at the camp with his ukelele and such was his repertoire of Formby songs on the instrument even the German guards called him "George". If ever there was a dull moment, or even if there wasn't, the section of the camp Eric was in would be filled with the great George's songs, such as "When I'm Cleaning Windows", "Leaning on a Lamppost" and "Mr Wu".

In the post-war years Eric has been involved in the National Ex-Prisoners of War Association and is president of the Notting-hamshire branch. He has personally arranged trips abroad to the camp sites in Poland, and anniversary parades in France. He and some of his comrades had their fair share of trouble on the route to freedom, with the advancing Russians behind them and the Germans retreating in front of them. Perhaps Eric can be per-suaded to relate his experiences in a more detailed way at some time through the medium of radio. His letter to me was a little difficult to decipher in parts, and as he said in signing off, "What a mix up, Bill; sort it out."

George "Wilf" Wyatt

Wilf was a miner by trade, had been since 1935, whose peacetime occupation had a significant bearing on his experiences in cap-tivity.

He was a gunner with the 51st Highland Division and part of the British Expeditionary Force in France, and was taken prisoner at St Valéry in June 1940. After being marched to Holland and then travelling by barge and train to Poland he spent the next two years being moved around the working camps, employed by the Germans on farms, building camps and constructing roads and railways. Although the working camps were much smaller than the base camps such as Lamsdorf, they were still prison camps. The soldiers would be taken out to their various jobs each day and brought back at night. In 1942 he was at a mining camp at Katowice.

We made our own entertainment, but not on such a grand scale as the base camps. A sergeant-major called Lindmeyer was responsible for producing our shows, and I was in the band and I remember one very successful production called *Paradise Alley*.

One of the strangest stories and perhaps the most touching happened at this camp and it involved a Polish girl called Halinka.

Halinka was employed to hand out the lamps to the miners when we went underground. I got friendly with her, and the friendship blossomed into a romantic attachment. We had to be very careful and discreet about our friendship, not only because of the German guards who were around us nearly all the time, but also because Halinka's father was a prominent member of the Polish Resistance Movement, who never knew when there might be a knock on the door from the Gestapo. If there had been and his daughter was linked with his activities and found to be fraternising with a British soldier, the whole family could have been in terrible danger.

In 1944 Wilf and some of the lads were moved to another mine about twenty kilometres from Halinka's home, but she kept in touch with him by simply walking past the mining camp occasionally and giving Wilf a wave, or just by seeing him on the other side of the "wire". On one occasion they even had a brief chat.

In 1945 he and another soldier, Eric Smith, decided to escape and take Halinka with them. The Russians by then were advancing on all fronts. Wilf and Eric managed to smuggle Halinka into various Polish communities until the Russians caught up with them and directed them to Krakow Airport where the RAF had a base. When they got there (by travelling on top of cattle trucks) Halinka and Wilf decided to get married. An RAF officer signed the permission note and a friendly priest in the nearby city agreed to marry them, and even found the accommodation for their wedding night.

We now made plans to get to England, but before going Halinka wanted to say goodbye to her parents, so we travelled back to her home a married couple, much to the surprise of her parents. After the initial shock they welcomed us with open arms, but alas our happiness was not to last long. The Russian occupation forces gave an order that POWs must report to their nearest military headquarters. Ours was at Krakow. I reported there and Halinka came to see me off (females were not allowed to leave Poland), and we were then to go on a four-day train journey to the port of Odessa. There would be a party of eight service men to each coach, so we decided to smuggle Halinka aboard. We were able to do this and then put all our greatcoats on top of her in the train to hide her. On arrival in Odessa she was held by the British Military Mission who had to escort her back home because of course she had no papers with her at that time. When she got home she was told to get in touch with the British Embassy, but there was no British Embassy there. Our world had fallen apart yet again.

However, Halinka was very determined, so she decided to make her way to Prague in Czechoslovakia. At the British Embassy there she was interrogated by a Major Wyatt. She said, "That's my married name." He seemed delighted to find someone with the same name as himself and he looked after her while she was in Prague, where she had to stay because she had no passport. Meanwhile I was on my way home from Odessa by ship via Italy, Gibraltar and finally Scotland. When I got back I reported my marriage to the British Red Cross but only received an acknowledgment. I subsequently heard nothing. Halinka had disappeared out of my life so quickly – or had she?

Imagine my surprise when on VJ Day 1945 I had a message at my home in Nottingham from the police in London to say that my wife had been put on the train and would I meet her at Nottingham Station? Halinka had got out of Prague and made her way to London and then contacted the authorities who knew of my letter to the Red Cross.

And they say there aren't such things as real fairy tales. This must be one of the happier, if not the happiest, postscripts to a soldier's five-year experience of captivity.

Cornelius Garvin

Peter Garvin's father, Guardsman Cornelius Garvin, was taken prisoner in 1940. Cornelius spent his captivity in Stalag IXC, Nordhausen. Peter told me:

My father wanted to get involved in the camp entertainment when it was being organised and set about trying to obtain an accordion. He heard that

190

the camp commandant was very anxious to get hold of some chocolate for his three children, which by 1941 and 1942 was practically non-existent in Germany. My father started collecting chocolate bars from his fellow prisoners who were getting them in their Red Cross parcels. He mentioned to the commandant that he was in search of an accordion and was willing to pay for it in chocolate. The commandant saw a solution to his problem and a deal was done. My father handed over two hundred bars of chocolate and in return received an accordion. Whether the instrument actually belonged to the commandant or whether he had obtained it from elsewhere was not clear, it was in my father's possession and that's what mattered.

The poster for one of the camp productions, *Robinson Crusoe*, has been reproduced.

Eric Smith

Eric was in the Royal Army Service Corps, Highland Division, when he was taken prisoner at St Valéry in June 1940. His first prison camp was at Schubin in the north of Poland, Stalag XXID.

We went out on working parties from here, first to a farm where we used to sleep in the cellars under a manor house, and after this we moved on to Poznan. This is where for me and a few others entertainment in captivity began, only on a modest scale, but it was a start. At yet another working camp south of Oppeln we were housed in a village hall-cum-theatre, and although the sleeping bunks were on the stage we felt we had to try and beat the blues we were all feeling by putting on a show, particularly as the temperature was well below freezing during our working day, laying sleepers on the nearby railway lines.

The blokes started to obtain some musical instruments, buying them with our *Lager Geld* (camp money). Our camp leader, Sergeant-Major Lindmeyer, was able to arrange this with the co-operation of the German commandant. We had a mandolin, banjo and drums, and my friend Wilf Wyatt managed to get hold of a trumpet. One bloke even managed to get a violin, but as he couldn't play it we had to suffer the caterwauling of his practising for several months, but we eventually had quite a good band.

Sergeant Lindmeyer was a great enthusiast and he got us all involved in producing a Christmas show which he had written; it was all light-hearted and lifted our general morale. We made a backdrop for the makeshift stage from a huge piece of hessian we borrowed (!) from the German railway line. The scenery was not very ambitious but it was artistically constructed and painted, and we even had a water scene which was a masterpiece. I made the wigs for the actors out of string from Red Cross parcels, and hats were made from papier mâché pulped with potato glue. At another camp we moved to we had lighting dimmers and other sophisticated stage equipment. A play, *The Monkey's Paw*, in which I played the son, was directed by Lindmeyer and was very successful.

I also wrote a story concerning Snow White and the Seven Dwarfs which we called *Snow White and the Seven Twerps*. [You may remember the same title was used at Lamsdorf.] The lad who was going to play Snow White got cold feet at the very last minute because he said the fellows were taking the mickey out of him. I took over the part, and I didn't ruin it. This was in 1943.

We moved again after this to work in a mine at Niwka which was a much larger working camp, and we were allowed to take our stage scenery and props from the previous camp with us. We soon got to work and built a good stage, putting on a lot of shows here. Lindmeyer wrote another show, *The Marriage Flame*, which had a prince and princess in the cast, while George Pearson was a wizard at making costumes out of almost nothing.

We moved on again in 1944 to a coal mine at Jaworzno, but after a short stay we were moved on to yet another one at Czeladz. I wrote and directed a pantomime here, *Dick Whittington*, and the most difficult costume in this was for the cat. It was made from a complete overall, and a balaclava provided the head and face, suitably painted, and the claws were made out of padded mittens. It really was a great success and ran until New Year's Day 1945.

Looking back it does seem amazing that in the circumstances we were able to put on so much entertainment. After all, we were all working hard during the day and until Red Cross parcels started getting through regularly we were hungry and under constant supervision of the German guards, although they were aware that the more recreation we provided for ourselves the less likely it was we would try and escape, so we weren't discouraged in our amateur dramatics. I think the authorities, particularly the older ones, liked seeing the shows too.

Eighteen days after the final curtain of *Dick Whittington* I decided to leave the hospitality of the Third Reich and made my escape with my friend Wilf Wyatt, arriving home in April 1945, as Wilf has already described.

Stalag Luft III

As I am sure everybody knows, *Luft* is the German for "air" so it is understandable that Stalag Luft III was a camp for RAF prisoners of war. Latterly it also housed some Canadian, Polish, Czech and American flyers. Luft III was in Sagan (now Zagan) in Lower Silesia. There was also a small compound for captured airmen in the huge Lamsdorf camp in Upper Silesia. Vic Gammon, who is now the Secretary of the Royal Air Force Ex-Prisoners of War Association, was a prisoner in Luft III and remembers some of the early entertainment in the camp. It was a little modest to say the least, with fairly simple pantomime productions, but the shows increased in professionalism as materials for lighting equipment, scenery, costumes and wigs became easier to obtain.

Vic said, "Actor Roy Dotrice was very much a part of the entertainment, playing the female leads in plays. He was really excellent and it was not surprising to me when after the war his professional career took off and established him as one of this country's leading actors." Dotrice's daughter, Michelle, has also carved out a career for herself in the theatre and television, and is perhaps best known as the wife of Frank Spencer (Michael Crawford) in *Some Mothers Do 'Ave 'Em*.

Peter Butterworth was another RAF prisoner who developed into one of the funniest comedy actors in the business as cinemagoers will have witnessed in the *Carry On* films and numerous television productions. I worked with Peter a couple of times on TV and he really made me laugh, and in pantomime he was such a funny dame. Peter was married to impressionist Janet Brown until his untimely death a few years ago.

Rupert Davies, the definitive French detective "Maigret" was an officer in the Fleet Air Arm when he was captured, and he subsequently joined the entertainments in Stalag III.

Cyril Aynsley, who eventually became the chief reporter for the *Daily Express*, was a leading man in several productions, including Shakespeare's *Merchant of Venice* in which he was a superb Shylock.

Another leading man was Peter Thomas, who eventually went into law and politics, becoming a judge, and chairman of the Conservative Party. He is now a peer, Lord Thomas of Gwydir.

Musical instruments became available through the YMCA and the Red Cross, and there were some fine musicians in the camp for the formation of a symphony orchestra under the very able direction of New Zealander Frank Hunt. It must be remembered that all the music had to be written out by hand, transcribed from gramophone records.

Young Denholm Elliott, an RAF sergeant pilot, was in the

smaller compound at Lamsdorf. One of the productions he was in was Bernard Shaw's *Arms and the Man*. Denholm told me: "In 1944 some of us formed a portable theatre which we carried around under cover of darkness. The reason for this was because Hitler had decided to ban entertainment in the camps for a while. At this time we were in chains from dawn to night, and the guards had to remove my chains when I went 'on stage' to perform, and on my exit they put them on again."

The sequence of events that led up to various prisoners being chained concerned the allied amphibian raid on Dieppe on the French coast in 1942, a raid that many thought, especially the German High Command, was a mini dress rehearsal for the eventual invasion of Normandy. Perhaps it was. The allies had many air and ground casualties but they also took a lot of German prisoners who were put in handcuffs during the journey back to Britain. A distorted version of this apparently got back to Hitler, claiming that the Germans who were taken prisoner had been thrown into irons.

I believe, and I'm sure there are millions like me, that Denholm Elliott is just about the complete actor. He has featured in major films, a list of which would fill several pages, since his screen début in 1945, and his television appearances, including his own season of plays, are numerous. This, coupled with his appeal to theatre audiences, has made him hugely popular on both sides of the Atlantic. Not bad for a young airman who performed in portable "fit-ups" in a prisoner-of-war camp.

Talking further to Vic Gammon, he told me his involvement in the camp entertainment was as producer. One of his productions was Gilbert and Sullivan's *The Mikado*, highly ambitious for a POW camp. "During the final rehearsals the German commandant refused to allow it to go on as he said it was an insult to their Japanese allies. But it did go on because we said we would change the title to *The Town of Titipoo*. The change of title seemed to satisfy the commandant and the production was quite a success."

Colditz

The late Major Pat Reid in his book, *Colditz – the Full Story*, mentions some of the theatrical activities in the castle fortress, including productions of *Gaslight*, *George and Margaret* and *Pygmalion*.

It was through the camp theatre, or at least underneath it, that Airey Neave and a Dutch officer made their escape to freedom, an escape that was engineered by Pat Reid. It wasn't during an actual performance, incidentally, as was first planned. Neave had himself been a member of the Colditz theatre players while he was there.

What an extraordinary life Airey Neave had: taken prisoner in 1940 during the defence of Calais; a successful escapee from Colditz; a prosecution lawyer at the Nazi war crimes trials at Nuremberg; an MP, and finally to die by an act of violence outside the British Houses of Parliament.

"Won't You Come Home Jim Bailey"

(With apologies to the song)

That song must have been Jim's family's theme song while he was in captivity. He was a regular soldier from 1939 to 1949 and was with the Royal Tank Regiment in the Western Desert when he was captured in 1942. First he was imprisoned in Camp PG73 near Bologna in Italy and then later transferred to Stalag VIIIB Lamsdorf in Upper Silesia.

The entertainment in the Italian camp was organised by a big Australian called Bill Gates. I asked Jim if he knew what had happened to Bill after the war and he told me he had become a BBC producer. This confirmed my first suspicions when I heard Jim mention his name and nationality. Bill Gates, or Big Bill as we called him (he was well over six feet), was a very well-known radio producer and, apart from other programmes, his voice was heard by millions of listeners when he announced his bi-weekly programme with "Ladies and Gentlemen, Workers' Playtime!". The half-hour shows were broadcast from factory canteens and suchlike, and were originated during the war by the BBC to help morale on the home front. There can be few British comedians, singers and musicians working at that time who, at some point or another, did not work for Bill on those shows. *Workers' Playtime*, which followed the twelve-thirty news headlines, was broadcast live, not pre-recorded. As a beginner you could ring Bill Gates and ask him if he had a vacancy in a programme and he'd say, "I'll try and sort one out," and he always did – he was a good friend to the "pro's". I did several radio shows for him, and the ten pounds didn't half come in useful. It meant the rent was paid for another couple of weeks.

However, back to Jim Bailey. Once he had arrived at Lamsdorf he was sent out in a working party to an industrial complex which was thought to be too far for bombing raids by British and American planes. Unfortunately the planes did reach that far, causing heavy casualties to the POWs working there.

Since leaving the army Jim has been responsible for the welfare of many ex-POWs and their families, achieving pension rights for them, for example. Jim is a colourful and friendly character, and has arranged pilgrimages overseas to Dunkirk and other venues over the years in his capacity as secretary of the Essex branch of the National Ex-Prisoners of War Association. Like other secretaries, Jim has been very helpful in putting me in touch with other POWs who had their story to tell about camp entertainment.

Jack Stedman

If you are able to get hold of a little book called *Louisa's Boy* (published by Tucann Books) it, perhaps more than anything else I have read, gives a true and sensitive account of what it was like for the very young men who went to war in 1939; young men who, like artisan Jack Stedman, were plucked out of the atmosphere of close communities and families and placed into a life that was completely alien to them.

Jack was illegitimate and lived with his mother and grandfather on a farm which was part of the Onslow estate at Clandon Park in Surrey.

He was part of the BEF in France in 1940 and was evacuated, only just, from Dunkirk, only to be captured later in the Middle East. This country boy has told the story of his simple family upbringing and extraordinary service career, and remembers with affection his less fortunate comrades. He gives great credit to the Red Cross and St John organisations for making life in POW camps bearable, and tells how the regular finale of the camp concerts, "Land of Hope and Glory", played by a single instrumentalist, sent the lads to bed happy. He says the guards often wondered what all the fuss was about when they sang it with great gusto and cheering.

Post-war, Jack worked for British Aerospace, and spent his spare time with his local cricket club, ending up as its president. In retirement he has worked tirelessly as one of the Welfare Officers of the Dunkirk Association.

Ken de Souza

There were a large number of POW camps in Italy, most of them guarded by brutal fascists. Even German soldiers had misgivings about some of what went on in these places.

Despite the normal (jolly) Italian temperament, camp entertainment was not encouraged. At Ascoli on the Adriatic coast this was certainly the case, at least to begin with. Ken de Souza describes the eventual presentation of theatrical productions there in his book *Escape from Ascoli*, published by Newton in 1989.

The most remarkable achievement of all was the camp theatre. The first production couldn't have been more ambitious. Producer Fred Hindle chose *The Desert Song*. First-class musical talent was unearthed, costumes were excellent and four men were found with a flair for assuming female roles. The stage "women" were so real that they had quite a stunning effect on POWs deprived of female company for a long time. The painting of the scenery, made from Red Cross crates, depended on two basic colour sources. Crushed anti-malaria tablets (yellow) and Italian substitute coffee which tasted like burnt acorns but made good brown paint, light or dark according to its concentration. Ambition begot ambition when later Frank Lazarre produced *Philadelphia Story*. With the ingenuity of the wardrobe master and his costumiers the costumes were always superb.

Ken de Souza endured one mercifully short, though quite horrendous experience during his captivity. He was a navigator in a Wellington bomber which crashed south-west of Mersa Matruh in the Western Desert after a bombing raid on Tobruk in 1942. After baling out he walked for a hundred miles, mostly at night, through German- and Italian-occupied Egypt almost to the El Alamein positions then in British hands, that had been consolidated by the Eighth Army ready for the push against Rommel's Axis forces. The walk was bad enough, although as Ken says, "The enemy was a little thin on the ground," but worst of all he was captured within striking distance of the Alamein lines.

After spending some time in captivity in the Western Desert he was then transferred by ship from Benghazi to Italy. That sea journey of six hundred miles was quite the worst time of his life, and I felt that just a small part of his account of it is worth recalling, if only to show yet another act of man's inhumanity to man.

I wondered how this huge crocodile of men could fit itself into just one boat . . . At six o'clock we began filing up the gangplank, a lengthy procedure for several hundred men of several nations . . . I tried to convince myself that the Royal Navy (active with submarines in the Mediterranean) would have been duly advised that this was a POW transporter and would refrain from torpedoing it.

Two fascist guards stood by the open hatch, impatiently urging us forward, menacing us with revolvers. The steady flow never faltered, the sick, wounded and half-starved moved into the hatch and down the steep companionway at the pace of the rest . . . Hal [his pilot of the Wellington bomber and close friend] slung his satchel round his neck, letting it hang behind him as he descended, rung by rung, into the darkness of the hold. I followed close behind him, just keeping clear of the feet of the man coming after me. When I got to the bottom Hal caught my arm and steadied me. I leant against a pillar, took a deep breath and looked around me. Only then did I comprehend the utter horror of the situation into which we had been cast.

The Indians had been packed in first and the place was filled with the babble of various languages. The gloom was the gloom of a hell-hole even though the hatch was not yet battened down; and the smell, even at this early stage, was the smell of several hundred close-confined human bodies. And still the pitiful human cargo was pouring in down the companionway!

With an outburst of shouting the hatches were slammed shut. We could vaguely discern the shapes of men still coming down the companionway. We had descended into hell, there was no doubt about that. Hell was a steel-plated dungeon seething with the damned, stinking in the airless heat. I lay motionless, eyes tight shut, and prayed. Whenever, as frequently happened, people stumbled over me, I said nothing, remaining completely inert.

With the deepening darkness, the stench from the already overflowing latrine-drums became ever more nauseating; and, because of the fearful overcrowding, every drawn breath was an effort . . .

Ken de Souza's subsequent escape from the POW camp in Italy and his deep friendship with an Italian family are recounted in his book. Back in England he became a school teacher, from which profession he is now retired.

Ernie Mack and Buddy Clive

Ernie Mack was with the 7th Armoured Brigade, part of General Wavell's army in the Western Desert in 1941 which completely outmanoeuvred their Italian counterparts and drove them back to Benghazi. This was before the German general, Rommel, arrived on the scene.

Ernie was part of the detachment of Wavell's army that was moved to Greece to help resist that country's invasion by the Germans. By the time Ernie's regiment, the 4th Hussars, reached Greece the German invasion was already well established in that country so it was a case of next stop Crete and a prison camp, Stalag XVIIIA Wolfsberg in Austria.

Among the 4th Hussars who didn't ever get away from Greece was "Buddy" Clive. He was the son of entertainers Connie Clive and Bobby Dunn, and later on, television and theatre audiences in this country and abroad were to know Buddy as Clive Dunn, Corporal Jones of *Dad's Army*. Clive, after some horrendous journeying and a spell in other encampments, finally joined up with his other mates in Stalag XVIIIA.

This was a fairly well-organised camp and entertainment was soon one of the recreations on the agenda. Clive took part in John Galsworthy's *The Skin Game* and then a production by the New Zealand padre of Ivor Novello's *Glamorous Night* and, as Clive said, "not a cut-down modest prison camp version, but a full-length-type Drury Lane version with orchestra, chorus and costumes".

Clive was dumbfounded when he was asked to play the female lead, the Gypsy Princess, originally performed in London by the lovely Mary Ellis. The most daunting thing about the part for Clive was that he was going to have to sing in a mezzo-soprano voice. However, he acquitted himself well, according to his old mate Dave Bradford who was responsible for the show's scenery, always a fine feature of the productions. Clive Dunn's life and all his theatrical activities before and after the war make fascinating and humorous reading in his autobiography *Permission to Speak* published by Century Hutchinson in 1986. Clive now lives with his wife Cilla and daughters Polly and Jessica in Portugal where they all run a restaurant.

Meanwhile, back at Stalag XVIIIA, Ernie Mack was producing variety and band shows which included excerpts from *The Desert*

Song and *The Student Prince*, comedy sketches featuring Ernie himself and a colleague, Ernie Carroll, billing themselves as "The Two Ernies". Mack also produced a seaside Pierrot show complete with wonderful costumes and traditional banjos.

After the war Ernie became a theatrical agent and impresario in Lancashire where he lives. He was recently the subject of a Melvyn Bragg documentary *The Impresarios* with his friend and colleague Billy "Uke" Scott.

An extraordinary coincidence took place in 1965 when Ernie took his wife to Austria to show her where he was held prisoner. On arriving at Wolfsberg station he hailed a taxi and, would you believe, the taxi driver told him he was one of the guards at the camp during the war. "I'm afraid I didn't recognise him," Ernie told me.

John Rix

To meet this chatty, friendly little man and his charming wife in their comfortable home in north-east London makes you realise how some people have the amazing ability to win through life's difficulties and come up smiling with little or no bitterness in their hearts. John was orphaned at a very early age, leaving a young family of children to be split up into various homes.

As I have said before, I do not want to repeat what has already been recounted in various books: the terrible ordeal the Far East prisoners of war endured, long marches on empty stomachs, standing for long hours in the blistering sun for minor offences, starvation diets (at times proving fatal) and much worse. It is, however, within this scenario that one realises just how wonderful it was that entertainment and other recreations could be organised at all under those conditions.

I was in the ARP until 1940 when I was called up and drafted into the 5th Beds and Herts Infantry Regiment. In 1941 we started on our travels to the Far East (we didn't know it at the time) via Canada, the Caribbean, Cape Town in South Africa, and India, landing up in Armanaga near Poona, the birthplace of Spike Milligan. Then a further journey round the islands of Sumatra to Singapore. The whole journey had been incredible.

We had been in Singapore for barely six weeks when the island garrison capitulated to the Japanese in February 1942. The island had one aeroplane, and the heavy guns were pointing out to sea. We did our best to resist but it was no use. The Japs entered Singapore on bicycles and all of a sudden their flags were flying from every building. The fifth column activities must have been going on for a long time. A whole Australian division was captured in Singapore, and if only the Japanese had realised how easy it would have been to land in Australia with that continent's lack of military resources things might have been very different.

When we were first captured we were force-marched to Changi Jail. Some were immediately put into working parties on the docks but there was no food to eat except limed rice which was for planting and not human consumption: the lime burnt the enamel off the bowls it was in, so goodness knows what it did to our stomachs.

We were then moved to Thailand to help build the Siam–Burma railway. Before we left Singapore we had to sign a document saying we wouldn't try to escape. Several hundred Chinese refused to sign and were all shot.

We eventually arrived at Chungkai which was the headquarters for the building of the railway and was just a short distance from the bridge over the Kwai. At this camp, although very weak from lack of food, the lads started to get a band together as they had managed to carry some of the musical instruments with them on the march. They managed to play Schubert's Unfinished Symphony written down on scraps of paper from memory. They were never allowed to play God Save the King. The camp was still being built when we arrived and they had just started on an amphitheatre so the Japs could show us propaganda films, but we were also given permission to use it for anything we wanted to arrange.

We had with us a chap called Leo Britt, who worked for the BBC after the war, and he started to organise our entertainment. He was marvellous. Somehow or other he produced an André Charlot 1929 success *Wunderbar* and it was really good under the terribly difficult circumstances. He then did a play called *Night Must Fall* by Emlyn Williams. There was a marvellous female impersonator called Bobby Spong, who was excellent in the female parts. Towards the end of the war Spong was rounded up with a lot of other soldiers to help with the labour force in Japan. Unfortunately the boat they were on was sunk by the US navy before it got there.

Some Dutch Eurasians were brought into the camp because the Japs wanted more workers as the British and colonial troops were getting too weak to work from dysentery and lack of food. These Dutch Eurasians loved dressing up and a lot of them were definitely pansies and I remember one scene they did in a show where there was a big flower on the stage and when it opened up there was this beautiful girl (boy) in the centre. All the time we were at Chungkai we all helped in putting on some sort of entertainment.

I also became a medical orderly in the sick bay helping a Dr Macarthur. He was an amazing man, and did some very complicated operations under primitive conditions. We had outbreaks of cholera, and we also had a lot of dysentery cases which we were able to alleviate with a few drugs the Japs gave us, one of which was aqua flavian enema. I remember we had a Major Swanton who was a bad case but he wouldn't take the enema, he said he wasn't having that thing put in him. Dr Macarthur told him he had to and he did. This major was the E. W. Swanton who until recently did the cricket commentaries and wrote about cricket for the newspapers. I often laughed when I listened to him on the radio. I also gave quite a lot of blood for transfusions at times. I must have had a good strain in my body to do this considering the lack of food.

The Japs treated some of the outside workers, Chinese, Tamils and Malays pretty badly if they got ill; it was awful. We used to work seven days a week nearly all the time, and then the atom bomb was dropped and all the Japanese disappeared, well most – some wouldn't believe Japan had surrendered.

We were eventually given instructions by messages dropped from the air to walk along the track of the railway we had been helping to build to a junction where we would be met by allied officers and escorted to Bangkok. When we got to the junction we saw a lot of Japanese soldiers who were half starved and ill so we shared our ration of chocolate and cigarettes with them. It seemed strange that these Jap soldiers who had been brutalising everyone until a short time ago should be treated to a few fags and choc-olates, but we just felt sorry for them.

From Bangkok we were flown on to Rangoon and put on a ship for Britain. It had certainly been an experience.

What an extraordinary comment for anyone to make after all the deprivation John and his comrades went through, but then he is a generous and warm-hearted bloke.

I wonder if anyone perusing these pages might be able to throw some light on my cousin's eventual death on the Burma–Siam Railway? He was Patrick Tobin of the Royal East Surrey Regiment. Originally well over six feet and fifteen stone, he was last seen weighing about six stone.

Alfred J. Cooper

Known to his friends as Fred, he was also imprisoned by the Japanese after the fall of Singapore, and subsequently got heavily involved with entertainment in captivity.

I was called up in June 1941 and drafted into a searchlight regiment, but I never saw a searchlight and was transferred to a "secret" radar base. In

September 1941 I was sent to the Far East, arriving in Singapore on November 28th. After we arrived events proceeded at a pace. On December 7th the Japanese bombed us, and three days later they sank the battleships *Repulse* and *Prince of Wales* that had put to sea three days before.

As the Japs were shelling Singapore I, along with others of my regiment, became part of an infantry brigade. They had forgotten to send any radar equipment to the island so we had no choice. Once the Japs had landed it was obvious we had no chance and a ceasefire was eventually declared. This was, however, ignored by a slightly mad major who dashed about saying, "Give them the cold steel, they don't like the cold steel."

Once we had been taken prisoner there started a ridiculous charade which, had the situation not been so sad, would have been really funny. The first thing the Japs had to do was to count us, so they lined us up in a field, and it soon became obvious they were very uneducated Japs because it turned into a real pantomime. They started to count us, but kept forgetting where they were and started to count again. Then some of them tried to rearrange us in groups of four, and we realised they couldn't even count up to four properly. They tried smaller groups, and we started changing places, and then they just gave up and started running about jabbering and shouting at one another. Eventually we were marched off to Changi Jail about twenty miles away. This was in February 1942. Changi had previously been a barracks housing the British Singapore Garrison; now the Japanese were in charge there.

Through a fall on some barbed-wire I was hospitalised for several weeks, and the doctor in the sick bay told me that someone from my home town of Hastings wanted to see me, a Norman Backshall, who was organising a concert party and would like my help. Norman had heard that I had been a hairdresser, and he wanted me to see if I could make some wigs for a show he was going to do. It appeared that he and the doctor who had been treating me for my bad leg, Jumbo Marshall, were in this show playing female parts and they wanted some wigs. (Incidentally, Dr Marshall's story was published by his wife Sheila after he died under the title *The Changi Diaries*.) My leg had taken a while to heal, but Jumbo had the idea of putting crushed M & B tablets into the wound, and then he did a skin graft in very primitive conditions. He said it was the first time he'd done a skin graft and would be good practice for him. It was all quite successful, I'm glad to say. Once I was completely fit I really got involved with the prison theatricals.

The show that was being produced was *The Dancing Years*. I had never actually made a wig, but I had had experience in cleaning them. First of all I made some skull caps and then I had the idea of using some plumber's jointing material we had found in the sick bay which I sewed piece by piece into the skull caps.

For make-up I ground down rice and coloured it with an anti-mosquito cream and liquid which was bright red. Mixing all this together we got rouge and lipstick. We were able to use the barracks cinema as a theatre and we found odd scraps of wood and other materials for making scenery. The paint for the scenery was made from the different shades of earth dug up from huge holes the Japs had bored in the ground for latrine pits. We boiled the bits of different coloured earth from the stratas of soil with rice-water, and hey presto we had a crude sort of distemper. There was an electrician called Ben Foster from Preston in Lancashire who created wondrous effects with lighting.

We used to ask the men in the camps if they could remember any songs or tunes right through, and then we would laboriously take them down on bits of paper. We also had a lad called Hugh Eliot who used to compose music on his guitar. The wardrobe department really excelled themselves, making very good costumes from some of the clothes left in the married quarters by the civilians who were evacuated before the Japs arrived in Singapore. Mind you, they had ransacked the place pretty thoroughly before we were taken there, but they did leave some of the ladies' clothes.

We really produced a lot of entertainment in both Changi and Karanji prison camps. A few of the productions we did included Ivor Novello's *The Dancing Years* in March 1943, *I Killed the Count*, April 1943, and a pantomime, *Aladdin*, in December 1943. Then Noël Coward's *Hay Fever* in January 1944, with *Private Lives* in November 1944. *Design for Living* in January 1945, Patrick Hamilton's *Rope* in March 1945 and Bernard Shaw's *Pygmalion* in May 1945, with several other productions in between.

Fred still keeps in touch with his friend Norman Backshall, a friendship that was forged in a prison camp in the Far East fifty years ago. He now lives in Coulsdon in Surrey.

Just as I have been exhilarated by some of the stories recounted to me by members of Stars in Battledress, the RAF Gang Shows, naval personnel and Combined Service Entertainers, who have all been a credit to those organisations, so also have I been humbled by the accounts of activities in prisoner-of-war camps. Perhaps astonishment is the right word for the wonderful resilience and resourcefulness of the prisoners in devising, under almost impossible circumstances, entertainment behind barbed-wire, particularly those captured during the Far East campaigns.

Without exception, the lads whom I have talked to have paid great tribute to the Red Cross, the Swiss intermediaries and other such organisations, for making life bearable and keeping their sanity, in most cases, intact while they were prisoners.

Index

205

STAN HALL

MARGARET COURTENEY

CHARLIE CHESTER

NORMAN VAUGHAN

DON SMOOTHEY